D0378727

COVENANT'S END

ALSO BY ARI MARMELL

Thief's Covenant

False Covenant

Lost Covenant

In Thunder Forged

The Goblin Corps

COVENANT'S END

A Widdershins Adventure

ARI MARMELL

an Imprint of Prometheus Books
Amherst, NY

Published 2015 by Pyr®, an imprint of Prometheus Books.

Cover illustration © Jason Chan
Cover design by Nicole Sommer-Lecht

Inquiries should be addressed to Pyr
59 John Glenn Drive
Amherst, New York 14228
VOICE: 716–691–0133
FAX: 716–691–0137
WWW.PYRSF.COM

19 18 17 16 15   5 4 3 2 1

Library of Congress Cataloging-in-Publication Data

Marmell, Ari.
   Covenant's end : a Widdershins adventure / by Ari Marmell.
      p. cm.
   ISBN 978–1–61614–986–4 (cloth)
   ISBN 978–1–61614–987–1 (ebook)
   [1. Fantasy. 2. Robbers and outlaws—Fiction. 3. Gods—Fiction.] I. Title.

PZ7.M3456Fal 2012
[Fic]—dc23

2015000416

Printed in the United States of America

To Arabelle and Rowan,
on behalf of two friends of mine who love you a great deal,
a gift of words. Hopefully only the first taste of many more to come.

PROLOGUE

She lived in a house. Just a normal, everyday house, so far as she knew, though any of Davillon's citizens who lived outside the Rising Bend district would have told her otherwise. Could have told her that the multiple stories and the high eaves, the glass windows and the broad gardens, all were signs of wealth and fancy. None of them *did* tell her, however, and she'd spent all of her eleven years in and around the better neighborhoods. She dwelt with her family, in ignorant comfort; just another willful, entitled child of the aristocracy.

She wouldn't be, for much longer.

Her name was Rosemund. Rosemund Seguin.

She wouldn't be that for much longer, either.

Rosemund wore her best that day. Her tunic of peaches-and-cream, vest of dark velvet, a full skirt very much like a grown woman's. And, of course, her favorite pendant, a gleaming silver swan. Wore her best, but certainly didn't act it.

"It's not *fair!*" It was a shriek, as affronted and accusing as only a child could make it. Through a film of tears that blurred her vision and pasted dark strands of hair to her cheeks, she searched frantically throughout the room, seeking some argument, some evidence, some leverage that would make her parents see reason. She saw only the ponderous old grandfather clock, the shelves of dinnerware and vases, the usual luxury of which, so far as she was concerned, the whole of the world consisted.

Only those, and the disapproving, currently despised faces of her parents.

"You said! You said I could! Weeks ago, you said!"

"That was before you snuck out in the middle of mass," her mother told her stiffly. "Again."

"But *everyone* will be there! I *have* to go!"

Her pleading gaze turned on her father, normally the easier touch, but tonight he seemed as merciless as his wife. "Maybe after this," he said in his gruff, pipe-smoker's voice, "you'll keep your promises."

"*It's not fair!*" Only the fact that her arm wasn't quite long enough to reach it, from where she stood, saved a fine set of lacquered ceramic tableware from shattering across the floor. "You said! You damn well said—!"

"Language, young lady!" the adults barked in unison.

A fourth, softer voice took advantage of the momentary lull. "What about me?"

Rosemund glanced back and down at a head of tousled hair and an outfit rather less well-kempt than her own. Frankly, she'd forgotten he was here.

"I was going to go, too," Rousel reminded them. "What about me?"

Their father stepped around the fuming daughter to the earnest son, reaching out to further ruffle his hair. "I'm sorry," he said. "But you're not old enough to go alone."

"I am, so! Why do *I* have to suffer because *she*—!"

The older sibling drew breath to protest, though whether she would have shouted down her brother for pointing out that she was at fault here, or would have used his disappointment as an argument against her parents, she hadn't yet decided. Nor, as it happened, did it matter.

"This is not open to discussion!" their mother roared. "Rousel, honey, I'm sorry you're caught up in this, but remember whose fault it is. Rosemund, next time you'll think before—Don't you walk away when I'm talking to you!"

And technically, she wasn't. It was really more of an awkward flounce than a walk. The young girl pounded up the stairs to her door, which she rather predictably slammed with sufficient force to shake the shelves below. A moment later, she heard Rousel's door down the hall do much the same.

But Rosemund wasn't *quite* done; she had one more thrust to get in. Hauling the door wide open, she shrieked, at the top of her lungs, *"I hate you!"* Again, Rousel was doing the same, following her lead, when she slammed the portal shut once more, satisfied that her parents must have heard that.

They did, of course, and though it hurt them, they salved themselves with the knowledge that it was just something children said. That she didn't really mean it.

Something else heard her, too. Something that reveled, basking in the knowledge that she meant every word.

❀

She wasn't sure what had awoken her.

Rosemund sat up, rubbing her eyes, to discover she'd dozed off face-down on her comforter, not having even changed for bed. The swan pendant left a faint imprint in her skin where she'd lain on it. Her tunic, vest, and hair were as mussed as she could ever remember seeing them. Not that she could see much, in the room lit only by the puddle of moonlight dribbling in between the drapes.

The house was silent; still. It always was, this time of night, but tonight the hush was heavy, oppressive. Nothing leaked in from outside, no wind or rustling branches, no birds or distant voices. The settling of the foundations, the creaking of old furniture, the mechanical *tick* of the clock's heavy pendulum—all sounds she'd never consciously noticed before, absences she all too keenly noted now.

Call out for her parents? The words jammed in her throat, throttled by fear, yes, but also a lingering wounded pride. Instead she slid to her feet and, after a minute spent fumbling to light the wick, slowly crept into the hallway with candle in hand.

It seemed . . . longer than usual, that hall. Her brother's room, mere steps away, was a distant blot, dark against light. The stairs were invisible, swathed in shadow. But of course, the hall *couldn't* have changed, that wasn't possible, had to be her imagination.

That or the candle's gleam remained duller than it should have. Was *that* possible? It sounded less preposterous than a growing hallway, anyway.

Bare feet on hard wood, and all in silence. No slap of skin on the floor, no creaking of the occasional loose board. Ghostly step after ghostly step, Rosemund proceeded, breath short, hand trembling. Until, finally, she reached the top of the staircase.

There the silence ended. From there, she could hear, however faintly, a sound from the floor below.

A faint, desperate whimper.

It must have taken a hundred years to descend the stairs.

The chamber below was dimly lit, ruddy embers in the fireplace peeking out from beneath gray coats of ash. Flickers and waves of crimson danced along the walls, casting everything in a nightmarish illumination.

She saw Rousel, huddled beside the old sofa, hands clasped, lips quivering.

She saw her parents, on their knees in the center of the room. Their clothing hung in bloody tatters, from where they had apparently been whipped again and again. Pillowcases covered their heads, and it was from beneath those that the whimpers and panicked gasps sounded. Their hands were bound behind their backs; with what, Rosemund couldn't see from here. And the air . . .

The air smelled heavily of cinnamon and sweets.

"Mama?" She was a babe again, barely able to speak. It embarrassed her, as only adolescents her age could *be* embarrassed, but she couldn't help it. Couldn't deepen her voice, couldn't steel her nerve. "Papa?"

The whimpers rose to muffled cries, fearful, warning. They must also have been gagged beneath the pillowcases, she realized, and then wondered why such a thought would even occur to her.

She drew nearer, edging around the room, trying to understand. When she could finally see her mother's hands, however, her confusion only grew.

Licorice. Her parents' wrists were bound, not with rope or chain or twine, but thick and twisted strands of licorice.

"Oh, you're here! Good. I grew bored of waiting."

Rosemund squeaked at the horrid voice. No, not voice. *Voices.* Two, speaking in perfect unison, perfect clarity. One, that of a growing boy, perhaps a few years older than she; the other, the rough, sandpaper rasp of a decrepit old man.

In the distance, as though responding to those voices, a chorus of children cheered her arrival.

He appeared from nowhere, between two flickers of the candle. Tall, lanky, he looked like a young man not quite past the edges of his maturity, perhaps only half again as old as she. But Rosemund wasn't fooled. She never doubted for one heartbeat that he was older, *far* older, than he appeared.

Dark, greasy hair hung in tangles to his shoulders. His tunic and leggings and vest had once been of finest make, richer even than her own, but now they were crusted with caked-in dirt and bore the rips and stains of careless play.

His right hand, tightly gloved in rabbit fur, clutched an old kitchen knife, nicked and scored. His left . . .

Oh, gods!

The thumb of his left hand was mundane enough, but the other digits were no fingers at all. Close to two feet long, each was a switch of freshest birch-wood, perfectly suited for welting and splitting the skin of disobedient children.

And his eyes, his eyes were glass. Perfect mirrors, reflecting the room and Rosemund herself, but *not* the other members of her family.

A single tear rolled down Rosemund's cheek, but she couldn't bring herself to scream.

"You called," he told her in his twin voices. "I came."

"Called . . . ?"

"Yes. Both of you. Quite distinctly. You said you hated . . . *them*." The revulsion in his tone was thick and viscous as he waved those fearsome switches at her parents.

Rousel sobbed from his spot across the room. "But we didn't *mean* it!"

"Of course you did." So matter-of-fact, now, the creature sounded; almost sympathetic. "All children do. Only for a second, perhaps. Only in the heat of the moment. But you do. You all do. And a moment . . ."

The ratty old knife flickered in the crimson light, once, twice. Blood stained the pillowcases from within, and the terrified whimpers ceased in a burbling choke.

". . . is all it takes."

The boy shrieked, sobbed, dashed to his mother's side and began shaking her, clutching at her, begging her to rise. But Rosemund?

Rosemund was horrified, of course. Grief-stricken. The tears ran unhindered down her face, now, dripping from her chin. At the same time, though it thrust a blade of shame into her gut, a tiny, hidden part of her offered a chuckle of relief. No more unfair punishments. No more stupid rules.

A tiny, hidden part, but not hidden well enough. That mirrored gaze flashed her way, and the creature smiled—gruesomely, impossibly, inhumanly wide. "Now *that's* what I love to see!" The fingers of birch reached for her, but rather than lash her skin, they wrapped comfortingly around her, guiding her gently to the stranger's side. This close, the scent of candies was almost overwhelming. "Come, child. Come meet your *new* family. You'll like them better. You'll fit in *so* well."

Another flicker of the light, and then there was only Rousel alone in the room, weeping over the still forms of his parents.

❊

"Gods damn it!"

Lisette Suvagne, the new master of Davillon's so-called Finders' Guild—and soon so, so much more—bolted upright, throwing off the luxurious down quilt under which she'd slept. Shaking not with fear but with rage, she swept her autumn-red hair back from her face and wiped the thin sheen of sweat from her brow. She knew the dream for what it was, just as she had the last time this had happened, and the time before. Knew that their connection allowed her to see, and what she saw was real.

Again. They'd done it *again*. It had been Embruchel this time; who knew which of them would slip the leash tomorrow?

She needed them, reveled in the power they granted, but this wouldn't do. They would kill, spread terror, everything she'd promised them and more, but not this much, not *yet*! Not everyone, everything, was quite in place.

"Gods damn it," she growled again, far more softly. "You bastards are *immortal*. Why the hell do you find it so hard to *wait*?!"

With a sigh, Lisette rose and began casting around the opulent chamber for her clothes. She needed to compose herself, grab something to eat.

And then to try, yet *again*, to explain the importance of "patience" to creatures of pure and unchecked whim.

Ah, well. It'd be worth all the aggravation when Davillon—*all* of Davillon—was hers.

❊

Lisette was not the only one in Davillon to wake in that moment.

Some distance across the city, in his dwelling chambers within the Basilica of the Sacred Choir, his Eminence Ancel Sicard, Bishop of Davillon, also sat upright out of a horrid dream. Groaning, he ran a few fingers through his pillow-matted beard before laying his head in his hands.

Confusing, unclear; a sequence of images, dark, disturbing, bloody. More a sensation than a sight, a cold and sick certainty that something was wrong, very wrong, in his city.

Not that he needed the dreams to tell him that. The Houses were squabbling, the Guard were dithering, and the rumors making the rounds were as horrid as they'd been last year, when the creature Iruoch had stalked the streets. Plus, Igraine was telling him of ever greater troubles in the criminal underworld as well. . . . It was no wonder his dreams were unsettling.

Except Sicard had been a priest long enough to know that sometimes the dreams of the clergy were no dreams at all. And if these were omens, signs, then something truly, impossibly, *inhumanly* awful was at hand.

It had been nothing shy of a miracle that Davillon came out of the last year so relatively unscathed. It seemed almost ungrateful to pray for another one so soon, but that was what his city required: another miracle.

Or maybe, he pondered, as the image of a chestnut-haired and darkly clad young woman floated to the surface of his sleep-addled memories, *just the return of a prior one.*

Unbelievable that he'd ever entertain that hope. She was rude, insolent, exasperating, unpredictable, and just talking to her was like trying to scoop up a squirming armful of puppies and eels. He'd shed no tears when he learned she'd left.

Still . . . *if she's coming back, I do rather hope it's soon.*

CHAPTER ONE

The days were oddly chilly, given that the calendar insisted mid-spring wasn't terribly far off. Not ludicrously so, not wrapped in snow as if winter had utterly missed its cue to depart, stage north. Just chilly. The breeze carried a subtle bite, the sort offered when the neighbor's dog was tired of your crap but hadn't *yet* reached the point of going for your throat. The rain, less frequent, fell in fat, cold drops when it came, liquid spiders scurrying down inside collars and boots.

The woodland creatures were confused, popping out of winter burrows one day and hunkering back down the next. Grasses grew, foliage sprouted, only to be uprooted or torn from branches by the wind and the rain. Along this particular length of highway, one of southern Galice's major thoroughfares, the road was more muck than dirt, and the leaves that had tried to grow on nearby trees lay scattered willy-nilly like a bunch of bleeding, groaning bandits.

A metaphor that would have made no sense whatsoever, had the road and surrounding woods not also been strewn with a bunch of bleeding, groaning bandits.

One solitary figure strode casually away from the human detritus, her boots crunching lightly in the cold muck. A dark hood, matching the rest of her traveling leathers, kept chestnut hair from roiling and coiling around her head in the breeze. For a time, other than those gusts and her own footsteps, the only sound to be heard was the faint jingling of the ratty pouch she weighed and juggled in one hand.

"I don't know, Olgun," she lamented to, apparently, nobody in particular. "This is barely more than the *last* group had on them. We really need to get ourselves accosted by a better class of highwayman.

What?" She cocked her head to one side, listening to a response nobody else could hear. "Oh, come on! I didn't hurt any of them that badly!"

Another pause. "Well, yeah," she admitted, "that probably hurt pretty bad. But he has another one that should still work just fine."

Widdershins—formerly Adrienne Satti, former tavern-keeper, former ex-thief, and soon-to-be-former exile from Davillon—continued along the path she hadn't, until recently, been sure she would ever tread again.

The way home.

"What?" she asked. Semi-violent imagery and an overwhelmed sensation ran through her mind; such was the "speech" of her unseen companion, a god foreign to Galice and who boasted, in all the world, precisely one adherent. "Well, how the happy, hopping horses am *I* supposed to know what's 'normal' here? We've only ever been on this road once before, and that was in summertime. Maybe this *is* the normal number of bandits along here. Or maybe, I don't know, maybe it's bandit season. That'd explain why we haven't seen many other travelers, yes? If the locals know when to stay off the highway."

With a frisson of both bemused and amused reluctance, Olgun pointed out the logistical paradox regarding the notion of a "bandit season" in which travelers remained home.

"Oh. That's a good . . . well, maybe it's *dumb* bandit season!"

Widdershins chose to interpret Olgun's subsequent silence as meaning she'd won that particular exchange. Olgun chose to let her. They were both happier that way.

Still and all, as the day aged and the road unwound beneath her feet, Shins had to acknowledge that something was definitely off. This was a major thoroughfare; even allowing for the unseasonable cold, even if the threat of banditry was higher than usual, such a total dearth of travelers was odd. They should be *fewer*, but they should not have been *absent*.

It was . . . off. And after the previous, oh, bulk of her entire life, the young woman had developed a healthy distrust of "off." Nothing about her posture visibly changed, but her steps grew softer and more deliberate, her attentions more focused on the world around her.

As she was so heavily alert for danger, however, it took a subtle nudge from her divine companion before she noticed the changing aroma in the air. The lingering breath of northerly climes and the first faint perfumes of buds and blooms gradually gave way to wood smoke spiced with roasting meats.

She was still a couple days from Davillon, so what . . . ?

"Ah."

A small cluster of buildings made itself visible as she crested a shallow rise. Nothing even remotely impressive, just a squat structure of wood with a couple of smoke-belching stone chimneys, and a few even squatter structures scattered around it.

Now that she saw it, Shins remembered it from her way out, last year, though only barely. At the time, she hadn't been in much of a mental state to notice anything at all, even had the place not been so forgettable. A simple trading post, taking advantage of the traffic Davillon normally received, distinguished only by its indistinctiveness.

Except . . . "Shouldn't it be empty? I'm almost positive that a road without travelers doesn't provide many customers. There could even be a proverb about it. Like the one about not licking a gift horse's mouth, or however that goes."

Olgun could only provide one of his "emotional shrugs."

It wasn't as though the trading post was packed to overflowing, but it clearly did a reasonable amount of business. Several horses—none of them having been licked, presumably—were tied at a post outside the main structure. A small gathering of people here, an isolated pair there, stood around talking, smoking, generally enjoying the evening's lack of rain. Shins received her share of curious glances, if only as a young woman (apparently) traveling alone, but otherwise nobody seemed inclined to acknowledge her arrival.

Not until she stepped up onto the rickety porch at the front of the central building. "Excuse me, *mademoiselle?*"

The man who'd addressed her was teetering on the precipice of old age, ready to fall at any moment, and clad in the sort of heavy, colorful fabrics that said "I'm a merchant who wants you to believe I can afford better than I actually can."

Shins's hand didn't drift to her rapier, but she suddenly became much more aware of precisely where it was. "Yes?"

"I'm just . . . if you've come this far traveling alone, does that mean the roads have grown safer again?"

She wasn't sure what "safer" meant, what she was supposed to compare to, but, "No, I don't think so."

"Still rife with highwaymen, then?"

Now she *did* allow her fingers to close on the hilt of her weapon. "Fewer now than before."

"Ah." The merchant's patronizing smile said, as clearly as any message from Olgun, that he didn't believe a word of it. "Well, thank you for your time."

A nod, and Shins pushed through the door, where the scent of cooked foods—as well as substantial amounts of travelers' sweat—dove into her nostrils like they were seeking shelter.

"How do you like that?" she asked, voice pitched so softly that nobody else could possibly overhear. "A girl could start to feel a bit mistrusted."

Olgun snorted, or made whatever the abstract empathic equivalent of a snort might be.

Square room. Square tables. Even squareish chairs. All creaking with years of use, all having absorbed so many odors in their time that they were probably made up of smells as much as wood.

It looked almost nothing like the common room of the Flippant Witch, but Shins still felt a pang of homesickness deep in her gut.

Soon.

It wasn't a tavern, precisely. The large common room was con-nected, via a wide doorway, to something of a general store. Drinks and food were made available here, yes, but as an adjunct to the shop rather than its own separate business.

About half the chairs were occupied, and about half the occupiers paused their drinking, chewing, or conversation—sometimes two or all three at once—to briefly examine the newcomer. Again her youth and sex drew a few second looks, but most of the patrons turned back to their own affairs readily enough.

Shins moved to the small counter beside the interior door, pre-suming that the young girl behind it served as barkeep. "Hi."

A saucer-wide stare and a breathy "Uh, welcome" responded.

Then and there, Widdershins firmly decided that the girl did *not* remind her of Robin. Mostly because Shins had no intention of allowing her to. Sliding two fingers into one of the many pouches at her belt, she produced a couple of the coins she'd, ah, liberated as compensation for the bandits' attempts to harm her.

"A mug of your best whatever this will pay for." Two thin *smacks* of metal against wood, and then Shins dug out a second pair. "And a plate of the best whatever *this* will pay for." *Clinks* rather than *smacks*, as she laid those two atop the others.

Blink. "Oh. Um . . ." Blink, blink. "Okay. Coming right up." Blink.

Widdershins wandered away from the counter, scooted a chair out from an empty table with one foot, spun it by the back, and dropped perfectly into it as the seat whirled past her. Studiously and smugly ignoring the bemused glances that brought her, she tilted the chair back, balanced on a single leg, and crossed her ankles on the table's edge.

"What? Oh, I am *not* showing off!" she protested. "I just . . . want to make it clear to everyone here that I can take care of myself. Can't be too careful, yes?

"No, it is not the same as showing off! The idea isn't to impress people, it's to . . . differently . . . impress people. For different . . . Oh, shut up."

For the next several minutes, Shins occupied herself by spinning her rapier and scabbard, balanced with one finger on the pommel, tip on the floor, just *daring* Olgun to say something about it. He didn't, but as she'd told him in the past, she could feel him laughing at her.

"If you don't stop that, I'm tying you to the post outside, with the horses."

The serving girl, or owner's daughter, or whatever she was, finally appeared beside the table with flagon and plate in hand. Here, in the open, her resemblance to Robin was rather lessened. She might have shared a slender build with Shins's friend, but the ruffled skirts and braided hair were about as un-Robin as one could get.

That didn't make the prodigal thief feel any less homesick, though.

"So," she asked just as the server made to leave, "what's with the crowd? I hardly passed anyone on the way here, and yet . . ."

"Oh! That is, um . . ." The girl earnestly studied the floor as she answered, perhaps expecting the flowers of spring to start blooming inside in an effort to escape the weather. "I really don't know if I should be spreading rumors on shift."

"Well, *I'm* not on shift," Shins explained patiently. "And it takes at least two people to spread a rumor, yes? So even though *you're* on shift, the rumor's not spreading on shift—or only half on shift, at most—and nobody can accuse you of anything inappropriate."

Olgun dizzily retreated to a far corner of Shins's mind and quietly threw a fit.

As for the barkeep, after a moment of slack-jawed gawping during which she couldn't find a single word—as they were, most probably, hiding in the corner with Olgun—she finally decided either that Shins's argument was convincing, or (more likely) that it was easier just to go along than try to unknot it.

"It's the monsters," she admitted in something of a stage whisper. Shins's rapier stopped spinning. "Sorry, what? Say again slowly, in small words."

"I know how it sounds," Not-Robin said, her head bobbing like a cork in boiling water. "But that's what we've heard. The road between here and Davillon—*all* the roads around Davillon—are cursed or haunted with monsters!"

"Look, there's apparently been a lot of banditry lately, yes? I'm sure that's—"

For the first time, the other's face lost all uncertainty, becoming a stiff, confident mask. "We know all about the bandits," she insisted. "Highway's lousy with them. But some travelers, some merchants, they'll chance it, you know? Robbers can't be everywhere, and some of the caravans are pretty well guarded. Many of them get through, come this far. But almost nobody's come back who tried to continue on to Davillon in the last few weeks, and those who did? Wasn't bandits who had them scared.

"So these days, travelers get this far and then start hearing the stories. Some try to keep on, and we mostly don't see them again. The others? They wait around here for a while, doing what business they can with us and with the other merchants, before risking the long road back to wherever they came from."

"If there *are* monsters on the roads," Widdershins said carefully, "why hasn't anyone dispatched any soldiers to deal with them?"

Not-Robin shrugged and headed back to her counter. "Rumor has it most of Galice's standing army's gathered at the Rannanti border," she said over her shoulder. "As far as soldiers from Davillon?" A second shrug. "Gods know what's going on in that city. Enjoy your meal."

Shins watched her go, then idly poked at the slabs of roast on her plate with a fork, as though trying to prod them into moving. "You don't even have a *face*," she groused, "so stop looking at me with that expression."

The tiny deity wafted a question across her mind.

"How the figs would I know? Doesn't really seem likely, though, does it? I mean, monsters haunting the highways of Galice? Come on."

Keeping his lack-of expression utterly neutral, Olgun dragged a pair of images through his young worshipper's vision. One demonic, one fae; both truly, deeply horrible.

Any appetite Widdershins had remaining dried up and blew away like a desiccated earthworm. "I didn't say *impossible*, Olgun. Just not likely."

The surge of feeling she got in response was apologetic, but not very. And if Shins were being honest with herself—something she tried to avoid doing too much these days, as a matter of policy, but couldn't seem to help—she *had* been a bit quick to pooh-pooh the notion. Often as she'd been scoffed at for trying to warn people about Iruoch, she ought to be a bit more generous with the benefit of the doubt.

On the other hand, she *was* smarter and less superstitious than most people, if she said so herself.

And she had, on more than one occasion.

"I'll be careful," she assured the fretting god. "Won't take anything for granted. But I'm pretty sure we can deal with whatever it is."

We are *going home, gods drum it!*

Widdershins attacked her food, then, more as a point of emphasis than because her appetite had returned. For some time, she knew only the clatter of tableware, the taste of beef not *too* badly over-cooked and not *too* heavily over-seasoned, and the background buzz of conversation.

It took her a moment to recognize Olgun tapping on her emotional shoulder. When she did, she felt his attention directed at a specific table behind her.

"Is it safe to turn and look?" she asked under her breath.

No mistaking the negative in his reply.

"All right." She examined the table before her. The plate was wood, the utensils unpolished. The ale?

Widdershins tapped the flagon with one finger. "Is the light right? Can you make this work?"

A *very* tentative yes, and an admonishment that he couldn't for long.

"It'll do."

Carefully, she gripped her drink, waited until she felt the familiar tingling in the air that heralded the god's limited magics.

This is going to be cold, uncomfortable, and really *embarrassing if Olgun's not able to manage it.* She thought of pointing that out aloud, then decided not to give him any ideas; he just might decide it'd make an amusing prank.

When the prickling sensation reached its apex, Shins lifted the flagon to eye level and tilted it completely horizontally.

For a few seconds, against all natural laws, the liquid within held fast rather than spilling, creating a dark pool into which she gazed. It wasn't much of a reflection, but it was enough for her to get the gist of what Olgun had wanted her to see.

A lone man sat at the indicated table, and—since her back was to him—he made no effort to hide the fact that he studied her intensely.

"Oh, for pastry's sake!" Shins sighed and lowered the beverage. "Ah, well. It's been a couple months since anyone tried spying on us. Guess we were due, yes?"

She wondered briefly what the stranger had seen of her trick with the ale, what he thought had just happened. Doubtless he'd assume the cup was empty, that any sense otherwise was a trick of the light.

A few more mouthfuls of supper, just to keep everything nice and casual looking. Next, with a deliberately inflated sigh of content-ment, she leaned back, once more tilting the chair until it balanced precariously on its back legs.

And then she allowed it to topple.

The room jumped around her as her perspective plummeted, but vertigo and Shins were old colleagues. She'd fallen into a backward roll and was again on her feet before the chair stopped bouncing. A quick pivot followed by a spin of the empty chair opposite the spy so that it faced backward, and she was settled again. She straddled the seat, arms crossed on the back of the chair, and looked straight into the man's ever-widening stare.

"Hi."

Then, under her breath, while the stranger struggled for words, "Yes, I *could* have just stood up and walked over, but where's the fun in—? Please, I didn't draw *that* much attention, only . . . oh. Well, there aren't that many people here, anyway. Besides, we caught him off guard, yes?

"You know," she continued, once more in a normal tone, "I'm pretty sure you're doing it wrong. If you mean to be eating, you should be putting something in your mouth, and if you mean to be talking, there should be sounds coming out. This empty chewing is just odd. You look like a fish."

"Uh . . ."

"A confused fish."

"I—"

"Trying to ask for directions."

"What are you *doing*?!" he finally managed to squeak.

Shins studied him, unblinking. Mousy brown hair, drooping mustache, clothes that wouldn't stand out even if they were on fire . . . basically, the sort of person who was *so* average, it made him distinct.

"I," she said finally, "I'm waiting for you to explain why you've been watching me."

"I—I don't know what you're—"

"Oh, for fig's sake, can we just not? How about you give me clear answers, and you won't have to live with all the mockery you're going to suffer after you've been beaten up by an adolescent girl in public."

His jaw clenched, causing his mustache to bristle as though it were an angry cat. Shins almost hurt herself swallowing a snicker. "What makes you think you'd be able to beat me?" he demanded.

Widdershins's answering smile was not only welcoming, it bordered on dainty. "Would you care to find out?"

Apparently he wouldn't; the stranger's entire posture slumped. "Would you believe I'm just taken by you?"

"Flattered, but no. You're not subtle enough to do anything less overt than leering, and I've *been* leered at. I know what it feels like, and you haven't left nearly enough slime on my back."

Olgun snorted, radiated mischievousness, and sent a crawling sensation of sticky wetness down the young woman's spine.

"*Quit it!*" Very tricky, getting the weight and emphasis of a shout into a whisper so soft it was barely a breath, but it was a trick she'd mastered a long time ago. Pretty much out of necessity.

Her divine partner's answer was, more or less, a chuckle.

The stranger hesitated a few seconds more. Then, with a resigned sigh, he reached into a pocket of his ragged coat and removed a worn sheet of parchment.

Squished, battered, folded, and refolded so often the creases were almost worn through, and soaked in the aromas of lint and stale sweat, it remained clear enough, once opened. The both of them took some time to contemplate, first the sketch and then one another.

"It's missing something," Shins said finally. "I don't feel it truly captures the inner me."

"Certainly didn't tell *me* what to expect," the man confirmed.

"Hmm." Again she turned her attention to the parchment, not the portrait but the text below. Her name, a brief list of the sorts of activities in which she might be involved—"*Petty* theft?!" she protested to Olgun. "There's nothing petty about them!"—and the promise of a small reward for any sightings or information regarding her, to be delivered to . . .

"The Finders' Guild? Oh, figs." Last she knew, Shins wasn't in any trouble with Davillon's thieves, but she couldn't readily come up with any *good* reasons they'd want to keep an eye on her.

"Where did you get this?" she demanded.

"Uh, been circulating for a couple months, now. In Davillon and all the surrounding towns. Actually were some going around earlier'n that, even, but those said deliver any information to a particular address in the Ragway District, rather than the Guild in general."

She was only half listening, now, her attentions fixed on a point hundreds of miles distant and a season gone by. The bustling city of Lourveaux; the strangers loitering about the tomb of Archbishop William de Laurent, as though waiting for someone; the spy she had believed, only learning otherwise much later, to be watching her on behalf of House Carnot.

Again she pitched her voice for divine ears only. "What do you think?"

Worry, suspicion, but tentative agreement. Someone watching for her on both sides of Galice? It seemed far too much to be sheer coincidence.

Snapping back to the present, Shins *clunked* a couple of coins onto the food-stained table. "It's not as much as they're offering," she said, tapping a finger on the parchment, "but you don't have to face a road supposedly full of monsters—or *me*—to collect."

Grimy hands twitched toward the silver, but the stranger stopped himself. "And, uh, what am I doing for this reward?"

"Finding any more of these that might be floating around this little trading post and burning them." It wouldn't accomplish much, she knew, but it might render this particular spot a tad safer if she had any need to come back this way.

Not that she planned to.

"Oh. All right."

"Incidentally," Shins added, interrupting him in mid-scoop, "it's probably crossed your mind to just take the coins and then not bother looking for any more of these posters. I mean, how would I know, right?"

"Um . . ."

"I suggest you consider the lengths that someone's gone just to keep track of me. And then wonder why.

"And *then* . . . ask if you're really sure I *wouldn't* know."

With that, she swept from the chair and the table. It was all nicely melodramatic and threatening, and she almost ruined the whole effect by bursting into laughter when Olgun suddenly filled her head with ominous operatic music. Fortunately, she managed to hold off until she was back outside.

"Was a little overwrought, wasn't it?" Still chuckling, she checked the overcast skies. Deciding she could still get a few hours' travel in before bunking down for the night, she turned her heels on the trading post and swiftly left it behind.

In the nipping winds and the shadows of the trees, however, her mirth scattered along with the stillborn leaves of early spring. Something was clearly wrong in Davillon.

"I mean," she told Olgun, "when *isn't* something wrong in Davillon? If nothing was wrong, we'd know for *sure* that something was wrong! But who the hens is so hot to find me? We didn't leave *that* many people still pissed at us! And even *I* can't irritate people from all the way across the nation."

A sigh, and then Shins stuck her tongue out at apparently nothing at all. "I set you up for that one, didn't I? Yes, I'm sure."

Olgun would have to have been a god of cats to be any more smugly pleased with himself.

"Yeah, yeah. Well, keep your eyes open. Or my eyes open, or your not-eyes open, or whatever it is you actually use to see. If you see. Did you know that, even after all this time, you can be very confusing?"

When no response beyond more amusement was forthcoming,

she continued, "Whatever. Be alert. There's something wrong at home, and there's supposedly something nasty on the road *to* home.

"I seriously doubt it's really any sort of 'monster,' though. I mean, most people go their entire lives without meeting one, yes? It's a pretty safe bet that you and I aren't going to encounter *three*."

CHAPTER TWO

"If you happen to think of it," Widdershins dully suggested to her unseen companion, "could you remind me, in the future, never to gamble? Or maybe talk?"

Olgun solemnly assured her he would take steps to ensure the former, but that the latter was beyond even divine intervention.

Shins nodded absently, having fully expected the retort; having invited it, even. The banter kept the both of them centered while taking in the tableau they'd stumbled over.

What had once been a large covered wagon lay beside the road, reduced primarily to planks and kindling. Here and there, though, protruded recognizable bits; a largely undamaged wheel, half of the driver's bench. The canvas tarp that had protected the vehicle's contents hung limp from a spur of wood, the heavy material rustling modestly in the wind.

It had, when intact, required a two-horse team to pull. One of those horses lay, still partly harnessed, as broken as the rest of the wagon. The abnormally cool spring meant that relatively few insects were out and about, but those that had found the equine buffet buzzed in offensive contentment.

Of the other horse, or any riders and drivers of a more bipedal nature, there was no sign.

Well, no sign other than the wide swathe of disturbed dirt and crushed underbrush where something had been dragged from the road.

Between that, and the almost comically large puncture wounds in the dead horse—it looked like it had been shot with multiple ballista bolts—Shins had pretty well given up on her earlier skepticism.

"Right. So. Monster it is, then."

Grudging agreement from her partner.

"But, hey, the timing couldn't be better. This had to have happened pretty recently, yes? So whatever it is, it's off somewhere. Busy. Probably not hungry."

Less grudging agreement.

"Perfect time for us to just continue on by, be on our way home in safety."

Emphatic agreement, now.

"No reason whatsoever for us to get involved."

Olgun continued to agree. Shins continued to stand at the edge of the road, gazing at the trail, and very obviously *not* going about her merry way.

"Yep. Going any minute now."

Air wafted over them. Insects buzzed. Feet failed to step.

Oh, figs. "We're both really, really stupid."

And back to grudging agreement again.

She hesitated a moment more, long enough to dig through her gear and recover the heavy pistol she'd confiscated from the first of the robbers who'd interrupted her travels. A quick juggle of powder and ball to load the weapon, and she was off, creeping low through darkening woodland.

Not her preferred environment, no, but avoiding protruding roots or loose leaves wasn't *too* different from creaky floorboards or crunching gravel. Between her own aptitudes and Olgun's assistance—warning her of an obstacle here, muffling the sound of a cracked twig there—her advance was quiet enough.

Her first hint that she was drawing near was the scent of smoke; rich, woody, redolent with roasting meat. It actually smelled pretty good, though Shins didn't have much of an appetite under the circumstances.

"Guess we know what happened to the other horse," she muttered.

Flickering lights, glimpsed through the foliage, guided her closer.

Widdershins ducked beneath a pair of crossed branches, dropped even lower so her crouch was more of a duck-waddle, and peered around a pudgy thumb of a stump.

A large campfire crackled angrily away, feeding on moist, snapping tinder that belched thick plumes of smoke in its death throes. Over the fire hung a primitive spit, little more than a branch on two rough Xs of wood. Shins couldn't clearly see the hunk of horse flesh dripping grease to sizzle in the flame, as it was already heavily blackened and veiled in smoke.

From across the encampment, a frightened whinny drew her gaze. The missing horse—a speckled roan, bits of its torn harness still wrapped around its chest—tugged frantically at the rope that bound it to a neighboring tree.

But if the horse was over *there*, then what . . . ?

Widdershins's gaze flickered back to the roasting meat, and she felt her stomach turn inside out.

"Olgun . . ." Barely a croak.

She felt the god's power tingling in her gut, settling it enough that the nausea wasn't overwhelming so that she could bite it back and not give away her presence with a loud retching. Even so, it was a near thing.

Then the *thing* whose camp this was tromped into view on the far side, actually shaking the nearby branches with each step, and Shins forgot about everything else.

It was no demon she'd heard described in sermons; no fae she'd run across in any fairy tale. More or less humanoid in silhouette it might have been—if overly, even obscenely, muscled—but it was anything but human. A single eye peered from furrowed brow; above, a lone horn curved upward, tearing leaves and twigs from the branches. Although difficult to tell in the firelight, it seemed the thing's skin was a deep russet; on a person, it would have suggested an exceedingly painful but slowly fading sunburn.

It smelled, even from this distance, of soured sweat and rotten breath. It wore only leather breeches, carried a primitive but brutal-looking spear, and *none* of these were the detail that first stole a reluctant gasp from her throat or set her gut to quivering all over again.

"Gods! The frog-hopping thing's got to be twice my height!" And that wasn't even counting the creature's horn. "What in the name of Khuriel's codpiece *is* it?!"

It was, in some ways, a useless question. Communicating through sensation and imagery as he did, Olgun couldn't really offer her an actual *word* for what they were seeing even if he knew it.

What he *could* convey was a sense of time. Of age.

Great time and age.

Before Galice and Rannanti and the other modern nations, a lengthy age of barbarism had engulfed the continent, perhaps the world. For centuries, violent tribes warred for territory, for supremacy of culture. It had been from these tribes that the 147 gods, those who would eventually make up the Hallowed Pact and bring about the rebirth of civilization, had come.

And earlier even than *that*, a millennium and more before Shins's own time, an age of myth. Legend spoke of great empires and warring kingdoms, magics far more potent and more common than today, and monsters the likes of which had never since been seen.

Shins didn't believe much of it. Nobody really did. But one tiny bit was true, apparently, since Olgun seemed pretty emphatic that this sort of creature was indeed that ancient.

"You don't believe this one's actually lived that long, though?!" she demanded.

No. No, he most assuredly did not.

"Then where the happy hens did it *come* from?" And then, "How do you even shrug without shoulders?"

To which, of course, Olgun only offered a second shrug.

"Whatever, then." She watched as the creature squatted beside the fire, winced as it poked at the cooking flesh, perhaps to see if it was done. Even crouched, it was markedly taller than she.

"I really don't want to fight that," she confessed. "So let's make this count, yes?"

The tingle in the air flared up as Shins raised the flintlock. Carefully sighting along the barrel, between grasping branches and the shadows cast by the dancing fire, she took a single, deep breath. . . .

Allowed Olgun's influence to tweak her aim, shifting the weapon a hair this way, then that. . . .

Thunder cracked; fire spat; smoke plumed. Through the dark and the sudden haze, Shins saw the creature's head rocked back by the impact. It screamed, hands flying upward to clutch at its temple.

And then, roaring like a tornado made of lions—and, though bleeding profusely, sporting a skull sadly lacking the hoped-for gaping hole—the thing bolted upright and charged.

"*Aaaaaaaaaaaaaaaaugh!*" Shins observed.

Rough bark chewed at her fingers as she scrambled madly up the nearest tree, empty pistol tumbling with a flat *thump* to the soil. She felt Olgun's strength supporting her own, tightening her grip, boosting her jump as she pushed off the trunk in a lunge for the next branch over. Slender boughs scraped at her face and arms, enough to sting, not remotely enough to stop her. From behind, the rending and tearing and splintering and howling rather efficiently announced her pursuer's approach where the darkness might otherwise have concealed it.

And about that darkness . . . "Olgun?"

Another tingle of the god's power and the world brightened, though it lost some of its sharpness and color. One more leap, so she could haul herself up onto a higher branch, and then Shins took the time to turn and look.

Although slowed by the need to circumnavigate or squeeze between the largest boles, the creature wasn't far behind. Most of the intervening branches, and even a few small trees, simply snapped and fell away as it thundered through them. The protruding horn occasionally snagged in the canopy, forcing the thing to twist and crouch, impeding it further still, but most of the time it, like the rest of the beast, just tore through whatever blocked its path.

Every few steps it thrust that massive spear up and out, stabbing into the darkness. It was a veritable battering ram, thicker than the scattered saplings; with Olgun's enhancement to her vision, Shins could still see dried blood—she chose to assume it was the horse's—clinging to the sword-sized tip.

A bough thicker than the one on which she crouched splintered and fell with the spear's impact, hanging loosely by a few thin fibers. With a sound something akin to "Eep!"—only less articulate—Shins leapt. Over the monstrous head and horn, though not as high above as she might prefer, she soared across the gap to the next tree over. There she swung clear around the trunk and began again to climb, seeking a perch too high for even this enemy to reach.

Olgun's doubt was a sheen of sweat, clinging not to her body but her soul. Shins couldn't honestly blame him; with a foe nearly twelve feet in stature, wielding a spear even longer than that, "too high to reach" was—so to speak—a tall order.

Every stretch, every heave brought an extra foot of height and a bit of swearing—well, "swearing"—to match. "Figs . . . figs . . . hens . . . figs . . ."

Beneath her, something growled. Shins froze, leaned left, and glanced downward.

It stood at the base of the tree, its one narrowed eye meeting hers. She could see it studying the length of trunk between them, deciding she was out of reach, if only just. It hefted the spear a time or two, perhaps debating whether to throw.

Then, grinning until the flesh around its horn rumpled like an unmade bed, it reared back, lifted a foot, and kicked.

The entire tree shuddered and jumped. Branches waved like drowning sailors, and Shins could only cling for dear life as bark bit into skin and her teeth clacked hard enough to grind cornmeal. She might have considered drawing her rapier and letting herself drop, hoping both to kill the thing and break her own fall by landing atop it, but the wicked horn made that a rather unenticing proposition.

A second inhuman kick. Shins slipped a few feet down the trunk with a brief squawk. A trickle of blood wormed its way out from beneath her left palm.

"O-o-o-lgun-n?" she asked as the shuddering faded.

She caught the first stirrings of whatever idea he meant to convey, a brief flash of imagery that had *something* to do with the branches around her, but whatever else he intended was lost in a silent shriek of panic. The tree shook yet again, but this time was different. The impact seemed somehow less solid, yet the vibration was just as violent. Once more, Shins could only clutch tight to the trunk and twist about to look down.

"Oh, *figs*."

The thing had turned the edge of its spear against the trunk. The massive tip was more than heavy enough to function as an axe, and while the surrounding trees provided limited room, the creature's strength was such that it didn't *need* much of a swing to build momentum. With that first strike, it had already gouged a larger gap into the tree than any human lumberjack could have managed in a half dozen blows.

Again it swung, and again, driving metal into wood. Shins tried to climb, but each impact cost her most of the progress she'd just made. She sought wildly for a safe spot on the neighboring boles, but the constant shaking kept her from planting her feet solidly enough to jump.

A fearsome *crack* sounded; the world began to tilt, just that much more with each subsequent strike; and in the end all Shins could do was scramble around the trunk so at least she wouldn't be crushed beneath the tree as it finally, ponderously, inexorably toppled.

Looking back on it some few moments later, the experience wasn't nearly so bad as she'd expected. The woods here were tightly packed enough that her tree lacked much room in which to fall. It plunged through a layer of canopy, ripping branches from its path, but lodged in the arms of its neighbors before its crown had traveled even halfway earthward.

On the other hand, it was still a sizeable tree, taking a sizeable fall. Already bleeding from a score of tiny lacerations and abrasions, Widdershins tumbled madly—head not only over heels, but also under, beside, and even cattycorner to them—thrown from the trunk by the impact. Only a desperate surge of power from Olgun allowed her to snag the nearby branches as she flew by, barely keeping herself from crashing through the canopy and breaking on the forest floor.

For roughly a decade or so, she just hung there, arms and legs wrapped tight around the thickest limbs, shuddering and aching over every inch. Wood and leaves crunched nearby as the creature prodded at the canopy with its spear, but the mess made by the falling tree, and the fact that Widdershins had managed to catch herself at a greater height than any normal human could have done, meant the brutal weapon thrust nowhere near her.

Her lungs burned, but she forced herself to take only soft, shallow, *quiet* breaths. Olgun's soothing touch washed over the worst of her cuts and bruises, but she knew she'd be feeling this for a couple of days to come. And still she waited, as the bestial grunts and the scraping spear grew faster and ever more frustrated.

Until, just as she despaired of it ever doing so, the creature offered a final sullen snarl and began climbing the fallen tree like a ramp, determined to find the hidden thief. It leaned sharply forward as it came, spear wrapped tight in one fist.

Which meant it did *not* have both hands available to grip the tree.

"Okay, Olgun. Now'd be a good time to impress me."

Her skin prickled, as though the air had filled with phantom bees. She felt the energies flowing through her, sensed every imperfection and every subtle sway of the branch beneath her, found her own weight fading as muscles grew unnaturally potent.

She also, beneath it all, felt the fatigue that Olgun struggled to hide, tugging at her bones and her eyelids as though it were her own. She'd asked a lot of him in a very short span of time; if this first attempt failed, the all-but-forgotten god might not have the power for a second.

So, one single chance to avoid a gruesome, agonizing end for both of us. Not something that happens to us just every day.

Only every fourth day, on average. Every third, tops.

Still she waited, bracing herself, letting the creature climb just that little bit higher. A moment more, just a moment, a handful of fluttering, pounding heartbeats . . .

Shins jerked her feet under her, rose, and lunged.

First the branch to which she'd clung, then the upper reaches of the fallen tree, passed beneath her. They waved, wobbled, threatened to spill her off, to turn an ankle or send her plummeting with every bend or imperfection in the bark. She had to narrow her eyes, raise her hands to ward the worst of the whipping foliage from her face. Agile as she was, as much of her life as she'd spent on tiny ledges or clinging to walls, she could never have managed more than a few steps without Olgun's aid.

The thing howled as it saw her coming, rising as straight and tall as it could on the precarious slope, spear held tight in both hands now, tip rising to meet her charge.

Pinpricks of Olgun's power beneath her boots, as though she left behind a trail of embers, she took two more steps and leapt.

It was impossible, what happened next, even for this incredible partnership of thief and god. Or it would have been, against any other, any human, any *natural* opponent.

But the creature's obscene musculature suggested an inhuman strength, and Shins now proved that theory right. With impeccable balance, she landed on the broad haft *of the spear itself*, and though the weapon bobbed downward at the unexpected weight, the monster kept from dropping it, kept it held close to horizontal.

She had only fractions of a second, but she needed less. Still at a full-out run, she closed half the remaining distance and leapt once more.

Everything slowed, or so it felt. The breeze fell still; the rustling of the leaves grew hushed. She saw the creature tilting back, fighting to keep its eye on her, to bring its spear up behind her in her flight.

Hands reached out, snagging the beast's horn. Her grip secure, Widdershins swung her feet forward, spinning around the horn like a dance partner, the entirety of her weight and her momentum hauling back on the creature's head.

Strong it might be, but it still required solid footing.

The creature rocked, dropped its spear in a mad scrabble for balance—and toppled, wailing, down the slope.

The first fall slammed its back against the trunk, bark and skin both cracking at the impact. The second—as it must have, given the curve of the bole itself—came when the creature slid off the side and plummeted to the earth. The *whump* when it hit was almost tectonic; breath blasted from its lungs, and its single pupil grew wide and unfocused.

Panting a bit, Widdershins huddled farther down the sloped tree, where she and Olgun had barely managed to right themselves before she, too, took a short journey in a bad direction. The fall hadn't killed the thing—she could see that even from here—but then, she hadn't expected it to.

It *did* appear stunned, momentarily, and that would have to do. After it practically shrugged off the flintlock ball, Shins had been unsure if her rapier had even the faintest chance of penetrating its hide.

If the thing would lay still for just a moment, though, it wouldn't have to.

Shins drew her sword, measured the distance between her new perch and the earth, and dubbed it workable. Then she plunged.

The inhuman thing thrashed once only as the steel slid through its lone eye and into the brain beyond.

Knees throbbing from the hard landing, shaking as the last of Olgun's energies faded and his fatigue mixed and mingled with her own, Widdershins straightened. She groaned once, low and quiet, then winced at the squeal of steel on bone as she yanked her weapon free.

"Okay, Olgun," she began, pressing at the twisted muscles near the small of her back, "what in the name of every god is going—?"

The body *melted*.

Like a snowman in the hot sun, but accelerated, the dead creature dissolved away in less than half a minute. Rivulets of liquid—well, liquid monster—dribbled away in snaking curves. From there it evaporated, forming tiny puffs and walls of mist before vanishing utterly.

Even stranger, however, the corpse very quickly split into two smaller bodies as it faded. Shins clearly saw the melting, dissolving substance form a pair of humanoid shapes, as though one had been standing atop the other in some sort of monstrous costume.

That was rubbish, of course; she'd seen enough, felt enough, to know the creature had been quite solidly real. Still, she clearly and distinctly saw what she saw.

"Olgun? What just happened?"

Confusion and bewilderment formed the bulk of his answer, but Shins could not possibly miss the fear mixed within—or, perhaps most importantly, the nagging sense of familiarity.

"You've seen this before?" she asked incredulously. The only thing she could think of that was even vaguely similar was a spell she'd experienced last year, allowing two people to share their strength, and even that was a far cry . . .

But no, Olgun hadn't meant anything that concrete. Finally, sifting through the sensations, she realized it was something about the magic of the creature—its basic nature, yes, but even more so its disappearance—that reminded him of something. It frustrated him more than a little that he couldn't place what it was.

"Come on," Shins told him, forcing a lightness she didn't feel. "Let's go collect that horse so the poor thing doesn't starve, and find somewhere to bunk down for the night. I want to make Davillon tomorrow, okay?"

Home. It was a lovely thought, one with which the tiny god firmly agreed. So they moved once more into the woods, each of them pretending not to know precisely what the other was thinking.

They both remembered, all too well, what entities of the supernatural the two of them had encountered in their time. Even if Olgun couldn't quite identify the magics he had sensed, if it was familiar to him at all, it was absolutely, positively nothing they ever wanted to face again.

CHAPTER THREE

Rain fell in fat, slow, cold drops, like snow or hail with second thoughts. It drummed on the leaves, drummed on the soil, drummed on Widdershins's sodden hood, until the day sounded as dull and gray as it looked.

"How about we trade?" she asked, tugging on that hood with one hand, the reins with the other. "*You* can wander around getting soaked, trying to figure out if you should be breathing the air or drinking it, and *I'll* ride around nice and dry in *your* head, for a change!"

And then, having gotten more or less the response she antici-pated, "Oh, shut up." She twisted to look back over her shoulder. "You! Tell Olgun to shut up."

The horse sneezed on her. Olgun howled, laughing until he couldn't breathe—which wasn't really an issue, since he *didn't* breathe, but was still saying quite a bit.

"Perfect. Just wonderful." Shins gave some thought to wiping the back of her tunic clean, but decided to just let the rain take care of it. "I hope you two will be very happy together."

Olgun continued to snicker, the horse continued to shiver and snort, and Widdershins continued to grumble as the road rolled on beneath feet and hooves.

Until, finally, the curtain of weather drew back enough to display the last winding stretch of highway and the glistening, rain-drenched walls of Davillon. High above, a tiny fissure in the lowering clouds allowed a single ray of sunlight to shine through, reflecting from the watery sheen to cast the city in a faint golden glow.

Shins, Olgun, and even—so it seemed—the horse stared in sheer incredulity. "You have *got* to be kidding me," the young woman said finally. "Olgun?"

All he could do was shrug those nonexistent shoulders. It wasn't him; it wasn't magic. Just a genuine, if dramatic—well, grossly *melo*dramatic—coincidence of the elements.

"Guess you're not the only god who *thinks* he's got a sense of humor." She sniffed once, almost haughtily, and resumed her trek—for about a dozen muddy, squelching steps. Then she halted again, squinting through the rain, raising a hand to protect her face from the moisture her hood failed to catch.

Was that . . . ? It was so hard to see—at this distance, only the pool of light she'd just scoffed at made it possible at all—but it certainly looked as though . . .

"Is it me," she asked softly, "or is the gate shut?"

The god's power surged, and the landscape seemed to flash by to either side. Her vision supernaturally sharpened, Widdershins could no longer harbor any doubt. The massive doorway into the greatest of Galice's southern cities was well and firmly closed.

Shins couldn't see the sun, of course; hadn't all day. Still and all, she knew her sense of the time couldn't be *too* far off. It was a few hours past noon, still early for the many merchants and shoppers who would stick around after the bulk of the markets had closed down, hoping to finagle special bargains for themselves. And that trade was fed, during all but the winter months, by a steady feed of goods from outside.

Never, in Shins's memory, had the gates been shut before dusk.

Nor was that the only abnormality she noticed, now that she could see. Sentries stood below, in and around the watch-house by the gate; and sentries stood above, patrolling atop the narrow wall. Just as always.

But their numbers were *not* just as always. Shins didn't bother doing a head count, but she figured there were at *least* twice as many soldiers on duty as she'd have expected; possibly nearer to three times. If the other gates were equally overstaffed, the thief couldn't imagine how the Guard could have enough other people on duty to even *begin* to keep the peace inside.

Then again, the sentinels clearly didn't expect anything remotely resembling "peace," either inside or out. Shins was accustomed to the traditional armament of the City Guard: a simple rapier and a so-called "bash-bang," a heavy pistol with a stock of reinforced brass rather than wood, to double as a brutally effective skull-cracker. And she did see those here, yes, but so, too, did she see guards wearing braces or bandoliers of additional, smaller flintlocks. She saw long-barreled muskets and gape-mawed blunderbusses; the wire-wrapped hilts of main-gauches or other secondary blades.

No enemy showed itself on the surrounding field, no damage scored the walls, but the men and women who stood watch appeared to be defending against a full-on siege.

"What do you think?" Shins asked, then shook her head almost before the image of the cyclopean beast faded. "No, I don't think so. I don't see any signs it's gotten anywhere near the city, and the Houses sure as all fungus aren't going to close the gates over a rumor. For pastries' sake, even if that thing or something like it *had* gotten here? My one shot couldn't drop it, but I'm pretty sure a whole fusillade or a cannonball would, yes?

"No, something else is going on here. That thing, or things, on the road was part of it. *Were* part of it? Does language have half-plurals? Anyway, that thing's part of it—too much of a coincidence for it not to be—but there's more.

"Heh. Mystery, confusion, and violence. Must be Davillon."

Still she stood. Studied. Soaked in the rain.

And then decided to play a hunch.

"Home!" She dropped the bridle and gave the roan a light slap on the haunches. "Home!" she shouted again.

Without a single look back, the horse trotted forward, head hunched against the weather, making for the gate.

The voices of the sentries rang out in challenge, falling quickly into a confused babble as they realized the animal was riderless. Several guardsmen braved the rain, emerging from the shack to examine the peculiar traveler.

And examine it they did. Shins had never observed as thorough a search of entrants to the city—human, animal, or vehicle—as she saw now. They removed the tattered bits of harness, checking carefully beneath. They examined the horse's teeth, its shoes. A short argument erupted, and only when one young sentry shuffled around, sullenly and nervously, to grip the beast's tail did Shins realize where *else* they were searching.

"I am going to turn away, now," Widdershins announced, as she did just that. "And *you* are going to swear to never, ever, put that image back in my head, or I will find a priest to bless a cabinet and so help me, I will lock you in a drawer."

She knew full well that Olgun's silence meant only that he was humoring her, but she decided it'd do.

The horse would be fine, if perhaps somewhat mortified. Either they'd find some kin to the owner, if the torn harness gave them enough to go on, or they'd take it for use by the city. Probably the latter. Shins didn't have any particular attachment to the animal, but she was still inordinately proud of having saved it.

So, what next? Shins was fairly certain that any search the guards subjected her to wouldn't be as—invasive—as the horse's. Nevertheless, they were clearly on higher alert, more meticulous about visitors, than she'd ever known them to be, and she wasn't keen on the notion of being interrogated in general, or in trying to explain her professional tools in particular. And that was assuming none of the guards recognized her. Widdershins wasn't precisely one of Davillon's most notorious criminals, but she *was* a known Finder, and she'd lost her only real friend in the Guard when—

No. Don't think of that right now.

Well, there really was only one option. If she wasn't willing to risk the procedure for passing *through* the wall, she'd just have to go *over* it. Not as though it'd be the first time.

"Aw, come on," she said to Olgun's surge of protest. "What's the worst that could happen?"

When his reply took the form of an image in which Widdershins was blasted clear off the wall by a volley of musket-fire, she merely grumbled something even the god could neither hear nor interpret, and wandered back down the road to wait for nightfall.

Heavily wooded as the region was, the grounds surrounding Davillon were largely flat and empty. What few trees remained all stood alone, or at most tiny copses, providing no hiding spot or significant cover for any attacking force. Not that Davillon had *faced* an attacking force since the nation of Galice was born, but one never knew.

During the day, approaching unobserved was quite impossible, assuming the sentries were semiconscious and had remembered to bring at least one eye with them that morning. At night . . . well, thanks to whatever had the place on such high alert, it was *barely* possible.

Men and women of the Guard walked the walls, stood by every gate, watching for any sign of movement, any conspicuous shape, in the shadows. Enormous lanterns stood at strategic intervals at both the top and the base of the wall. Contained within a mirrored shell, essentially a vertical bowl, they shed their illumination in only a single direction, a beam rather than an aura. These slowly rotated, sweeping back and forth across the open terrain. The arc of each lantern overlapped with the next, ensuring that no stretch of earth remained in darkness for more than a minute or so. In her younger thieving years, Shins had heard rumors that the Guard possessed such capability, but the equipment hadn't been used in generations.

Until now.

Of course, those defenses and that system had been designed to detect approaching enemies—plural. A single figure, clad in dark hues to match the gloom, possessed of any real speed and halfway decent luck, could pass between the shifting beams with little difficulty.

"You know," Shins sub-vocalized as she leaned against the great stone wall, listening to the steps and the voices above, "if they'd just randomize the lights a bit, not run them through those same arcs all the time, they might just . . . what? No, I don't want them to catch *us*! I meant for, you know, *other* people! Dangerous ones! It's definitely a problem they should fix . . . *later*.

"Well, yeah," she continued as fingers and toes found purchase that most people would never have seen, let alone been able to use. Her ascent was swift and silent, not much louder than a caterpillar making the same journey. "I *do* think the laws should only apply to other people. I mean, you know that *I* can be trusted, but we don't know that about anyone else, do we? Frankly, with all I've done for this city, they really should have thought of that themsel—"

Olgun's silent squawk of warning froze her in place, a bit more than halfway. She pressed herself tight to the stone, willing herself to be a lump of rock. Above her, a bit of scraping and slow breath suggested that one of the guards had chosen almost that exact spot to lean against the parapet and stare out into the darkness. He had no cause to glance straight down—but if, by ill chance, he did, there was nothing even Widdershins's skills could do to hide.

Her fingers and calves began to burn, then threatened to shake. She'd intended the various nooks and crannies and imperfections in the stone to support her just long enough to catch hold of the next. Now that she was trying to support her weight at a standstill, those niches weren't nearly as large or as secure as they had been.

"Olgun . . ."

The tension in her digits eased with the rush of additional strength, but she'd only bought herself moments. She was just about to ask the little god to do something a bit more dramatic—make the guy think he heard something elsewhere, perhaps, or set off a nearby firearm to draw attention—when the problem solved itself. The sentry heaved a phlegmy sigh, hawked up and spit something over the edge—missing Shins by about the distance of a housefly's sneeze—and wandered off to resume his patrol.

"You're getting too old for this," Shins whispered. Then, at Olgun's protest, "Well, *one* of us clearly is! And it can't be me, because I'm younger than you are!

"What? Don't be silly; of *course* gods age! If you didn't, you'd be too *young* for this, and you're clearly not."

At which point Olgun firmly decided that more important things than this conversation demanded his full attention.

Another tense moment, as Shins waited for Olgun's "all clear," then slowly peeked over the parapet. This stretch of walkway, startlingly dark behind the focused lanterns, indeed looked and sounded empty. The young woman scrambled over and across, quite steady despite the rain-slicked stone and occasional puddle collected earlier that day, and rolled over the barrier on the opposite side. Only then, once more affixed to the wall as if glued, did she look around to get her bearings.

"What the hopping . . . ?!"

At the base of the wall, more of those focused lanterns shone *into* Davillon, illuminating the approaching thoroughfares. Fewer than their counterparts above, a small group of guards stood watch inside the main gate, just as alert as the others, despite facing what should have been a safer direction.

"You're supposed to be able to do the impossible, yes?" Shins whispered finally. "So do it. Tell me one way this could possibly indicate anything *good*."

Olgun, as she'd anticipated, had nothing.

"Figured. All right, try this one. What do you think the odds are that this *isn't* related to the Guild hunting for me? Because I don't think numbers actually go that low."

Scurrying down the rest of the way and slipping unseen into the shadows across the road proved uncomplicated enough. Just as well, really, since Shins had proved utterly incapable of keeping her mind on the task. Even as she vanished into the winding streets, leaving the wall behind, she grumbled and fretted about the mysteries surrounding her, here in this city that was feeling ever more unfamiliar and ever less like home.

Perched on a window ledge that might well have given a cat pause— or at least required cat paws—Shins watched the small squad move on down the street below, their boot heels shouting a peculiar sort of *click-splash* with every step. She was only vaguely aware of chewing a lock of her hair, a habit she thought she'd shaken a year ago.

"How many patrols is that?"

Olgun indicated there had been six.

"Really?" Shins began idly peeling splinters off the edge of the rough wood beneath her. "Feels like twice that." But then, six was still three or four more than she'd have expected to see in the brief span since she'd entered the city.

Peering from inside the mouths of alleys or from atop small, rundown buildings, Shins hadn't really gotten a good look at any of them until the fourth such group. Up to that point, she'd been intensely curious as to how the Guard could possibly field so many soldiers at once, especially given how many were stationed atop or along the wall.

Then that fourth patrol had passed directly beneath a streetlamp, answering the thief's question and presenting her with a whole new host of worries.

The light shone, not on the black and silver of the Guard, but on tabards of sky-blue and white, colors Shins recognized immediately as belonging to House Poumer.

Private armsmen. The city government had either called upon house soldiers to assist in keeping the peace, or the Houses had elected to do so and the city had been powerless to prevent them. Either way, it explained the extra manpower but raised a whole legion of additional questions that Shins would really rather not have considered.

Plus, the last time she'd dealt with private house guards, back in the Outer Hespelene, it had not proved a pleasant experience.

"Olgun, what the happy hens is going on here?" And then, "Yes, I *am* going to keep asking. And you're the one with knowledge of the ages, so you tell me. How many ways *are* there to say 'I don't know'?"

Only when the patrol had been lost to sight for a good few minutes did she descend to the street, making her way deeper into the neighborhood. The place deteriorated with every additional step. Staircases sagged; garbage grew thick along the roadway; cobblestones became ever more sporadic, finally giving way to hard-packed dirt; and the air gradually yielded to what certainly smelled like the various internal gasses of a dog's back end.

It didn't turn her stomach any less than it would someone else's, but it was a familiar, homey sort of nausea.

Not that her destination was really "home," but it'd do in a pinch.

Widdershins had very seriously considered heading straight for the Flippant Witch. *That* was home, so far as she was concerned, and she was greatly anxious to see old friends. Ultimately, it was vanity that got in her way. She'd been traveling for a very long time, and her clothes were near to demanding that she pay rent. Better to wash up and change first, lest Robin and the others mistake her for a vagrant or perhaps something from beyond the grave.

She'd let many of them go after taking up ownership of the Flippant Witch, but Shins still maintained a few boltholes throughout Davillon: cheap, rundown flats where she could store funds and equipment or spend a few nights where nobody would know to look for her. It was one of those—not directly on her route to the Witch, but only moderately out of the way—that she approached now.

When she reached the building, her eyes only lightly stinging from the local miasma, it looked much as it always had. The external staircase sagged a bit more than it used to, maybe, and even more of the windows were boarded up, but otherwise little had changed. The façade was just as grimy as ever, but that was fine; Shins was pretty sure it was load-bearing dirt, anyway.

The framework creaked alarmingly with every step she took—and that was *with* Olgun's assistance!—but Shins reached the third floor without incident. She pushed through the outer door, which was connected to only a single hinge, and that more by sentiment than genuine attachment, and entered a hallway made almost entirely of rickety. The cobwebs, she was sure, were primarily for the ambiance, as most spiders had too much self-respect to live here.

"Be it ever so horrible . . ." Shins began, before a flicker of someone else's curiosity stopped her. "What?"

Then again, "What? No, nothing. How can you smell *anything* over all the garbage and apathy? Ugh. I guess you'd better give me a hand, then. Or a nostril. How would you even describe helping someone to smell something? Has anyone before us ever even *needed* to describe helping someone to smell so*ghaaaaoourghthkt!*"

Said noise was, most probably, caused by the letters attempting to flee Widdershins's head. The stench of the building, the neighborhood, the streets, had been bad enough already. Now, after she'd felt the familiar tingle of her partner's power, it flooded her nose, her mouth, her lungs. She felt as though she'd just tried to inhale an athlete's armpit. Through a used diaper.

Before the horrific fetor could reach her gut, an event that could only have resulted in the addition of yet another foul odor to the hall, Olgun narrowed the scope of his "nasal assistance." Just as he'd aided her in the past in focusing in one particular sound or sight, so now did he sweep aside any extraneous scent, if only briefly. Widdershins slowly straightened, sniffing like a curious kitten.

"Yeah, something definitely doesn't belong here. It's almost . . . I'm not sure. Floral?"

Tentative agreement from her partner.

Whatever that scent wafted from, it wasn't in the hallway proper. The bouquet was such that, even over the other lingering odors, Shins wouldn't have needed Olgun's help to detect it if it were.

Inside one of the rooms, then.

She crept by a few of them, past doors that were no more than uneven slabs of half-rotted wood, nailed to makeshift hinges, until she arrived at one in particular. One that hung just a few inches open, when she *knew* she'd securely latched it last time she was here.

Shins was angered at the invasion of her sanctum, confused as to how anyone might have found it, but she wasn't at all *surprised*. Soon as she realized something was out of place in one of the apartments, she knew which it would be.

Rapier unsheathed and at the ready, Olgun's senses reaching out to warn her of any threat she might miss, Shins nudged the door open a hair more and slipped inside.

Basically a room and a half, the flat was largely open, with only a smattering of furniture. It was the perfume that hit her first. And it *was* perfume, that scent; she could tell, now that it was stronger, more direct. Too much and too spread out to be the lingering traces of someone who'd passed through, or even the result of a spill. No, this strong, this evenly spread—someone had very deliberately sprinkled perfume across the place.

So what did you not want anyone outside to smell, you motherless frogs?

No enemies by the door or lurking in the shadows with a pistol, and a quick Olgun-enhanced glance revealed no tripwires or other booby traps. Safe from any immediate danger—probably—Shins crossed the room, heading for the nook in which her bed, chests, and various accoutrements awaited.

No ambush. No trap. So far as she could tell, no theft, and anyway, the only stuff worth stealing was carefully hidden away. So what the—?

Shins smacked a palm to her mouth to keep from shouting aloud. There was someone—some*thing*!—in the bed.

Unwilling to give the intruder more time to react, Shins turned her startled jump into a forward leap, coming down beside the mattress. Her rapier was already winging outward when Olgun's cry of alarm actually registered. She couldn't quite cut her thrust short, but she did manage to twist her wrist aside, so the blade punched into the filthy pillow rather than the . . .

She gawped downward, leaning on the rapier's pommel, her throat working silently.

A corpse. Someone had intruded into Shins's apartment—well, one of them—for apparently no other purpose than to lay a corpse atop her mattress, head propped on pillow and blankets tucked neatly under its chin.

"Well, we. . . . It's about time to buy a new set of linens anyway, yes? Or steal. Yeah, maybe steal a set."

Olgun allowed her to go on, and Widdershins was grateful that he pretended not to notice the tremor in her voice.

She'd been around corpses before, far too often—had even made some herself—but rarely any that were this *mature*. Clearly the perfume had been intended to ensure nobody discovered the body early; the floral scent might have been odd, but a rotting cadaver would eventually attract attention even in this rundown pustule of a building.

But it was almost unnecessary. The body smelled more of dirt and dust than decay; whoever this poor guy might be, he'd clearly been dead for well over a year. Little remained but shriveled, parchment skin coating brittle bones. He'd been someone of means, or of import; that the skin remained relatively whole suggested the use of preservatives and embalming agents that simply weren't affordable to any but the aristocracy. Even had she lacked that hint, Shins could tell—as badly decomposed as they were—that the burial clothes had been of the highest quality.

"I don't get any of this," she confessed to her god, turning her back on the bed and its vile occupant. "I mean, it's some kind of threat. That much is obvious, yes? But what? And . . ."

Olgun tugged at her awareness, trying to get her attention, but in her preoccupation she shrugged it off without noticing.

". . . from who? Most of the people I've pissed off would just try to hit me with something heavy. Or set me on fire. Or . . ."

The god was all but waving his arms and shouting now, which was impressive for an entity without limbs or voice.

". . . hit me with something on fire. And for pastry's sake, *how*? How did they find this place?! How did they know—?"

A crackle of power raced through the air around Widdershins as Olgun literally dragged her attention over to the bed. It was, as best she might have described, like he had threaded a hook through her senses—not her eyes, but her *sight and hearing themselves*—and yanked her around by them.

"*Ow!* Dogs grommet, Olgun, what are you—?! What? No, I think I've gotten as close to that corpse as I'm going. . . . Oh, for . . . *fine!*"

Grumbling furiously, as much to distract herself from the fear and revulsion, Shins moved to the bedside and leaned over, studying the body far more intently than she preferred.

"All right, I'm here. It's . . ." Something tiny and black, with far too many legs, skittered out from a rent in the leathery skin and vanished behind the bed. "Show me what you think is so hopping important," Widdershins demanded through clenched teeth and a sudden sweat, "or I am walking out of here."

With a startling gentleness, given his earlier insistence, Olgun guided her focus to the head.

It meant nothing to her, initially. The rictus grin and gaping sockets were utterly unrecognizable as whoever this might once have been. The face, if face it could still be called, meant nothing.

At this distance, though . . . at this distance, there was something about the overall shape of the head. Something nagging at her, scratching at a door to awareness that she abruptly knew she did *not* want to open.

"Olgun . . ." She was pleading, and she didn't even know what for. Waves of caring, of sympathy, washed over her, and broke against the rock-hard tightness in her soul.

It was then, only then, that she noticed—that she allowed herself to notice—the dull and faded colors on what remained of the corpse's finery. What had once been a deep red, a dark blue, a wine purple.

A scream pierced her ears, so loud it was agony; her throat burned, rough and raw, but Widdershins lacked even the facility to put those facts together, to recognize the cry as her own. Like a madwoman—no, not "like," for in that moment, she *was*—she yanked the sheet from the bed, sending it fluttering across the room. She clawed desperately at the corpse's hand. Patches of papery skin flaked off in her fingers, drifted to cling to her clothes, and she didn't care. She was beyond disgust, beyond revulsion, beyond everything but the hunt she wanted so terribly to fail.

It didn't.

The ring slipped from the body with a faint pop, taking the finger with it. And there it was, embossed into the signet, just as she'd known it would be, needed it not to be.

A lion's head in a domino mask.

Trembling violently, spots dancing before her eyes, Widdershins staggered back from the bed. From the bed and from the body of the kindest man she'd known, her adopted father in all but name, Alexandre Delacroix.

CHAPTER FOUR

She couldn't breathe. Couldn't think. Primal screams and wracking sobs, a wounded animal lashing out at anything within reach. Jagged rents in her glove, and the flesh beneath it, wept crimson runnels down her fingers to splatter across the filthy floorboards. It barely registered at all, and when it did, she only vaguely made the connection between that pain and the jagged hole punched into the flimsy wood of the wall.

Her gut burned, hot, corrosive. The room tilted, until she couldn't understand how she failed to tumble and slide across the floor. She spun, trying to toss her sword across the chamber, but either the twist itself or the fact that she succeeded only in yanking herself sideways by a scabbard still firmly fastened to her belt sent her reeling to the floor. There she lay in a gangly tangle, chest heaving, face drenched with sweat and tears. The shrieking had finally subsided, replaced by soft, mewling, primal sounds.

Only then, finally, was she able to feel Olgun's touch, his frantic efforts to reassure her, to calm her. Even without the need for words, with the emotions washing directly through her, they felt distant and meaningless.

Until she sensed the tiniest flicker of the fury beneath it. A divine rage, feeding off of and feeding into her own, roaring just below the surface. A rage that Olgun fought tooth and nail to control, to hide from the reassurances he offered her.

And *that* was enough. If he could make that effort for her, she could do it for him. She took no peace from it, no comfort, but what it could provide her was *control*.

Clutching the furniture, her breath coming more slowly albeit still in ragged gasps, she staggered upright. A careful check of her sword, and her injuries, first. Then, gaze carefully averted, she felt around until she located the ring. Shaking its gruesome burden free, she wiped it clean on one corner of the sheet and slipped it on her own hand. With the glove, her finger was large enough to wear the band with little chance of slippage.

Only then did she allow herself—or was it force herself?—to look once more over the bed. Emotion roiled up inside her again; she clamped down, hard, nearly suffocating before it subsided.

"I'm going to find whoever did this to you, Alexandre. And I'm going to kill him."

Widdershins had never been casual about death. She'd killed, yes, but only under the most violent or extreme of circumstances. Yet her promise here was cold, as matter of fact, as stone.

She very carefully latched and locked the door on her way out, though she knew it wouldn't stop anyone sufficiently determined. Scuffs and whispers sounded from the other flats as she passed down the hallway. The morbidly curious, no doubt, their attention drawn by her earlier screams, but wise enough not to open their doors until they knew the place was safe.

Safe as it ever got, anyway.

One door did open, just a crack, revealing only blackness and the dull yellow-white reflection of a single curious eye. Shins snarled something, deep and unintelligible, and it quickly slammed shut.

Back down the stairs, not pounding or stomping, no, but certainly without her earlier caution. They quaked, groaning with the effort of clinging to the wall against which they'd sagged for so long. Shins didn't notice, didn't care.

The sky above, the one time she glanced upward—searching, perhaps, for guidance—held no stars. Just gray on black, a night choking on clouds. The moon, presumably bright and crisp beyond the overcast, was to her nothing more than a careless thumb-smear of lighter hue against the darkness.

It felt appropriate. The world tonight *should* be shrouded, shadowed, black as Widdershins's thoughts and intentions.

"I don't know!" she snapped at an almost tentative question from her partner. She knew, could hear it in his not-voice, that he forced himself to calm, shared her fury but held it at bay so he might balance out her own. To continue feeding her some measure of control.

Her reaction even to that, though understanding and even grateful, was tinged with irritation. She *wanted* to lose herself to her anger, or part of her did; felt that it might just be the only way, in the long run, to stay sane.

"I don't know," she repeated—more calmly, if only by a sliver. "I don't know who would, or who *could*. How they knew about the bolthole, or my connection to Alexandre. And no, I don't have the first idea how we're going to figure it out. But purple, steaming pits, I *am* going to find them, no matter what it—"

"You, there! Halt where you are!"

Had the racket she'd made up in the apartment carried? Had someone in the building actually gone for help? Or was their appearance here sheer happenstance? Didn't really matter, she decided. Whatever drew them, here they were: a half-dozen guards, tromping around a distant corner and down the street toward her.

And they *were* proper guards, this patrol, not private house soldiers as some of the prior squads had been. During most of Shins's life, that wouldn't have been a good thing, but at the moment, it made them a tad more predictable, if nothing else.

Actually, come to think of it . . .

Shins held her hands to her sides, not a posture of submission or surrender, and not only made no effort to flee into the Davillon night, she actually began walking *toward* the oncoming guards!

"We'll let them do some of the work for us," she responded to

Olgun's bewildered squawk. "I doubt they'll find anything, but if they're taking care of all the little details of an investigation, we can focus on more important stuff." Much louder, she politely announced, "I'm so glad you're here, officers. I need to report a crime."

"In this neighborhood? Who doesn't?" They crashed to a halt a few arms-lengths away. Their leader, the absolute spitting image of what a guard "should" be—his black and silver tabard flawless, his medallion of Demas polished to a shine, his hair and thick mustache meticulously trimmed—advanced an extra step and touched a finger to the wide brim of his hat in a polite but perfunctory greeting. "Kindly identify yourself, mademoiselle?"

"Clarice deMonde," she responded immediately. Not one of her usual or preferred aliases, but it *was* the false name under which she'd rented this festering roach-trap of a flat. And her preferred alter ego, Madeleine Vallois, wouldn't have been caught dead *thinking* of a neighborhood like this one, let alone in it.

Granted, *any* false identity would have been more believable if she wasn't still wearing road-dusted leathers, but . . .

"And what appears to be the trouble, Mademoiselle deMonde?"

"Well, uh . . . Constable . . . ?"

"Lieutenant," he corrected.

When it became clear that he was not, in fact, going to append a name to that title, Shins continued. "Right. Lieutenant, someone broke into my rooms and left . . ." She choked off, very much *not* part of her act, overwhelmed again for an instant at the thought of Alexandre's desecrated rest.

In that window of opportunity, one of the younger guards called out. "Excuse me, Lieutenant Donais?"

The patrol's commander sighed and only half turned. "Can this wait, Constable? I'm just in the midst of something."

"Uh, I don't think so, sir." Clearly tentative, nervous, but he didn't let that stop him. "Please, sir, I just need a moment."

"Very well." Another cursory hat tip—more of a hat nudge, really. "Your brief pardon, mademoiselle."

"Of course." She barely waited until his back was turned before calling on her god in the faintest breath. By the time Donais had reached the young soldier who'd called to him, Shins was able to hear their words clearly, despite the distance and the low whispers.

"Sir, I think it's *her*!"

Well, figs. That wasn't a hopeful start.

The lieutenant, it appeared, had little more idea of what his underling meant than Shins did. "Her who, Constable?"

"From that notice Maj—I mean, Commandant Archibeque was passing around a few weeks ago. She's wanted . . ."

What? I shouldn't still have any warrants!

". . . for murder," the young constable concluded.

Shins's throat did something that, as best she could tell, was an attempt to swallow her ears in shock.

"Now that you mention it—" Donais began.

I don't think I'm going to stick around for explanations, the thief decided. "Olgun? Bang."

At the rear of the patrol, one unfortunate soldier's bash-bang discharged; it'd been trickier than normal, as the hammer wasn't cocked, but Olgun had long since mastered the technique. The flintlock launched itself from the bandolier, going one way, while the ball tumbled off in the other. Slightly singed by the flash and startled so severely his first child would be born quivering, the constable screamed, high and piercing.

More than enough, the lot of it, to attract the sudden and complete attention of every man and woman in the patrol.

Widdershins bolted like a kicked cat, her skin humming and prickling with Olgun's magics.

Her tenth step (or so) came down on a remarkably solid chunk of nothing whatsoever. Boosted by her deity's will, she leapt from that impossible spot, easily clearing the first floor of the nearest building. Tucking in tight, she landed snug in a windowsill of the second floor, arms outstretched to grab the edges, toes barely finding purchase between the edge and the old wooden boards. The entire ledge groaned, and she could feel it starting to shift beneath her.

The soldiers, of course, had turned their focus back toward her, but as of yet, between the distraction Olgun had arranged and the utter impossibility of what they'd just witnessed, none of them had managed to target her.

"If *that* bothered them . . ." she whispered. "You ready?"

Rather than provide a stationary target for even a heartbeat longer, she jumped without waiting for Olgun's reply.

Not up for the third (and uppermost) story; not back to earth; not even for the ramshackle house across the street. No, Widdershins launched herself sideways, paralleling the wall to which she'd just clung. Propelled by her own acrobatic skill and a helping of divine might, she would easily clear the building's corner, leaving her with nothing to grab onto, nowhere but the open street to land.

Except she and Olgun had other ideas.

Just as she started to clear the wall, she slapped both hands against the corner. It was an impossible grab, should have been nothing more than her futilely smacking the wall as she hurtled past. Using a variant of the same trick he'd used many times to give her an invisible leg up, Olgun braced her fingers against the stone, *just* enough so that—flat and straight as they were—they managed to find purchase.

A hard yank, also augmented by her guardian deity, and Shins flipped around the corner, heels over head—a somersault turned on its ear, performed sideways in apparent defiance of gravity and momentum both.

Even Olgun couldn't defy said forces for more than an instant, though. The trick had yanked Shins out of the guards' sights (and line of fire) far faster than they could have anticipated, but not even she could regain a hold on the wall after that. Teeth gritted, she braced herself, twisting so that at least she landed on her feet when she struck the roadway. Ignoring the protests in her knees and the burning ache in both arms, she took off at a dead run. A quick left, as soon as she'd cleared the dilapidated structure, and then another after that, found her standing directly behind the spot the guards had been gathered only a moment before.

They, of course, having given chase, were now on the other side of the building, wondering where their quarry could have disappeared to.

Wondering what else could possibly go wrong, and why everyone seemed to have it out for her—even more than usual—Widdershins disappeared down the nearest side street, casually but carefully making her way toward the busier parts of town.

She needed time to think. Needed to know what in the name of Banin's belt was happening in this madhouse of a city. Needed a chance to rest, and to talk to a friendly face.

And with everything else going on, that could only mean one place.

❋

Even the Flippant Witch had changed.

Not from the outside, no. It remained the same old structure, battered and worn but determined to keep on keeping on. Light glowed between the slats of the window shutters, smoke dribbled from the chimneys, and the muted hum of conversation reached her even from across the way.

Initially, it seemed as though things were far better than when she'd left. Even if she hadn't seen the constant comings and goings through the tavern's front door, it was quite apparent that the place was far more crowded, doing far better business than she'd seen in the months prior to her departure. In a Davillon that had apparently lost what remained of its mind, Shins was delighted to see that Robin had, to all appearances, turned the place completely around.

That notion, and the resulting grin, both lasted just about as long as it took her to mount the steps and enter the common room itself.

It *was* packed; it *was* busy. But not at all in the way she remembered from the good old days. The scents of various libations, though always strong, now utterly choked out everything else, including the aromas she should have smelled from the kitchen. People were drinking more and eating less, and had been for some time. The place was uncomfortably warm, despite the chill air outside, and there was a sourness to the stench of sweat that Shins's recollections did not include. Even the conversation was wrong. Loud and boisterous as always, yes, but heavier. A false note here, a spark of anger there. Most of these people had come to escape their lives, not to carouse and catch up with friends.

A few faces brightened as they turned her way, old regulars happy to see her, raising hands or tankards in greeting. Those Shins returned with a smile almost alarming in its cheer, so frantic was she to find *something* familiar.

The bulk of the throng, however, tossed her the same glance they offered any other newcomer and sullenly went back to their cups. That the strangers didn't recognize her was to be expected, but more than a few regulars, those who hadn't offered their welcome, turned away just as swiftly.

How could they fail to even *recognize* her? Had they changed so much—or *she* changed so much—in less than a year?

Olgun's presence calmed her, a feeling very much like a comforting arm draped around her shoulders. She *probably* wouldn't have just turned around and left without it—but she couldn't swear to it.

Still, she might well have considered getting out, had a particularly friendly face not finally presented itself.

"Gerard!"

The burly, red-bearded barman—a fixture of the Flippant Witch since its earliest days under Genevieve Marguilles, before even Robin had been employed—peered curiously around the cluster of customers gathered before the bar. Too chaotic to be a queue, too narrow and winding to be a mob, it was effectively a "smear." Yes, a smear of patrons.

Gerard leaned around that smear, seeking the source of that call; when he saw her, Shins figured it had to be the beard itself that kept his jaw from swinging freely before dropping to the floor.

Maybe he braided it.

"Shins!" He waved her over, utterly losing track of the drink he was pouring at the time. Pushing, ducking, squeezing, elbowing, and occasionally Olgun-ing herself a path through the busy common room, Widdershins didn't hear whatever complaint the patron had made to Gerard regarding his lapse in attention, but she arrived soon enough to hear the tail end of the barman's reply.

". . . to own the place, you jackass! So unless you want a permanent ban—not to mention," he added with a meaningful gesture toward the thick cudgel he kept for emergencies, "a permanent *bang*—I suggest you take a few steps back, ponder our wide selection of fine aperitifs, and give *long* thought to what you want to order!"

She'd made it back behind the bar by the time Gerard had wound down, and the customer had huffed away, doubtless determined to go somewhere else to drink until it occurred to him just how much walking and how much not-drinking that would entail.

"Fine aperitifs?" she asked, eyebrow migrating upward.

"Yeah, well." Gerard shrugged. "Figured the big words would keep him off-balance, and it sounded better than 'our intestine-abrading fire-piss.'"

"Oh, what are *you* snickering at?" she demanded quietly in response to Olgun's burst of amusement. "You don't *have* intestines, and you don't piss! At least, I assume you don't. Do you? Because considering where you live, ew!" Then, to Gerard, "I was sort of looking for a middle ground, yes? Somewhere our drinks are neither ambrosia *nor* arsenic."

"You'll need to hire on a barman with a more sensitive palate, then. Or at least a broader vocabulary."

They stared, smirked, burst into a hearty laugh, and came together for a mismatched hug almost in perfect unison.

"I'm glad you're okay, Shins," he breathed into her ear.

Shins could only nod, overwhelmed. She and Gerard hadn't been *that* close, but right now the heavy squeeze, musky and alcoholic scent, even the tickling of beard against her head, were far and away the best welcome—the *only* welcome, really—she'd received thus far.

At the same time, while she'd no doubt at all that the embrace was heartfelt, and while she was hardly the foremost expert on Gerard's body language, his posture felt a bit guarded, his back stiff. Sooner than she might have preferred, he slowly disengaged, returning to deal with the ever-growing rumble of irate patrons.

"So, um. Business seems . . . good," she said weakly.

Pouring drinks and passing them on with a facility Shins never had mastered, Gerard responded over his shoulder. "Like this most evenings, these days. Bad times . . . well, the right *kind* of bad times," he corrected himself, referring, Shins knew, to the Church-driven recession of a while back. "They're good for places like ours, since folks drink more. Sounds hard, but that's the nature of things."

"It's not just the Witch, then?"

"Far's I know, every tavern in Davillon's raking it in."

"Gerard, what *is* happening in Davillon?"

"Politics. Crime. Superstitious rumor. Same as always, just . . . more of it."

Shins tapped a fingertip against her cheek, somehow felt Olgun doing much the same. She knew she could get a clearer answer out of the barman, and knew just as well that he'd resent her trying. This wasn't turning at all into the homecoming she'd anticipated.

And that made her even more apprehensive to ask the next question.

"Where's . . . ?" She swallowed, feeling a sudden burning need for one of the mugs Gerard was topping off. "Where's Robin?"

Was it a product of nervous imaginings, or did the man's back stiffen further at the sound of that name? Shins felt her heart begin to pound.

"Upstairs. The bigger bedchamber, one that you used to use."

The young woman almost melted all over the floor, so frightened had she been—given his reaction, and how unusual it was (or at least had been) for Robin not to manage the night shift herself—that Gerard's answer would be something far worse. She started for the far stairs . . .

"Shins?"

She glanced back, at a face shifted dramatically from rigid to sympathetic. "A lot can happen in almost a year. You should maybe . . . temper your expectations a little. I'll have a cup of something ready for you if you need it."

On the edge of losing it now even more than she had been, Olgun's efforts to calm her somewhat sabotaged by his own concern, Shins bolted up the steps, leaving a shuddering, dust-shedding staircase in her wake.

CHAPTER FIVE

She knew Robin must have heard her pounding up the steps. The whole tavern, if not the whole *street*, probably had. And she *absolutely* knew her friend had heard the knock on the door, because Robin had very distinctly called out, "Come in!" in a voice that Widdershins had forgotten how much she missed.

And for no reason she could put words to, no emotion she could identify in the swirling morass of all the others, Shins had to wrestle with the urge to run away. "Olgun, what the figs is wrong with me?"

She knew his response—which translated, if loosely, to "How much time do you have?"—was meant to cheer her up, or at least distract her from the bundle of nerves that now occupied most of her body. "Appreciate the thought," she told him, "but I think I'm kind of uncheerupable right now. And don't even *try* to tell me that's not a word! I dare you to find a better way to get that point . . ."

Enough. She was stalling and they both knew it. One very deep breath, and Widdershins pushed the door open with an only marginally unsteady hand.

"Hi, Robin."

The next few endless seconds were the strangest thing. For Shins, it was almost as if she viewed the tableau through a cracked sheet of glass, emphasizing this image, this movement, this part of the room, this *detail* over that.

Robin first and foremost, of course. The younger woman's features had gone slack, as though not merely shocked at what she saw but still uncertain she was truly seeing it. The freckles dusting her skin like confectioner's sugar were lighter than Shins remembered, her hair a bit longer. Perhaps most peculiarly, though, was her outfit. Never in Shins's life had she seen Robin in anything but drab tunic and trousers, the sort of clothes easily mistaken for a boy's at any distance. Tonight, her blouse, though still loose and simple, was a soft, lush green, and she wore a peculiar skirt, one that wrapped twice about her waist before fastening, of such deep crimson it was almost black.

Gaze directed, almost guided, to the perimeters of the room. All the furniture had been moved from how Shins remembered it. The bed was now turned sidelong to the wall against which it stood, rather than head-first; cheap wardrobe, cheap desk, also as far to one side as the chamber would permit. The result was a gaping open space in the center, several paces across.

And only then, as Shins believed her bewilderment had reached its peak, did she even notice the third person in the room!

Taller than Robin, she was, at a guess, probably closer to Widdershins's age, maybe older. Her hair was the sort of blonde that the old tales might have called gossamer or moonlight, but for which Shins was quite content with "blonde." She wore what looked very much like a fancier version of Robin's own clothes, topped with a tightly laced vest of black.

"Who . . . ?" Shins actually felt dizzy, turned her focus back to Robin, again began to ask, "Who . . . ?" And only then did her brain finally register the room's final surprise.

Robin leaned on a thick cane, her fingers going bloodless, so tightly were they pressed into the wooden grip.

Shins was not, quite clearly, the only one overwhelmed. That near-deathgrip suddenly trembling, Robin stumbled. Her old friend gasped, moved to catch her, but the stranger reached her first. She wrapped an arm around Robin's waist, steadying her, and even when the younger woman stood upright once more, the other kept a gentle, supporting hand on her shoulder.

Finally, it appeared Robin had pulled herself together, at least enough for words. "Widdershins?"

Shins almost broke, then and there. The thick concoction of doubt and fear, delight and hope, hurt and yearning and, yes, anger . . . it was a toxin, leeching into her heart, her lungs, her soul. Crying openly, she all but threw herself into her friend's arms, slowing only at the last second as she remembered Robin's unsteadiness and her cane. The stranger, once she was certain that Robin was not, in fact, to be knocked from her feet, glided a few steps backward, her own expression a blank mask.

And for a few intense, glorious moments, the two old friends held tight to one another and wept together.

Only for a few moments. Robin pulled back without warning, so quickly that it was Shins's turn to stagger. She caught herself, looked into her friend's face, jaw already moving to ask a question . . .

She saw, though Robin's face was wet with tears, that her lips had gone flat, her eyes flinty.

"I'm glad to see you're not hurt," the younger woman said in a near monotone. "We've been worried for a long time."

"Robin? I—"

"Did you just get in, Shins? You smell like a used saddle."

It was just the sort of comment Robin *would* have made in good humor, but there was nothing behind it here. These were the motions, and she was determined to go through them.

"Robin?" Shins tried again. "Are you . . . not happy to see me? Did I do someth—"

The other woman, standing back and silently seething this whole time, erupted. "Did you *do something*?!" Shins actually jumped at her voice, found herself backpedaling as the stranger advanced. "How can you even ask her that?! How *dare* you ask her that?!"

"What are you *talking* about, you crazy—?"

"Faustine," Robin said at the same time, but the woman didn't hear her.

"You *abandoned her*!" Faustine accused, her finger an angry dagger jutting at Shins's chest. "You were her best friend, her only family! The only one that made her feel *safe*! And you just walked out, leaving her to wonder if you were ever coming back, how she was going to make it, if you were even alive or dead! You selfish, heartless—!"

Shins saw nothing but fire, heard nothing in the pounding of her ears except the roar and crackle of that flame. Not since Aubier, where she learned her self-loathing anger and Olgun's own fury had enflamed one another, had she felt anything close to such rage. She hadn't thought herself capable of it, anymore, but here it was, sucking her in, wrapping its ugly tendrils tight about her.

She lashed out, fast and brutal, a blow that might well have caused this Faustine severe or lasting injury. Even as she attacked, however, Olgun was there; Olgun was always there, ready to save her from any danger. Even herself.

Flowing as if through a burst dam, a torrent of emotion crashed through her burning anger. Dredged from the depths of her mind, the nesting place of dreams, they flooded through her, summoned and guided by her own personal god.

And Shins knew—she *remembered*—with whom she was truly furious. Why Faustine's words had so viciously stung.

Because Widdershins had long accused herself of precisely the same thing.

No way, in that fraction of a second, for her to halt the strike she'd begun. Between her own reflexes and Olgun's aid, however, she was able to slow it, flatten her palm, transform what would have been a bruising, possibly bone-breaking blow into a vicious shove. The woman staggered back almost to the wall, nearly toppled, gasped in pain as she clutched her chest, but nothing more. Nothing worse.

"You have no idea!" Shins screamed, her fists tight and shaking. Even in her tirade, though, she couldn't miss Robin limping clumsily, awkwardly to Faustine's side. "You have no hopping idea what

I'd been through! What I'd seen! What I'd *lost*! I *had* to get out for a while! I *had* to—"

This time, when Faustine interrupted, her voice was calm, almost soft, yet wrapped around a core of jagged iron. "Had to walk away from someone who counted on you, someone who'd seen just as bad? Had to make sure that *she* lost someone, too?"

Shins felt Olgun stepping in again, ready to calm her down despite the ever-heating furnace of his own anger, but this time it wouldn't prove necessary. Faustine's words were a thick coat of frost filling Shins's, heart and throat, ice that even her lingering fury couldn't melt.

"Who *are* you?" she demanded when she finally could choke out a few words. "Why are you even *here*?"

It was Robin, however, who answered. Very deliberately, like a performer on stage, she transferred her cane to her other hand so she could wrap her right arm around Faustine's waist. "Faustine, this is Widdershins. You kind of figured that out. Shins, this is Faustine. My girlfriend." The words were an announcement, yes, but also a challenge, a gauntlet thrown at Widdershins's feet.

Shins, by this point, was beginning to feel as though she and her language skills had perhaps become separated, having lost track of one another back when they were being pursued by the guards. Her eyes blinked, her jaw went slack—or maybe it was the other way around; she was befuddled enough that it could have been—and yet another moment passed while she struggled to remember what her voice was for and how to use it.

"Girlf . . . what do you mean, girlfriend?"

"What does it *usually* mean?" Robin retorted. Then, as Shins continued to stare, unable to absorb so much at once, the younger girl sighed, wrapped her arms around Faustine's neck, and pulled her down until their lips met. Faustine stiffened, at first, quivering as though she wanted to run, then all but melted into the kiss.

"Sorry," Faustine muttered as they finally came up for air. Her face was flushed so deeply she looked more floral than animal. "I'm . . . still not used to other people seeing . . ."

"Shh. I know." Robin, still holding the other woman tight, turned again toward Widdershins. "Is *that* clear enough?" she demanded, somehow defiant. "Or do I need to slide her hand up my skirts?"

"Robin!" Faustine shouldn't have been able to go any redder, but she managed. It was a miracle enough blood remained in the rest of her body to keep her standing.

Widdershins's own shock and bewilderment, however, blew violently apart, a heap of leaves and twigs in a gale. She'd overplayed it, Robin had; she was *too* challenging, *too* hostile.

"You *want* me to have a problem with this," Shins accused. "You want me to be upset. Why? So you have another reason to be angry with me?"

"That's horseshit!" Robin's expression twisted, angry and ugly, but she also blushed faintly and couldn't quite seem to meet her friend's gaze.

With a final off-kilter frown at Robin, Faustine said, "It's not like she *needs* another reason, Widdershins."

"Why?! Look, just because I—!" Gently, perhaps even tentatively, Olgun directed her thoughts back to Robin's cane.

"I'm an idiot," Shins whispered. This time, Olgun didn't even make the obvious retort. "What happened, Robin?"

The girl wilted. Eyes downcast, she shuffled backward to sit in, almost fall into, the nearest chair. Still studying the floor, she hiked up her skirt—that skirt Widdershins had thought, from the moment she arrived, was so out of character—practically to her waist.

"Gods . . ." Hardly helpful, but Shins had no idea what else to say.

Robin's right thigh bore a grotesque wound, one Shins knew even at a glance must have been inflicted by some sort of blade. For all that it had scarred over, it clearly wasn't terribly old. The flesh, still faintly reddened, puckered and wrinkled around it, somehow obscene in its contours and bulges. The whole patch of flesh cratered inward a bit, as though a bit of the tissue beneath had just given up entirely and atrophied away.

"For days, nobody could tell us if I would live or die." Her words were bitter, throat-stinging and eye-watering, equal parts rotten horseradish and bile. "It was weeks before I could even start to walk. I'm *never* going to run again, Shins. I can't stand through a full shift downstairs. It burns with the slightest touch or change in the weather. They tell me that'll probably fade one day. *Probably. One* day."

"Oh, Robin. I'm so—"

"Don't you dare. Don't you *dare!*" She was on her feet again, however shaky, and Shins honestly expected the cane to come hurtling at her any second. "This is *your fault!*"

"That's not fair! I know that if I'd been here—!"

"*Fair?!* Gods dammit, Shins, this was directed at *you!*"

Shins couldn't tell whether she or Olgun was the more stunned, the more paralyzed. ". . . what?"

"This was a message for *you*. Because nobody knew where to find you. I was just *honored* with the task of playing messenger.

"If you'd been here—if you'd been *standing with your friends*, instead of turning your back on the people who . . ." The tiniest choke interrupted, but Robin fought past it. ". . . the people who love you, this would never have happened!"

The atmosphere in the chamber had long since melted to liquid, then frozen to glass. Now it shattered, every shard a blade, every blade slicing clean across thoughts and dreams and memories. They bled as fiercely as any physical wound. Widershins had no memory of choosing to flee, no memory even of the tavern as she passed through, or the peculiar response she must have gotten from Gerard as she flew by. She couldn't even make herself care, when the thought finally occurred, that she might well be committing a smaller echo of the same sin for which she'd just been fearsomely rebuked. She knew only that every breath, every heartbeat, brought her closer to falling apart, and she *could not* be caught in Robin's accusing stare when it happened.

She felt Olgun's presence, of course, as she always did, but she could take no comfort in it. No, not so; she perversely *would* take no comfort in it, refusing to acknowledge his gentle but insistent tug. She could not let herself be soothed by anyone else—not even a god—who relied on her. It felt wrong. Dishonest.

Water on cobbles and mud *between* cobbles sprayed from beneath her heel with every heavy step. Frigid as it was, she welcomed the predawn rain, even yanking her collar loose so it could wash over her neck, her shoulders, her back, as well as through her hair, across the upturned face she aimed stubbornly at the clouds.

It felt clean. Smelled clean. It was the only thing tonight that had.

She stood, still, soaking, letting her thoughts run away in rivulets like the dirt of her journeys. Until, when it was already so close that any enemy could have done her serious harm, she heard the splashing steps of someone's approach.

Her rapier had cleared the scabbard up to the tip before Shins realized precisely who she was looking at.

"You have a *lot* of gall," she spat at the other woman, whose own blonde hair was now plastered flat to her scalp and shoulders. "What the hopping hens do *you* want?"

"You actually do say that," Faustine marveled. "I thought she was exaggerating."

"Why didn't you warn me she was coming?" Shins hissed at Olgun while waiting for the woman to say something that actually mattered. The little god, who'd been trying to get her attention for some time now, huffed off to go grumble in some metaphysical corner.

"Look, Shins . . ."

"No. Uh-uh. Nope. Only friends get to call me that."

The small cascade of water shifted as Faustine raised an eyebrow. "Because 'Widdershins' is so much more formal?" Then, when Widdershins refused to respond, "Can we at least go back inside to talk?"

"Feel free."

Faustine sighed, a sound stolen away by the weather long before it could reach anyone. "Widdershins, you . . . we think you may be in danger."

"And you came to bask in it, yes?"

"Oh, gods dammit! Robin's angry! She's in awful pain, body and soul. But she wouldn't want you to be hurt, and you know it!"

"Do I?" She'd meant it as a challenge, but it emerged a plea.

"Of course you do. Robin loves you, Widdershins. Your leaving couldn't have hurt her so badly if she didn't."

Shins nodded dumbly. Though still unwilling to go back inside the Witch, she at least stepped into the doorway of a building across the way, motioning Faustine to follow. The overhang couldn't keep the rain completely off them, but it was better than nothing.

"And why do *you* care if I get hurt?" she asked. No challenge or confusion, this time, just honest curiosity.

"Because she does."

A second, firmer nod. "She doesn't know you came after me, does she?"

"No. And she'll be upset when I come back soaked. But she *would* have thought of this, if she was clear-headed, and she'd have wanted you to know."

"All right. I'm listening."

"Your friend Renard?"

Shins couldn't quite hold back a crooked half-smile, thinking of the strutting, peacock-ish fop of a thief. So full of himself, yet the most stalwart friend and mentor—well, former mentor—she could have asked . . .

The smile fell as though the rain had washed it off her face. "What about him? Did something happen?"

Faustine actually took Shins's hand in her own; the thief stiffened but forced herself not to pull away. "We don't know," she admitted. "He always came by the Witch regularly. Said it was just because he could drink for cheap, but Robin and I both knew he was checking up on her.

"Couple of months ago, he came by, fretting like I've never seen him. He told us something was wrong. Something in the Finders' Guild."

Ah. Funny how they keep popping up, yes?

"He didn't say much," Faustine continued, "just told us to start being extra careful. Said things were getting rough, and he didn't know how much he could protect us.

"That was the last time he came by with any regularity, Widdershins. And he hasn't shown up at all in weeks. We figured, you've *already* had problems with the Guild in the past, so with gods-know-what going on . . ."

Shins had to swallow twice before she could answer, clearing her fear for Renard from her throat. "Thank you," she said, only slightly grudgingly. "I . . . don't suppose you know what he meant by 'getting rough'?"

"He didn't say specifically," the other woman answered. "But between Robin's place at the tavern and my job—I'm a local courier— we both hear things. Lots of things.

"There's a lot going wrong in Davillon right now, and part of that is the Finders' Guild. They've gotten brutal. Vicious. And overt enough that everyone's scared. I mean, they were always dangerous, but now it's like they're shedding blood for the *fun* of it!"

Shins pulled free of Faustine's grip and began to pace—which, given the size of the canopy, meant basically one big step in each direction. It was a testament to how distracted she was that she didn't start to feel really, really foolish.

"Doesn't make any sense," she muttered, a sentiment to which Olgun could only vehemently agree. "What's the Shrouded Lord thinking?"

A particular doubt took root in her mind, planted by divine effort, and blossomed.

"You think so?" Then, answering herself before he could, "You may be right. I can't imagine why he'd change so much, but if he's not in control anymore. . . . But who in the Guild would be so . . . ?"

So completely, so abruptly did Widdershins freeze that Faustine jumped. The cold, the wet, the world, even the deep ache of Robin's reaction to her homecoming, all of it was gone. There was nothing for Shins, nothing around her, nothing *to* her.

Nothing but a gaping darkness and a slowly growing ember of pure, murderous hate.

Robin's wound was a message. A message for Widdershins.

The wound in Robin's upper thigh.

And the Guild had turned suddenly sadistic, brutal . . .

"Who attacked Robin?"

Shins didn't know what she sounded like, but it couldn't have been pleasant; Faustine actually retreated a step. "Wh-what?"

"The attacker. The one who stabbed her. Who was it?"

"We . . . we don't know . . ."

"Describe her!"

Faustine squeaked something only marginally intelligible. Then, "It was a woman! She was fast, so impossibly fast! We didn't . . . I couldn't see her face, not in her hood, but her hair was an almost brilliant red. . . . Wait. How did you know it was a 'her'?"

But Shins was no longer listening to anything but the voices in her head, her own and Olgun's both.

Lisette.

She had wondered, on and off. After the men she'd had to kill in Castle Pauvril—not in self-defense, as she'd done before, but coldly, deliberately, for a greater good—the guilt had almost crushed her. And though she'd hoped she didn't have it in her at all, she'd wondered, idly, in the days that followed, what it might take for her to kill, to *murder*, without remorse.

Now, she knew. Now, Widdershins not only *could* kill, she swore she *would*.

And just this once, she would revel in it.

CHAPTER SIX

The weather had finally—if only partly—cleared, sometime around midmorning. The rain deteriorated into a soupy fog, the kind that, though more subtle than any precipitation, still managed to soak through and moisten just about everything.

It was more than enough to prevent Widdershins's drenched clothes and hair from drying out, and she was starting to feel a bit chafed. She could only imagine how bedraggled she must appear; probably looked like a drowned scarecrow.

Still, cleaning up and changing remained out of the question. She'd been halfway to one of her other boltholes after her talk with Faustine when several questions, previously held at bay by shock and anger, had finally returned to her mind. Questions that Olgun not only couldn't begin to answer but that—judging by the radiating waves of shame—he felt should have occurred to him earlier, too.

"How . . . ? Olgun, how . . . ?"

The words chewed through her mind, even if they refused to reach her throat. *How had Lisette known of her connection to Alexandre?!*

The Taskmaster had been present during the Apostle's rampage, if not particularly involved. Could she have heard something? Something linking Widdershins to Adrienne Satti, the girl she once was?

But then, if Lisette knew that, why not spread the word? She'd have a lot more people looking for Shins, that way.

"Okay," she breathed. "We'll come back to that." Mostly because if she remained focused on it now, she might just panic. "Let's look at more practical stuff."

Practical stuff such as . . . *Leaving alone the question of how she'd found the various boltholes, how in the name of Banin's backside had Lisette known* which *of them we'd use when she returned? Even* I *didn't know! How had she known where to leave the bod—Alexandre?*

That Lisette was, indeed, the one responsible, Widdershins never questioned. The timing and the sheer inhuman cruelty of the act both fit too well. Their first question, in turn, had led god and worshipper both to another, even more awful.

What if she hadn't *known which apartment to pick?*

Shins had immediately changed course, crossing half the length of Davillon. First to a smaller cemetery, where the Guard buried their own when no family plot or crypt awaited. Then here, to a much larger graveyard, on whose winding paths Shins had walked so many times.

The plot was unrecognizable when she finally reached it. The many flowers and flourishing vines, growing things that never faded in even the harshest winters thanks to Olgun's divine touch, had been ripped from their roots and left to rot. The stone itself was defaced, cracked across the front by some sort of hammer or heavy blow. And, just like the grave of Julien Bouniard—the reason she'd gone to the smaller cemetery that morning—this one wore a thick layer of soil clearly fresher and far more recent than it should be.

As though the burial had occurred weeks ago, not well over a year.

The desecration, too, appeared roughly that old. The interior of the broken stone remained bright and relatively clean; those portions of dead foliage that hadn't rotted or blown completely away were slowly decomposing into soggy sludge.

Shins knelt beside the grave, her knee sinking into the mud with a sort of *squelch*. She carefully lifted the rotting remains of what had been a lush rose, held it briefly in her palm before squeezing shut her fist and letting it dribble between her fingers. Even the rage she'd been stoking had faded, leaving nothing but an empty, numbing chill.

"Olgun? Groundskeeper?"

She felt a faint tug, nodded, and rose to follow.

He wasn't that hard to find, though; Shins probably could have managed it without Olgun's hints. Opposite the main gate, the cemetery's far end had been recently expanded. The earth still showed a few open wounds where the walls had been partly dismantled and moved, and whole rows of graves were obviously fresh. The caretaker—for that is what Shins assumed the ashen-haired older man in the beat-up woolens to be—leaned wearily on a spade and watched a band of workers digging up yet another new plot some yards distant. Shins didn't envy them their task, not with the earth both drenched by the weather and packed down hard by so many feet over the past weeks. The scent of loam in the air was so thick, Shins was surprised it didn't disturb the occupants.

She made no effort to conceal her approach, and the groundskeeper turned to greet her at the sound of her footsteps. "What can I do for you, madamois—?"

"The Marguilles grave. What happened to it?"

"Happened? I'm afraid I don't know what—"

Widdershins heaved a sigh so deep, it could itself have come from one of the coffins. "Are we really going to do this? Genevieve Marguilles was my friend. I've been to her graveside more times than you could count without undressing. So spare me the fake ignorance, yes?"

Straightening to his full height, he scowled down at her. "As we're digging so many new plots," he said primly, "we decided to take the opportunity to touch up a few of the older ones, where time and weather had begun to—"

"The face-saving cover story now? What, do you have a checklist to run through? Just tell me the truth, for figs' sake!"

"Stop interrupting! Mademoiselle, I don't know where you learned your manners—"

"Her body's missing, isn't it? Someone dug her up. And this cemetery's not the only place it happened."

The panic in the old man's eyes and the brief stammer before he could manage an indignant "I've never heard such nonsense!" were more than evidence enough.

"Thanks," she called as she began to walk away. She'd covered perhaps three or four paces when he called out to her.

"Mademoiselle, wait!" Although tempted to ignore him, she stopped long enough for him to catch up. "Please," he said, hoarse and quiet. "I've no idea how you found out, but you *can't* tell anyone! Everyone's scared and upset enough as it is. If word of *this* should spread . . ."

"How bad *are* things?" she asked. Then, at his baffled look, "I'm only just back in town." She waved a hand at the new expansion. "Frankly, and no offense, but yours isn't a business I like to see thriving."

It was his turn to sigh, that peculiar mix of exasperation and sorrow that only people old enough to speak seriously of the "good old days" could muster. "Crime's gotten awful, the Guard can't handle it, and the house soldiers 'helping keep the peace' are sparring with political rivals as much as anyone else. I've never seen the like. And that's not even counting . . ."

"Counting what?" she prodded when it became clear he had no plans to continue.

"Oh, the usual rumors. Sort you get every time there's civil unrest. Only, well, there's an awful *lot* of them this time."

Teeth grinding in her impatience, she prodded again. "Rumors of?"

"Well, some folks are saying that there's something *supernatural* stalking the streets. Lot like it was last summer . . ."

Olgun gibbered something that even Shins found incomprehensible.

"Uh, thanks," Shins said again to the groundskeeper, then broke into a steady jog, headed for the gate. She swiftly left the old man behind, shouting after her not to tell anyone.

"Yeah," she muttered, "*that's* a good way to keep a secret."

More frightened blather from her god.

"Oh, calm down! It's just another of Lisette's tricks. Taking advantage of something she knows frightens people. Vile, nasty frog of a woman. I should have killed her the first time."

Quivering, almost childish uncertainty.

"Well, maybe it is. But even if she found a way to summon something, it still starts and ends with her. This is *not* going to be like Iru—like before."

Olgun didn't sound—well, feel—convinced, but he let it drop. Instead, after Shins had cleared the gate and made an abrupt turn down a nearby road, he wafted a question across her mind.

"No!" She skidded to a halt, took a moment to catch her breath, which had abruptly grown sharp and ragged. "No," she repeated, "we are not going anywhere *near* any of the flats. We already know what we're going to find there, and I can't . . . no. No place to sleep, and no *time*. You'll just have to keep me going until we're done."

Perhaps she *was* being foolish, at that. Gods knew she could use some rest after the last couple of days, and while Lisette was no great threat one-on-one—Shins had full-well proven that once already—there was no telling how hard she might be to *get* to.

But Widdershins absolutely could not face the idea of returning to any of her boltholes. The thought of having to confront Gen or Julien, finding them in the same state as Alexandre . . . no. She'd had far, far too much. She was tired of death.

Well, except for one upcoming death in particular . . .

❀

Widdershins sat on the wet rooftop, legs dangling off the side, and carefully cleaned the diluted blood from her rapier with a bit of torn cloth. Beneath her, in an alley ankle-deep in old rainwater and the "juice" of various garbage heaps, groaned and whimpered a trio of disreputable men who would all live—assuming none of their injuries grew too badly infected—but would probably never walk normally again.

She hadn't *meant* for it to go this way. Once night had again fallen and she'd succeeded in locating a roving gang she recognized as Finders, the plan had been for Widdershins to tail them, observe all she could about the new behaviors of the Guild, hopefully eavesdrop enough to learn some of what was going on in the halls of underground power.

Said plan had survived exactly as long as it took the robbers to find their first victims. When it became clear that the young couple's money was not all the gang was after, that they wouldn't be content without bloodshed or even worse, Shins hadn't been able to stand by.

The result, thanks to the element of surprise and Olgun's power, had been three mangled Finders and three healthy people—the couple and the fourth man of what had been a quartet of brigands—fleeing into the night.

"Wasn't an accident," Shins explained to her curious partner, shifting along the ledge in a futile effort to find a spot where she could still observe the wounded below yet wasn't soaking her backside in a puddle. "I wanted him to get away.

"Oh, I did *so!* Why would I make up—what?! Right, like I'm going to lie to make you think better of me. You already *know* I mess up a lot, so why . . . wait, that's not what I . . . oh, horsebubbles."

After a few moments, when the tiny deity finally stopped laughing, Shins continued. "*As* I was saying," she growled, "I don't think he got a good look at me. He just knows *someone* turned his friends into a hedgehog's bedsheets. Since these guys aren't really in any good shape to talk to me, and they probably don't know much anyway, I figure, let their friend come back with someone more important and less, um, bleedy.

"And don't even *think* of trying to tell me that's not a real word, either. You don't talk. You don't *get* a say in how words work."

This continued for some time, punctuated by the moans from below. Shins was just in the process of actually defining the word "word" for Olgun's edification when he abruptly alerted her to someone's approach.

"All right. If you'd be so kind?"

The night grew brighter, the sounds sharper. She could hear them clearly, now, the slap of boots, the dull thump of sheathed blades against hips and thighs. "Heh. Guess they're coming prepared. I wonder how many people he *said* it took to flatten his team?"

Olgun snickered.

The gang finally reached the alleyway, led by the man who'd escaped earlier. Shins got ten at a quick head count, more than she really wanted to take on even with Olgun's help. More to the point, though, she also *recognized* one of those heads: bald as a snake's bottom, sitting atop a leather-clad body built more like a bear or a gorilla than a man.

"Well, well. Taskmaster Remy Privott, himself. I guess not *all* the gods are annoyed with me yet."

She merely sniffed, then, at her own god's response, which translated roughly to *Give them time.*

It really *was* a stroke of luck, though. Second only to the Shrouded Lord—or the woman who'd taken his place, presuming Lisette hadn't drastically rearranged the Finders' hierarchy—the Taskmaster would be privy to nearly everything happening within the Guild. She just needed the opportunity to ask the right questions. . . .

She grinned, wide and vicious, as a thought occurred. "Your ears are still better than mine," she whispered. "Are there any Guard or house patrols nearby?"

Considering how many she'd seen the prior night, she'd have been surprised if he told her there weren't.

She was not surprised.

"All right. Wait for it . . ."

At Remy's gruff instruction, several of the Finders moved deep into niches between buildings, kneeling to check on their injured compatriots. Several others stood at the mouth of the alleyway, hands dropping to the hilts of daggers, swords . . . or flintlocks.

"That one," she whispered.

The weapon all but detonated, the catastrophic misfire warping metal and splitting the wooden stock clear from end to end. The explosive *crack* echoed through the Davillon night, as did the piercing shriek—more startled than pained but certainly made up of both—from the man who owned the gun.

Every man and woman in the alley had spun about or leapt to their feet, weapons drawn and hearts pounding. Remy wasn't even remotely finished cursing when, even without the divine aid that Widdershins enjoyed, the lot of them could clearly hear the shouts and rapid steps of an approaching patrol, drawn by the gunfire.

Shins knew exactly what was coming next. She was counting on it.

"Scatter!" the taskmaster hissed. The Finders obeyed, vanishing —alone or in pairs—in every direction. And it was, indeed, *every* direction. While most of the group remained on the streets, several of them began scaling the sides of nearby structures, as others sought shelter within.

Only one of them mattered.

Remy scrambled up the building next to the one on which Shins was perched, accompanied by a scraggly, unshaven thief who would have to clean up to aspire to "weaselly." With impressive stealth, they jogged along the rooftops at a low crouch, hopping the narrow gaps between neighboring eaves, leaving the scene rapidly behind.

Widdershins found it laughably easy to keep up.

It would have been nice if the taskmaster had scampered off alone, but apparently her luck wasn't to be *that* good. Now she'd have to *make* him alone.

"Ah, well. What's one more injured thief? Safer streets, yes?"

Olgun pointed out that she really didn't need any *more* enemies in the Guild, but since she was already quite well aware of that, she ignored it. Instead, she said, "Going to need some extra speed and a boost here."

The next obstacle Remy and his companion would have to clear was a street, not an alleyway, albeit a narrow one. It was a tricky jump to make, but not *too* difficult, certainly not for men with their training and experience.

Just as the two of them neared that edge, Widdershins's run turned into an impossible sprint. Inhumanly steady on the rickety roof, hair and hood flying behind her in the wind of her own motion, she closed the distance in a matter of heartbeats. When her quarry leapt, she was only steps behind them.

She felt Olgun's presence beneath her, propelling her up and out with her last step so that she soared through the open air, higher and far faster, than the others. She tucked her knees tight to her chest, giving herself just enough room to pass over the head of Remy's companion.

Then, still in midair, she kicked down hard with both feet.

The not-quite-weasel screamed at the sharp impact on his shoulders, the bone-shaking jolt as he was suddenly propelled downward. Shins's kick did *not*, of course, substantially alter his forward momentum, so that same scream ceased just as abruptly as he slammed face-first into the wall just below his intended landing point.

Neither that impact, nor the subsequent fall, should prove fatal, but when he finally woke up, he was going to seriously envy his friends back in the alley, who had merely been stabbed a few times.

Given the Guild's recent activities and behavior, Shins found herself remarkably guilt-free regarding the whole endeavor.

Thanks to Olgun's divine boost, Shins landed on the far roof a fraction of a second ahead of Remy. It was more than enough, especially since his brain still hadn't fully processed what was happening. The young woman dropped into a low crouch and spun, one leg extended, sweeping the larger man's ankles out from under him even as they had just begun to touch down. The taskmaster toppled forward—no, more than toppled, practically pivoted in space, so that he slammed to the roof face and chest down, his legs protruding over the edge. Shins gave him a helpful nudge with the toe of her boot; not enough to send him over, just to make him slide, forcing him to clutch at the rooftop with both hands to keep himself from a painful plummet.

He could, of course, have hauled himself back up—Remy was nothing if not a powerful man—had he not looked up to find the tip of Widdershins's rapier hovering about two inches from his nose.

"As I don't actually have any plans to stab you tonight," she told him, "I'm going to be very put out if you impale your face on my sword. Talk about rude."

"Well," he wheezed, wincing at what she had to assume was a spreading pain in his ribs, "I wouldn't want to put you out, would I?"

"Exactly! It's so nice to understand one's colleagues."

"I'm sure. When did *you* get back in town?"

Widdershins's gawp of disbelief was only partly exaggerated. "Really? *That's* the question you want to lead with under these circumstances?"

Remy started to shrug, then froze as he slid a few more inches back with the gesture. "I don't figure threatening you's gonna do me any good right now—though you *are* going to regret this—and you're going to tell me what you want when you damn well feel like it, anyway."

"Fair." Widdershins dropped to her haunches, her blade still steady. "I think you know my first question."

He didn't even bother to equivocate. "Yes, Lisette's back. And yes, she's in charge now."

"What happened to the old Shrouded Lord?"

"Gods only know. I. . . . Look, if this is going to be a long talk, can I pull myself up? My arms hurt."

"I guess you'd better make sure it's *not* a long talk, then."

The taskmaster growled at that, but they both knew it was empty.

"The Shrouded Lord?" she prompted.

"Yeah, don't know. She says he's dead, but . . . she's avoided talking about who was under the mask, and she gets pissy—pissier—if he comes up in conversation. So maybe he's not as dead as she wants.

"Might as well be, though. He's out, and she's already purged most of the Finders who were specifically loyal to him."

"Uh-huh." The tip of the rapier twitched. "I can't help notice that didn't include *you*."

Somehow, without shifting his grip, Remy managed to look as though he wanted to shrug again. "I do my job. I'm loyal to the Guild, not any one person."

"Uh-huh," Shins said again. "Also you didn't want her to open you up like a chest of drawers and reorganize your insides by color and size."

"There was that," he admitted.

"So she took the Shroud, then?"

"Nah. Seems happy enough running shit as herself."

For the first time in the conversation, Shins found herself taken aback. "I thought the priests would've mandated it. It's a requirement, yes? To honor the Shrouded God?"

"Yeah, about that? Lisette's also purged the ranks of senior priests. Thinks she's got her own way of doing things in mind."

She wanted to turn to Olgun, ask him what the frogs was going on, but she could feel his confusion as intensely as hers. Lisette had always been a fanatical worshipper of the Shrouded God, a zealous follower of his teachings. What could have changed?

A faint groan, clearly unintentional, pulled her thoughts back to Remy. "Almost done," she told him, sympathy just *dripping* from every word. "Why all the bloodshed all of a sudden?"

"Orders." His breath grew more labored with every word. "She wants . . . people afraid of us . . . wants bodies in the street. Seems to be trying . . . to stir up the Guard and . . . the Houses both. No idea why."

"Because she's nuttier than a squirrel's larder." Even as she said it, though, something about it nagged at her. Lisette *was* crazy, always had been, but there was always purpose behind her actions. "All right, last question. Maybe. What are your orders regarding *me*?"

"Locate . . . follow and watch. Nothing . . . else."

Makes sense, given that the posters offered a reward for information about me, not body parts.

"You think Lisette wants to kill me herself, yes?"

"Maybe. Or she's got . . . some other scheme in mind. Either way, she wants you alive . . . for *something*."

"Well . . ." Shins stepped back from the ledge, instinct and divine intervention all but painting her in shadow, leaving enough clear space for an exhausted, shaking Remy to haul himself up. "It'd be seriously inconsiderate to keep her waiting."

CHAPTER SEVEN

Thick blankets of fog rolled in, but by the time Widdershins approached the Ragway District, they'd begun to dissipate. All that remained were thin tendrils and small accumulations of a lighter mist, seeping up from between the cobblestones. The ghosts, perhaps, of yesterday's storm-drenched passersby.

The shops and houses grew steadily more worn, more rickety, in some cases absent entirely. It was rather like walking through a mouth of bad teeth. Didn't smell much better, either. No sewers, here. No street cleaning. No comfort. No hope. Not in Ragway.

Widdershins didn't notice. She'd been through the district too many times before.

The building was an old, brick-shaped thing, supposedly the home of insurers and pawnbrokers barely breaking even. More or less everyone in the city knew the place's true purpose, though.

She knew she was watched by at least three separate sentries, even if she hadn't spotted them yet. It didn't stop her from striding right to the front door and knocking like the gods' own tax-collector.

"It's called being *confident*!" she breathed in reply to Olgun's observation. "Not *cocky*. Well, yeah, that's because I'm *not* worried."

I'm not. *This isn't the Apostle and his demon, or Iruoch, or even Fingerbone with his weird goops. It's just Lisette!*

Footsteps sounded behind the door, followed by the sound of a latch disengaging.

I'm not worried. Then, aloud, "Uh, but be ready to run anyway."

A panel in the door slid open, granting Shins a view of deeply shadowed eyeballs—and them, in turn, a view of her.

Given their sudden, almost comical growth, the young thief had to assume she'd been recognized.

"Widdershins," she announced casually. "To see Lisette Suvagne. I have an appointment."

The panel slammed shut, and for some time there was silence nearby. Thunder and a howling wind both cracked that stillness at one point, but far in the distance, well beyond the walls of Davillon.

"Sounds like tomorrow's going to be unpleasant," she casually observed. Her partner didn't reply.

Footsteps again, and for all her bravado, Shins tensed. It wasn't impossible that the door would open onto a bristling array of flint-locks and crossbows, and she needed to be ready to . . .

But no. The door *did* open, revealing only two young thieves, similar enough in appearance that they might have been brother and sister. He wore mostly browns and grays, she deep blues and crimson, but both were heavily armed—and both kept their weapons sheathed.

"Follow us," the woman said. "We'll take you to her. You're going to have to surrender your blade, though."

"Only if you're prepared to accept it handed over point first and very, very fast," Shins replied, smiling prettily. "Possibly more than once. Not saying you're clumsy, but it can be a tricky sort of thing to hang onto."

After which, following a minute's energetic discussion between the two Finders, Shins was ushered *back outside* and left to wait while the sentinels returned to Lisette for additional instructions. She managed to wait until she'd heard the door latch and the footsteps move away before she cackled aloud.

"I don't think the old snake's going to like having to repeat herself," she told Olgun.

Indeed, when the door opened once more some minutes later, the woman was holding a hand tight to a bloody nose and lips, while her partner, or brother, or whatever, sported what was already proving to be a dark and nasty black eye.

"I'm not sure your new boss is a very nice person," Shins observed. The others merely glared and turned their backs, confident that—or else not caring if—Widdershins would follow.

"And you called *me* cocky!" she quietly crowed—yes, she'd learned how to do that—to her god. "Look at Lisette's arrogance! The only way she even had a chance was if we had to fight our way through the whole hopping Guild to reach her! Now? Ha!"

Indeed, Shins was feeling better than she had at any moment since she discovered her flat had been . . . profaned. She'd handily beaten Lisette once already, and she and Olgun hadn't worked together as smoothly then as they did now. Even if Lisette had spent every intervening minute practicing, she didn't stand a chance.

Alert for trap or ambush, just in case—though she was fairly sure she'd encounter no such thing—Widdershins followed her guides into the winding tunnels that were the true headquarters of the Finders' Guild.

And toward one of the few violent clashes, in a lifetime full of them, she was actually looking forward to.

❋

Onward and downward. Through a complex of deliberately twisting passageways, as though someone had dropped a platter of wet noodles; past chambers both open and sealed, of purposes both blatant and hidden. Shins couldn't help but glance sidelong at the darkened chapel, that oddly shaped room with the heavy portals and the fabric-masked idol of the Shrouded God. Glance, and shiver at the memories of the statue's awful curse.

And all of it swimming in a miasma of breath and sweat, wrapped in a chorus of whispers and snickers, beneath the fascinated stares of scores of Finders. Some moved cleanly aside, some bristled and threatened first, but all cleared the path walked by her two guides.

Most recognized her, either personally or by description. Many of those offered vicious grins or contemptuous sneers; Shins never had been one of the more popular members of the Guild. Some, however, couldn't quite seem to meet her eyes, or cast their looks with a furtive discomfort.

They're afraid. And not of me.

An ember of doubt tried to ignite in the primal reaches of Widdershins's mind. She swiftly crushed it out.

It's just Lisette.

Still, "You *are* memorizing the way out of here, yes? This place still confuses me."

Olgun assured her that he was, which meant the uncertainty she felt in him had to be caused by something else. "What's bothering you?"

But to that, he could offer no clear answer.

The door to which the two thieves finally led her surprised Widdershins not at all. This was the audience chamber of the Shrouded Lord, or at least it had been. Of course the usurper would rule from here.

"I think I can find my own way from here, thanks," she said to her guides. She was a tad taken aback when they both nodded and stepped aside. Shrugging, she pushed the door ajar and slipped through.

The most notable aspect of the room was that she could *see* the room. The Shrouded Lord had always kept it full of rolling, incense-perfumed smoke; vapors that blended to near perfection with the tattered storm-cloud fabrics that made up his own uniform, as well as the sheets draped over the desk. The effect had been a ghostly—if also scratchy and irritating—fume wherein the Shrouded Lord was only another partially formed apparition.

Now? It was just a room, an office much like any other in the Finders' Guild's upper ranks. The walls were a bit soot-stained, perhaps, but the massive hardwood desk was a thing of art, the chairs arrayed about it soft and welcoming, the single bookcase loaded to groaning with stacks of papers and parchments. The braziers, which had once spewed that thick incense, now served as the resting places of pricey oil lanterns, brightening the room rather more evenly and cleanly than torches ever could.

And that was everything, really. Everything save the office's lone occupant.

"Took you long enough," Lisette complained, rising to her feet behind the desk. "Hello, little scab."

If anything, she looked even meaner than Shins remembered. Her face had hardened and sunken with age; the younger thief likened it to a plow protruding from her thick mass of crimson hair. Her lips were thin, her teeth exposed in a tight smile that had nothing whatsoever to do with friendliness. Otherwise she looked normal enough, clad in greens and blacks, topped with a vest that so perfectly matched her hair it *must* have been custom made.

She wore no weapon to be seen, but Shins wasn't foolish enough to assume she had none ready behind that monstrosity of a desk.

"I'm surprised, Lisette. I figured you'd have spruced this place up once it was finally yours, make it more you. This . . ." She indicated the desk and bookcase. "This doesn't even come *close* to tasteless."

"Oh, and I'm so *deeply* sorry to have disappointed you," Lisette replied. "I did *think* of doing a more substantial redecorating, but it didn't seem worth the effort. I don't intend the heart of my domain to remain here for too long."

"And where do you expect to be ruling from, Your Malignancy?"

"Wherever I choose. City Hall, perhaps. Or maybe Luchene Manor? I've always rather liked the look of that place."

Widdershins felt her grip on the conversation beginning to slide, or at least cause rope burns. "You—"

"Honestly, though, at the moment I'm thinking the Basilica. It's such a nice place, and it would certainly send a message, don't you think?"

"You think you're going to run the whole *city?*" It was almost a squawk, so incredulous was Widdershins. Then, at the other woman's casual shrug, "You're even crazier than when you left! For pastry's sake, you couldn't even run a conspiracy within the Guild without being exposed."

For the first time, Lisette's false smile slipped into a more honest sneer. "Yes, and whose fault was that?"

"It's about to be mine again, you dog!" The lingering shreds of Olgun's unease vanished beneath a surge of fury; Shins had her rapier in her hand without ever consciously choosing to draw it. "You should have stayed away, Lisette. You should *not*. Have touched. My friends."

"The living or the dead?" the former taskmaster asked dryly.

"And you *really* shouldn't have just let me walk in here." Widdershins's tone could have frozen the remaining oil in the lanterns.

"The truth is," Lisette continued, "I gave serious thought to torturing you for a few months after you got home. You have so many weaknesses, little scab. But, well, I have a *lot* to do, still. So, alas, I decided to deny myself the pleasure of a slow revenge.

"That does *not* mean," and now that tight, ugly smile was back, "I wasn't going to allow myself a *personal* one. Really, you think I'd have gone to all that trouble to extend my invitation with Genevieve's, Alexandre's, and Julien's rotting, vermin-eaten carcasses if I was just going to have one of my people kill you? You. Are *mine*."

The room had been clearer, under its old cloud of smoke, than it was now beyond the blazing red in Shins's vision. "You didn't have a chance against me even *before* the limp, you snake!"

"Whose limp? Mine? Or Robin's?"

Shins lunged.

The sharp tingle of Olgun's power and she was airborne, clearing the space between herself and her enemy in a single leaping step. Her front foot landed atop the desk as she thrust, the tip of her rapier a bolt of steel lightning, tracing a line between the two women faster than the human eye could possibly register.

It never even came close.

Lisette *folded* out of the way, leaning far enough at the waist that the blade passed only through empty space. Then, whipping her body around so she now bent forward rather than back—without straightening in between!—she slammed a backhanded fist into Widdershins's ankle.

The impact knocked the young thief's foot completely out from under her. She crashed down on the desk, chest first, a burst of air blasted from her lungs. It was sheer luck, or perhaps quick thinking from Olgun, that kept her fist clenched around her rapier.

She wasn't sure what had just happened, only that she had no time to ponder it. Her god screaming a warning at her, she punched down with both fists—one empty, one wrapped about the sword hilt—propelling herself back and upward, off the desk to land in the center of the chamber.

A heavy bladed dagger, clutched in Lisette's fist, sank into the hardwood where Shins's back had just been, scarring the wood and utterly blunting the tip.

"Do you have any idea," she shrieked, hurling the ruined weapon aside, "how much this desk is *worth*?!"

"How did you do that?" Shins demanded, shocked to her core and starting—far, far too late—to feel the first genuine stirrings of fear.

Lisette's answer was almost a purr. "There are powers in this world, you damn fool. Powers greater than you can imagine, and powers more than capable of concealing themselves.

"From you *or your wretched, insignificant pet of a god!*"

The words were weapons, rocking Widdershins, stunning her—and Olgun, too—far more than any physical blow. Her mouth opened, but she couldn't force whole concepts to pass through it.

"What . . . ? How . . . ?"

But Lisette was already moving. This time it was she who landed atop the hardwood, and though Shins was far too taken aback to be certain, it looked less like she had jumped and more as though she had simply lifted both legs, at once, high enough to reach the desktop. She wielded a rapier in one hand, a new dagger in the other, and Shins hadn't even seen her draw. Lisette froze for an endless instant, crouched atop the desk, and then her legs straightened in a tremendous leap.

Passing within a rat's knuckle of the ceiling, she soared over Widdershins's head in an arc so impossible it almost hurt to see it. By any natural law, she should have struck hard against the stone ceiling, or else covered perhaps half the room, at most, in her flight. Instead she landed at the far door, having already twisted to wind up facing her opponent.

"Are you beginning to understand," Lisette hissed, exhaling pure malevolence, "how badly you fucked up in coming here?"

"I think so," Widdershins said through a wan, sickly smile. "So, time to call it lesson learned and go our separate ways, yes?"

"Ah, yes, I well recall the famous Widdershins's wit. But no, my mocking gutter bitch, we're not done. I have so much yet to teach you!" Rapier and dagger swirling around past one another, Lisette advanced.

"Olgun . . . ?"

Another surge of divine power, and the older woman's foot caught on an up-curled edge of rug. It should have sent her tumbling into the waiting chairs, granting Widdershins a second or two of opportunity to try to get past her, make for the door . . .

It didn't happen. Even as the toe of Lisette's boot made contact with the heavy weaving, the rug twitched, yanking that awkward fold from her path before it could begin to trip her up.

Olgun gibbered, and Shins felt a very great deal like joining him. Palms sweating, heart pounding, she retreated toward the desk.

"Such childish little tricks you two rely on," Lisette taunted. "Not much more than divine sleight of hand. Would you care to see something . . . rather more interesting?"

"If it's all the same—" Shins's reply began with words; it concluded in a terrified cry, hers and Olgun's both.

Still spinning, Lisette's weapons advanced, suddenly seeming to attack Shins from all sides. *Yet Lisette herself hadn't taken another step.* It was impossible to see for sure—the whirling steel, and her efforts to either dodge or parry it, occupied the entirety of the young thief's attentions—but she swore her enemy's arms had simply reached across the intervening space, lengthening to compensate. Every time she allowed herself a fraction of a blink to look past the weapons, though, to actually try to *study* those arms, she couldn't quite focus on them. As though she tried to examine them through tears and a thick heat haze.

The superhuman speed with which Olgun infused her limbs, the extra warning he gave, the manipulations of chance that ensured her rapier was so often in place to catch an incoming attack—only these had kept Shins alive thus far. Her entire body was drenched in sweat, now, her arms stung from half a dozen tiny cuts where she hadn't *quite* moved fast enough. She couldn't recall ever growing so tired, so swiftly, or feeling Olgun falter so soon in his own exhaustion.

What was *she? What had Lisette become?!*

The incoming blades froze, and then Lisette was standing *directly before her*, as though her arms had resumed their natural length and pulled her forward to match, rather than recoiling.

Or at least that's what Shins assumed later, when she had a moment to gather her thoughts. Now, all she saw was a sudden blur, the vicious leer, and then searing pain as Lisette slammed her forehead into Shins's face.

She'd tried to turn aside, to avoid the blow she'd somehow known was coming. All she'd accomplished was that her nose *might* be broken, rather than assuredly was; it was something, but between the throbbing agony and the horrid sound of *something* going crunch, it didn't mean much.

Olgun guiding her arm more than she herself was, Shins twisted her wrist inward and stabbed awkwardly, struggling to thrust with a rapier at a range where a far shorter blade would have proven far more effective.

Still, clumsy a strike as it was, it should have connected. Before the tip could cover those mere inches of distance, however, Lisette simultaneously dropped the rapier from her right hand and tossed the dagger from her left. Neither hand *remained* empty, however, as she caught the dagger in her right, *and grabbed the blade of Shins's rapier* in her left.

The sword just stopped; she might as well have stabbed an oak tree. That the grip was impossible, that no human hand was strong enough to arrest a thrust like that—let alone do so without slicing open her palm and fingers—wasn't remotely surprising, not anymore. In fact, Widdershins had just enough time to think a bitter *Of course* before Lisette plunged the dagger into her body.

❁

Olgun did for her everything he could. Had the blade struck precisely as Lisette intended, punching into Widdershins's liver, the young thief would have died in agony, excruciatingly slowly, but not slowly enough for the tiny god to make any real attempt at healing the damage. At saving her.

Instead, with the last of the power he could muster, he deflected the steel, just the slightest angle. The result, instead, was a gut wound.

Meaning that Widdershins would still probably die in agony, excruciatingly slowly, but it *might* buy Olgun enough time to patch up the worst of it before that could happen.

Might. *If* he was even given the opportunity. If the red-haired monster didn't just finish her—finish *them*—outright.

Because whatever else, Olgun knew damn well that his powers were drained, that he could do only so much without Widdershins's will to channel his own. That he couldn't protect her any further.

In the deepest confines of the young woman's mind, the frightened, grieving god wept.

❀

A piercing scream, a sob, a plea, all that and more. Shins fell back against the desk, felt the steel slithering from her flesh, then crumpled into a tiny ball on the floor, arms clutched tight to her stomach. Her sleeves were already soaked in thick, warm blood, but she didn't notice. Didn't notice she had fallen, didn't notice she still screamed and cried.

She had been stabbed before, in her life of conflict. Had strips of skin torn from her by the clinging fingers of the creature Iruoch. Had even been struck in the gut before, with a hammer wielded by a man large enough to make the Taskmaster, Remy, look like Robin.

She had never felt *anything* to match this.

Her world was fire, agony and nausea and terror. In that moment she would have done anything, given Lisette anything she could possibly have asked for, begged Olgun to kill her, *anything* to make it stop. Would have, had she possessed the presence of mind to try, but even that was denied her.

Around the edges of her awareness, she almost thought she felt the faintest tingling, a sense that Olgun was doing what he could for her injury, but it wasn't enough, not nearly enough. Her body spasmed, wrenching muscles, as though sharply tugged inward by the wound itself.

"Please . . ." She'd no idea what she begged for, exactly, nor to whom. Possibly to Lisette herself, and Shins couldn't even find it within her to be ashamed at the thought. "Please . . ."

And all the gods be praised, the pain *did* begin to fade! She believed, at first, it was her imagination, or perhaps her mind shutting down. A chill spread through her body, from the wound outward, and where it passed the torment eased—sort of. It didn't go away, not exactly. Rather, it felt like the seeping cold formed a wall, a barrier of ice and numbness, between the agony and Shins herself. It was still present, still raging, but somehow the worst of it failed to reach her.

Widdershins vomited a gout of bile-tinted blood and then stared up at Lisette in utter bewilderment.

The older woman was cloaked in ribbons of nothingness, maddened worms of shadow that slithered and humped about her.

One of those lengths of shade had snaked its way between them, caressing the edges of Widdershins's wound, doubtless the source of that frigid relief.

"We can't have you overcome yet, little scab," Lisette taunted her. "Not until the others have had the chance to meet you."

"O-others?"

"Oh, yes. They've been almost as eager for this as I have."

Those writhing shadows erupted to either side of Lisette, somewhere between a billowing cloak and widespread wings. The lanterns flickered and dulled, the light itself seeming to recoil, and the air was abruptly redolent with cinnamon and vanilla and other sweets.

From within those shadows, an array of figures formed.

The first was a silhouette only vaguely human, a lithely muscled man with skin the mottled colors of a stagnant marsh and the legs of a giant frog. His head was bald, and the corners of his lips reached all the way to his ears. Even in her state, Shins shuddered at the thought of that mouth opening wide, and of what might lie within.

He—it?—was followed by a young woman, pirouetting on long, slender legs. She was clad in a dress of leaves, and her hair was red— not the simple ginger of Lisette's own, but as deep and rich as rose petals. Her eyes, when she paused in her twirling to glare at Shins, were tree bark, and the fingers of both hands were long rosebush stems with vicious thorns.

And finally, the last, though this one was accompanied by his own entourage. Lanky of form and greasy of hair, he looked no older than Shins herself, yet there was something of the ancient about him. His left hand boasted long, slender switches where its fingers should have been, and his eyes were mirrors in which Shins saw her own reflection, but not Lisette's.

Crawling at his heels, moaning with every breath, were half a dozen children—or child-shaped creatures. Their flesh was maggot-pale, their eyes no more than gaping hollows into a seemingly endless darkness, their jaws distended around long and jagged teeth. They wore only old and tattered rags, all save one: from her neck alone dangled a silver pendant, badly tarnished, in the shape of an elegant swan.

Through it all, Olgun shrieked his fear and his warnings, to which Shins could offer no response at all.

"My dear friends, this is Widdershins," Lisette announced grandly, "to whom we owe thanks for bringing us together. Widdershins, these are my new friends. Do you understand why they're here?"

It wasn't, even in her current condition, hard to puzzle out. "Iruoch . . ." she whispered, blood dribbling from one side of her lips.

As if in response, somewhere off in the distance, in a direction that had nothing to do with any compass, an entire chorus of children babbled.

"Very good," the older woman congratulated with joviality so false it should have qualified as counterfeiting. "They're not *really* here, of course. Iruoch was invited, however accidentally. My friends were not, and the Church presence is still a bother to them. We're taking care of that, though, aren't we, my dears?"

The ghostly children cooed; the trio of fae nodded in unison.

"In the interim, they ride the magics they've bestowed upon

me," Lisette continued, now clearly bragging. "Lets them manifest in Davillon for small periods of time. And they *so* wanted to be here for you, specifically."

Shins figured she was supposed to ask why and kept her teeth clenched tight. She wouldn't offer the satisfaction.

"For the same reason," Lisette said, as though she actually *had* asked, "we've eased the pain of your injury.

"Part of our bargain is that I let them in on the fun, you see."

The adolescent-looking fae with the reflective eyes advanced, then, the lashes on his left hand twitching, *writhing*, living tendrils of inhuman hatred.

"I wonder," Lisette pondered aloud, "if their tender ministrations will kill you before you have the chance to bleed to death. I wonder if they'll feel it when a god *dies*."

Not like this. It wasn't supposed to go like this. I'm so sorry, Olgun . . .

The vile creature raised its hand to strike, but Shins couldn't even see it through her tears.

CHAPTER EIGHT

This time, the dream was different.

Bishop Sicard awoke screaming, his cheeks glistening and his beard soaked with tears. Still he'd seen no recognizable images, gleaned no clear meaning from the baroque nightmare.

He knew only that somewhere, someone suffered. Somewhere, the world teetered on the verge of losing something infinitely, irreplaceably precious.

Again Sicard buried his face in his hands. And for long minutes, grieving for he knew not what, the holy man wept.

❋

She couldn't remember her name, for even the *concept* of name, of self, had fallen away. If her whole world had become agony before, now there was no such thing as "world." No consciousness.

No awareness.

No memory.

Not even a desire for it all to stop, because she couldn't recall that there ever had been, or ever could be, anything else.

She screamed, a constant, despairing keen, with no realization that she had ever *not* been screaming. Body, mind, and soul, she began to break, fractures running ruthlessly through her; fractures that, if permitted to widen, could never possibly heal. Still she didn't care, because she didn't even know she *could*, and beneath her, all around her, the abyss gaped, nearer, ever nearer . . .

Something else? Was there something else? She'd lost the very notion of "else," but it came slowly trickling back as she heard it. Not in her ears, not only in her mind, but somewhere betwixt and between.

She screamed—and he screamed with her. The agony was not hers alone; he suffered, as she had never, ever known he *could* suffer.

He?

Olgun!

Olgun? Then that would make me . . .

Opening her eyes in that moment was the second hardest thing Widdershins had ever tried to do.

Remembering Widdershins, *being* Widdershins, was the hardest.

But she was. And she did. Because he needed her to.

She saw only the floor on which she lay, dark stone covered in dust and grit; and in the corner of her vision, a blurry lump, only slightly brighter in hue, that might have been the leg of a table or a . . .

Desk. The Shrouded Lord's desk.

As if that single second of sight had opened her other senses as well, the room rushed in on her. She remembered where she was. She smelled the years of boots treading across this stone, the lingering residue of the incense that used to fill the air, smelled—and tasted— the blood and worse that trickled from between her lips.

She heard Lisette, gloating at how she'd found something so much better than the "weak, cowardly god" who'd abandoned her when she needed him most; how her allies would render the Church as impotent as the Shrouded God.

She heard the distant laughter of children, cooing and cackling, and—more closely—the breathing of the child-sized creatures actually present.

And she heard the faint whistle of the creature's switches in the air before they landed again across her back.

Oh, gods, it hurt! Again she screamed, without intention, and it was only the howl of Olgun's own pain that kept her from slipping back under. No individual stroke was nearly so bad as having been stabbed in the stomach, but they just. Kept. Coming. She could feel her skin welting, opening, bleeding, burning.

They were more than whips, more than just injury. It was *unclean*, a physical and even moral degradation. The magics contained within were poisonous, unholy, *obscene*.

Which, she realized in the portion of her mind she'd managed to wake up, explained Olgun's response. He didn't just experience the pain through her, as he normally would; wasn't just afraid, for himself or for her. He actually *felt* the lash of every "finger," his essence torn and abraded no less than her own skin.

She wondered, with a horrified shudder, if her god had *ever* experienced direct pain like this. As awful as she felt, at least it wasn't a *totally* unprecedented experience for her! Poor Olgun . . .

The creature raised its hand yet again, Shins began to tense in anticipation of the next blow—and Olgun *whimpered*.

Absolute fury, molten, searing, coursed through Widdershins's veins. Her scream grew louder still, tearing at a throat already savaged by stomach acids and bile, but no longer was it a cry of pain.

The fae torturer's lashing digits descended once more—and Widdershins, impossibly, rolled to her feet to meet them.

It wasn't that she'd somehow ceased to feel the pain. It roared over her, flames licking from her gut and her back, digging white-hot blades across every nerve. What survived of her clothes were drenched in blood, shreds caked tight to her skin. And it was only that blood, still thickly oozing over her stomach, that prevented her, when glancing down, from spotting bits of herself that were never intended to see the light of day.

None of that had gone away. She hadn't escaped anything. Shins knew full well that nothing but a stubborn anger kept her body from giving out beneath her like an empty sack.

But in that single, liberating moment of fury, she didn't *care*.

Lisette and even the fae, almost comically astonished, seemed unable to react. Shins's fist closed tight around three of the creature's switches, squeezing them into a thick bundle, and yanked him off balance. Still shouting in a voice growing ever more hoarse, she allowed her entire body to follow her arm in a forceful spin, hauling as hard as she could. Her enemy stumbled as she pivoted, almost staggering into her from behind, when the elbow of her other arm shot backward, cracking him hard across the bridge of his nose.

The fae, she knew from her own experience, weren't particularly susceptible to injury. She knew, too, that her divine connection to Olgun made her a partial exception to that rule.

Howling in pain, the creature threw her off, launching her across the chamber. She slammed into the far wall and collapsed in a boneless heap, every nerve screaming, the whole world flashing, sparking, strobing. Still, she saw blood—or a thin liquid that was *probably* blood, though it more closely resembled a wet and runny water-based paint—trickling from her tormentor's nose.

And, she noted when her vision began to clear, from the noses of his various child-sized companions, as well.

The distant children ceased their laughter. The fae, masters and minions, stared at Widdershins as though not entirely sure what it was they were looking at. Lisette gawped, at a loss for words for the first time the young thief could ever recall.

Through a mask of blood, coating her lips, staining her chin, welling up through her teeth, Widdershins tossed them all a broad, unwavering smirk.

They were going to kill her; she couldn't even hope otherwise. She had absolutely nothing left to fight with. They might even break her, first.

But she'd tainted it for them. They'd hit her with everything, buried her under tortures and torments, and she'd still bloodied them. Their perfect vengeance, their easy victory, was neither. Not entirely.

It was, under the circumstances, the best she could ask for.

Apparently, Shins wasn't the only one in awe of her own efforts. After a moment's hissed discussion between Lisette and her allies, the fae faded away. Once more they were only shadows, collecting around the flame-haired thief, and then even that thin veil was gone. Just Lisette, again—albeit Lisette with a whole array of inhuman magics.

"I'm impressed," she said, striding across the room, her steps a slow drumbeat as she neared. "Honestly, I am. I keep reminding myself not to underestimate you, and still you keep surprising me."

A pace or two from where Shins lay, she stopped, dropping into a crouch so they might better see one another. "You're still more dangerous than you should be," Lisette observed. "And while it's not exactly my usual way of doing things, even *I* think that degree of determination and sheer gutsiness should be rewarded.

"So no more torture, little scab. No more pain." From the back of her belt, she produced a small flintlock. Beneath her thumb, the *click* of the hammer locking into place was deafening. "Time to end it. Maybe you can go see your little god."

The barrel, so tiny from any other angle, gaped open like a darkened cave when viewed face-on. Battling every remaining instinct, Shins refused to shut her eyes.

Everything happened so fast, once the first *bang!* finally sounded, that it took Shins far more concentration than it should have to realize she wasn't dead.

The first was a gunshot from *outside* the chamber, echoed and amplified by the enclosed confines of the hallway. Lisette jolted back, startled, standing upright . . .

The second *bang* blew the heavy door to the Shrouded Lord's former sanctum clear from its frame.

Only Shins's position slumped against the wall, beside that

door—or former door—saved her from the blast, as she was certainly in no condition to have avoided it. Already battered into uncertainty, her mind and senses threw an absolute fit. Her vision strobed again, offering only quick, still images of everything happening around her; her ears rocked from ringing to utter silence, allowing only the occasional sound in through their drunken staggering.

Dust and tiny shards of stone raining down, the petrified remains of a refreshing spring rain . . .

Plumes of smoke rolled through the empty doorway, a choking, searing cloud . . .

Lisette heaving herself back the length of the room, snagging the desk with one hand as she rolled across it, hauling it over with a strength she simply could not have possessed and then taking cover behind . . .

Guns roared; geysers of splinter or dust erupted where lead balls flatted against wood and stone . . .

Voices shouted behind the smoke, the words tumbling over and wrestling with one another, and Shins understood none of it, wasn't entirely sure what it was . . .

Blood seeped across the stone floor from uncounted open wounds, and Shins watched it, fascinated by every ripple, struggling to recall why it was important . . .

Another detonation, louder than any flintlock, and the chamber filled with smoke, smoke of briny scent and peculiar violet hue.

That's not right. The smoke here's supposed to be gray, yes? To match the Shrouded Lord's . . . shroud . . .

More yelling, more gunfire, a touch of prayer . . .

Prayer?

She was sure she knew what was happening, if she could just have a moment to tell herself, to *think*, to—

"I've got her!" Hands closed around Shins's upper arms, hauling her upright. She decided, somewhat dreamily, that it was a good thing she didn't know if she ought to fight or not, since she really *couldn't*, anyway.

"Who've y'got?" she mumbled, then cried out as an arm brushed against one of the open welts across her back.

An indrawn hiss sounded from the figure holding her upright. "Good gods, Widdershins. What did they do to you?"

"Bad things," she replied with a fervent nod, before bursting into tears.

The other voice quivered, as though on the verge of joining her. "Come, dear lady. Let's get you out of here." Then, in a much louder shout, "Fall back! The smoke's not going to impede the bitch for long!"

"The hell do you *think* we're doing?!" someone else called out, followed by an abortive shriek and a sudden, sickeningly wet thump.

"You're right," Lisette growled through the obscuring haze, from precisely where the prior call had come. "It won't."

"It doesn't have to," the man—definitely a man, she'd decided—holding Shins muttered. She felt herself being half-guided, half-dragged, from the room. More than once she stumbled . . . No. No, she was essentially in a single long stumble in which she occasionally managed a halfway steady step. Each time, her supporter's grip tightened or shifted to catch her, and each time she winced or gasped or wailed in agony.

"For the fucking gods' sake, someone help me with her!"

Someone slipped beneath her other arm, balancing her between the two of them, and their pace increased dramatically. Every step, every jostle, every moment was a new blade of anguish, but Widdershins gritted her teeth and let herself be carried along, slowly reawakening.

The hall was choked with smoke, but not nearly so badly as the chamber had been. Olgun's touch, shaky but as comforting as ever, hummed around the edges of her wounds, worked at shoveling the thickest of the cobwebs from her mind. And finally, she began to more clearly make out what was happening around her.

The man on her left, the one who'd only just appeared, she didn't know, though the general posture and shabby upkeep said "Down-and-out thief" to her. But the other, shorter one . . .

Well, though he currently lacked his accustomed ostentatious hat with even more ostentatious feather—which he would no doubt claim he had plucked from the tail of a phoenix—she could not possibly have failed to recognize the ornate mustache or deep-blue eyes, to say nothing of the bright-blue and white and yellow and violet of the tunic and half-cape.

"Renard?!"

Her old Finders' Guild mentor offered a genuine smile between harsh gasps for breath. "As ever and always at your service, Lady Widdershins."

Had her arm not already been around his shoulders, and were she not currently being dragged at a near running pace through the Guild's chapel, she could have hugged him.

Wait. The chapel*?! Why the—*

But Shins received her answer before she could ask. Several more of who she presumed were Renard's people waited therein, standing perhaps a third of the way around the chamber from the idol of the Shrouded God—around a gaping trapdoor that Widdershins had never known existed!

"Bwuh?" she inquired.

"I know every secret of this place," Renard said as he gestured for the others to clear a path. "This was the nearest hidden ingress to where I figured you would be. Well, the nearest one I trusted, now that Lisette knows of the concealed passage from the Shrouded Lord's chamber itself."

"Let us," a rather more imperious voice insisted, "save the questions and answers until we're clear. If that's all right by all of you?"

Shins craned her neck, wincing at the pain. Almost beside them was a dark-haired, dark-skinned, darkly-clad woman, of sharp and almost-but-not-quite regal features.

Igraine Vernadoe, priestess of the Shrouded God. Widdershins realized it must have been she who'd been praying earlier.

"Didn't know you cared," Shins managed with the faintest smile.

"I could still be talked out of it," Igraine warned as she dropped through the trapdoor.

Renard followed, and the next moments were sheer torment as several hands clasped Widdershins's body and—gently as they could, which under the circumstances wasn't very—lowered her down. Renard took one of her arms again, Igraine the other, and they proceeded down the cramped, dust-choked, web-bedecked passageway at what could, at best, be described as an impatient shuffle.

"Others not . . ." Shins gagged at the sudden inhalation of dust, sneezed hard, and spent the next minute or so waiting for the world to stop spinning beneath the onrush of pain from her injuries. "Not coming with us?" she finally croaked out.

"I still have a few people loyal to me left in the Guild," Renard said, drawing an unexplained glare from the priestess. "That's how I knew you were there, dear lady; they dispatched a runner to me the instant you arrived. If all went as planned, in the chaos of the incursion, nobody should be able to identify them as having assisted the 'invaders.' They should have been able to reseal the trap, too, so that the bitch and her people can't follow us."

"And," Igraine added as they passed one of the old wooden support struts, "if they do appear to have found the tunnel, we have other safeguards in place."

Following her gaze, Shins noted a parcel of some sort tied to the beam. A parcel with a fuse protruding from it.

"Notice there are no torches or lanterns?" Renard asked. "Very sensitive fuses. Bring a flame anywhere near them, and . . . loudness ensues."

Shins blinked, felt Olgun doing . . . whatever his equivalent of blinking was. "But I can see."

"Luminescent fungus. Deliberately cultivated long ago. Of course, anyone who finds the tunnel but doesn't know about that is going to assume they require a torch . . ."

"Got it. Thereby loudness."

"Precisely."

Shuffle. Shuffle. Step.

This is actually starting to hurt a little less. "Thank you." Heartfelt but silent, audible to no mortal listener. A warm glow, hesitant but growing stronger, in response.

Stumble.

But only a little less.

Shuffle. Shuffle.

And only then did her mind begin finally to catch up with the events of the last few minutes.

Wait one frog-hopping minute! "I *have people still loyal to* me . . ."? *Not us.* Me.

"How do you know Lisette knows about the escape tunnel in the Shrouded Lord's office?"

"Renard . . ." the priestess warned.

"Oh, what difference does it make now, Igraine?" he grumbled. "I know because I used it to get away from her the first time. And it was a near thing, believe you me."

Shins could only shake her head, which—under the circumstances—didn't accomplish much save to drag her hair through the wet blood across her back, and then brush the tips across the pair helping her. "Renard Lambert. The Shrouded Lord. I have to confess, I didn't see that coming."

"Anonymity is the whole point," Igraine groused. "Or it's *supposed* to be."

"Does it really matter anymore? I'm not in charge. There *is* no more Shrouded Lord. And even if there ever is again, we both know it won't be me, not after Lisette took over on my watch. No way the priests would allow it."

Shins heard a low mutter from the woman to her left, but it certainly didn't sound like a denial.

"I wasn't a good fit, anyway," he admitted to Widdershins, shifting her weight on his shoulders a bit. "I'm not ruthless enough. Never have been. The Finders might have been a little nicer under me, but they also weren't nearly as profitable. Even if Bitch Suvagne hadn't returned and yanked the rug out from under all of us, I probably only had a couple of years left before I was replaced. A process, I should hasten to point out, that I might or might not have survived.

"No, when all this is over, someone else gets to take up the burden. I'm done with it."

"*Someone* obviously thought you were right for the position," Shins said after another moment.

"How do you mean?"

"A position that powerful, where being imposing is basically your *job* . . . ?"

"Yes?"

"Well, they *clearly* waived the height requirement for your sake!"

Igraine's normally tight expression shattered in a burst of laughter, however reluctantly. Olgun joined her, though only Shins knew, and after a prolonged gawp, so did Renard himself.

When he'd calmed again, he squeezed Widdershins's shoulder, as lightly as he could manage. "You've been missed, my dear. And I think Igraine and I both needed that. Hasn't been a great deal to laugh about these days."

Shins elbowed him—so weakly it really wasn't much more than a faint brushing, but all she could manage for the nonce. "If you've been trying to lie low," she scolded, "those colors aren't exactly the most inconspicuous. You look like a birdhouse. Without the house."

"I do not, alas, dress so fashionably on a daily basis under the circumstances. Tonight, however, was a special occasion."

"I can't imagine why," Igraine interjected. "It's not as though you needing to be rescued from obscene quantities of danger is an uncommon occurrence."

"Hey! I resent that uncomfortably accurate assessment! Guys . . . Renard . . ." The passageway tilted, perhaps attempting to buck her off, and her head and body began once again spinning in multiple directions at once, including a few she'd never heard of. "I need . . . I need a few minutes. I'm sorry."

"No apologies." The priest and the former Shrouded Lord carefully sat Shins down on the gritty floor. Renard swept his half-cape from around his shoulders and draped it across hers, so she need not lean her lacerated back against the unyielding and rather dramatically dirty wall. She offered him a soft smile and a grateful nod; even that was nearly enough to make her topple over, vomit, or both.

Renard's fingers twitched with every wobble, reaching to catch her. "Gods, you . . . Igraine, can't we do something? I don't understand how she's conscious, let alone at all mobile!"

"Well, we all know Widdershins isn't a normal girl, don't we?" The priestess knelt, gently prodding at the younger woman's injuries. "If she . . . Heavens and hells, you should be dead!"

"It's almost . . . hurtful how many people . . . seem to think that of me," Shins gasped, flinching at every poke.

"I have some clean rags, enough to slap a few makeshift bandages on the worst of these, but—"

"Just keep me from . . . falling apart for a few days."

"Olgun can handle the rest?" Igraine asked. Then, at Widdershins's start, "This entire city is in turmoil, not just the Guild. I've been spending a great deal of time consulting with His Eminence Sicard. I have a much better understanding of your—situation—than I did."

"Sicard has . . . a big mouth."

"I'm sure you'll have your chance to yell at him."

"Can we," Renard begged, "discuss this someplace where we can all be a bit less filthy and bleeding?"

"You're starting to talk like her," the priestess accused.

Shins snorted, winced, tried to think of a term to encompass both, and gave up. "He should be so lucky." Another rough gasp. "He's right, though. It shouldn't be too hard to get to the Witch from why are you all giving me that look?"

Indeed, not only could she see it from her two fellow former Finders, she felt it from her third companion as well.

"Widdershins," Renard pointed out gently, "the very first place Lisette is going to try to find you would be . . ." He finished with a shrug, clearly feeling it unnecessary to spell out any further.

Shins wondered if she had enough blood left to blush. Her cheeks certainly gave it a solid effort. "I knew that," she grumbled. "I just wanted to see if *you* remembered."

"I know I'm going to regret asking, but why, by the entire Pact, would *I* have forgotten?"

"Well, you and Igraine are both all blurry, and have been since you showed up. How am I supposed to know what *else* might be wrong with you?"

Renard and Igraine shared a wry and somehow vaguely resigned glance. "It's like you foresaw the future," the woman said blandly.

Shins's own expression, however, had fallen dramatically. "We still need to go, though," she insisted. "If Lisette shows up and I'm not there . . . Robin, and the others . . ."

"You're in no shape to help them," the foppish thief replied.

"No, but *you* are!"

"Shins—"

"Look, you and Igraine and the others have been in hiding for a while. You have safe houses and message drops, yes? So she and I'll find somewhere to hole up and then let you know where. But I need you to do this!"

She can't get hurt because of me. Not again . . .

"Okay, but . . . Igraine can go just as easily as I can. I'll take you to—"

"No. Robin, may—need a lot of convincing just now. And she knows you. She trusts you. Ish."

"Trustish?" Renard protested, his tone forced and weak. "I don't believe that's in any way a legitimate word."

"And now you're talking like someone *else* I know," Shins sighed, ignoring Olgun's own somewhat strained chuckle. "Renard, there's nobody else. I'm running out of allies. I can't ask the Guard to protect her. Even if anyone there would listen to me, I'm wanted for killing . . . actually, I have no *idea* who the figs I'm supposed to have killed!"

"I'd heard that you were wanted," he told her thoughtfully. "But I'd not been able to learn why. Only that the word comes down from on high."

"Lovely. And today was going so well. Point is, it has to be you. It needs to happen this way. *I* need for it to. Please."

"Oh, just go," Igraine ordered. "We both know you're going to give in eventually, so why waste the time?"

"You'll take care of her?" the former Shrouded Lord almost begged.

"No, I'm going to knock her over the head, steal her purse, dump her in a kennel somewhere, and run off to Rannanti with the proceeds." Then, when the two thieves stared at her, "Get out of here, Renard."

After one last moment of reluctant fidgeting, he got. For a minute or so after *that*, the women just sort of studied each other.

"It took both of you to get me this far," Shins said finally. "Can you get me out of here on your own?"

"You'll have to take more of your own weight. But I'm stronger than I look."

Shins forced herself to her feet, almost gasping in relief as a tiny current of Olgun's power ran through her. With his help, she *could* take more of her own weight.

Barely.

She chuckled, even as she caught herself with one hand against a support beam before she could stumble. "I think it's more important right now," she commented through a tight grin, "that you be stronger than *I* look."

Igraine clucked her tongue once, adjusted Renard's cloak around Widdershins to hide the horrid bloodstains and the immodest rips in her tunic, and then wrapped her own arm about the younger woman's shoulders.

"I've seen half-drowned kittens," she said as they began a slow, unsteady walk toward the passageway's end, "that looked stronger than you do."

Widdershins managed another polite chuckle. "So where *are* you taking me? The Basilica?"

"No. Suvagne knows that many of the Shrouded God's priests are among Renard's allies. She'll have people watching. Besides, there's as much unrest in Sicard's ranks right now as there is everywhere else in this godsforsaken city. Actually," she admitted, "I'm not entirely *decided* on where to hide you. I'm not sure any of our Ragway safe houses is secure, and the others—"

"That's okay," Shins interrupted, almost brightly. "I know where we should go!"

"Of course you do. Why do I just know I'm not going to like this?" the priestess complained.

"Because you don't like anything."

Silence, for a time, save for the shuffling steps.

Not, obviously, a situation Widdershins would let stand indefinitely. "Igraine?"

"Hmm?"

"Only *half*-drowned? Really? I'm improving faster than I thought."

"Shut up and walk."

CHAPTER NINE

"Of all the plans you've ever hatched," Igraine growled, peering around the shadowy street corner at their startlingly well-lit destination, "this one is inarguably one of the most *Widdershins*."

"Oh. Well, thank you!"

"That wasn't a compliment!"

"You think not?" Shins sniffed "Shows what you know. *Nobody* plans the way I do!"

"Now *that*, I agree with."

Widdershins scowled, shooing a few early-season flies away from the drying bloodstains peeking around the edges of Renard's cape. "Look," she explained, and not for the first time, "it's perfect. He's probably not even *in* Davillon! His family's got no properties or interests here, so when things started getting bad. . . . But I'm sure he's kept the rent on the place. He'd want to make sure he didn't have to live in the 'squalor' of a *regular* house if and when he returns, yes? So it should be empty, and there's no chance anyone'd think to look for us *here*!"

"That's because we're not going to get in the door without being stopped and reported! I'm covered in dust and cobweb from the tunnel, and you look like a raw fillet trying to rise above its station!"

The younger woman drew herself up, proud and straight, and then slumped again with a wince at the tug on her slowly scabbing wounds. "I've gotten in there before!" she protested.

"Uh-huh. Through the front entrance?"

"Well, no . . ."

"And how many walls are you going to be climbing in your *current* condition?"

"Oh, come on!" Shins protested. "We just need a diversion of some sort."

"Hmm. All right. You pass me the cloak, so your wounds are obvious, and then go collapse in the street. Then, when everyone's gathered around you . . ."

"Yes?"

Igraine offered an almost helpless shrug. "I'll leave."

Widdershins's first comment was directed at Olgun, not the priestess. "How do you snort like that without a nose?" Then, more loudly, "Cute plan."

"I thought it had some charm to it."

"May I," Shins asked haughtily, "make an alternate suggestion?"

"I was almost certain you would."

It didn't require much, all in all. A nearby stable provided the raw materials. ("Raw materials," in this instance, meaning "horses.") A bit of shouting and arm-waving bolstered by a surge of artificial panic from Olgun, and the beasts began rearing and screaming, agitated without quite being alarmed enough to injure themselves.

After that, as the building's private guards and those few people out and about in the street gravitated toward the commotion, it was simple enough for Igraine to help Widdershins stagger away from the stable, as though she'd been injured by a frenzied hoof.

And then they really did just walk through the front door.

The one and only time Shins had previously visited the Golden Sable, she hadn't seen the entryway, the open lobby, the broad halls. Carpet, thick and lush enough to warm a bear in winter, led to a series of doors here, a massive staircase there. Clean-burning lanterns of polished brass and scintillating crystal held the shadows at bay to all but the deepest corners. Several servants in livery or other fine outfits looked down their noses at the shoddy pair, but none of them said a word. They all had their own duties to think about, and probably assumed Shins and Igraine would be hearing an earful from their own employer soon enough.

Three flights up, several corridors in, and they finally halted at what Widdershins *believed* was the proper door. (Having only ever entered the suite via the window, and never having set foot in the rest of the building, "believed" was as certain as she was getting, and "guessed" was probably a more honest assessment.)

"This place is unbelievable!" Igraine sounded almost offended rather than impressed. "This is an *inn?*"

"Not exactly," Shins said, hesitantly kneeling beside the door and fumbling for the last few picks that remained hidden in her belt and boots. "The Golden Sable's sort of long-term manor-sized suites for the high and flighty who aren't in town often enough to be worth buying something more permanent. Comes complete with servants, if you don't have your own. The Davillon Home for Wayward Aristocrats."

"However often the Finders hit this place," the other woman muttered, "it's not enough." She started, then, and the faint *clank-slosh-fwump* as Shins took a swig of something from a faceted crystal decanter, then set the vessel down beside her as she worked. "Where in the Shrouded God's name did you get that?!"

"One of the aforementioned servants. He was too busy sneering at us to pay attention to the contents of his tray.

"Oh, don't give me that look! I have so much dried blood coating my mouth and throat, I couldn't even smell the frog-hopping stables! It's pure luck I'm even still able to *talk*!"

"I don't know if 'luck' is the word I'd have—"

"Shut up and have some brandy."

Igraine did nothing of the sort, instead looming over Shins's shoulder and wincing at the occasional *click* within the lock. "Do you want me to do that?"

"I'm a little better at it than you are," Shins insisted, tongue slightly protruding in concentration as she worked the tumblers.

"You're also injured," the priestess pointed out.

"That's why I'm only a *little* better at it. And there's that look again. You're going to get bored of it *eventually*, yes?"

"Not at this rate."

"You're way too uptight about this." Shins leaned back in triumph as a much heavier *clank* announced the lock's unconditional surrender. She reached up, using the latch to heave herself to her feet as she slowly, silently began to open the door. "I told you, he's not going to be here."

"And if you're wrong?"

"Then we reason with him. I'm not exactly his favorite person in the world—or even in this hallway—but he *can* be reasoned with. We*aaaaaughk!!!*"

Something yanked the door away from her, taking her already precarious balance with it. Shins crashed headlong to the carpet, unable to catch herself or even to react at all, save to bite back a whimper at the renewal of agony across her back and stomach. Inch by inch, she twisted her neck until she lay on her cheek rather than her aching nose, struggling to see.

What she saw was the unwavering tip of a rapier, some few inches from her eyeball, and the onyx-haired, hawk-featured man standing at the other end of it.

"I suggest," said Evrard d'Arras, "that you start reasoning."

❀

She squirmed, occasionally thrashing, caged by shackles of fever between waking and sleeping, dreaming and thinking. Sweat plastered the light sheets to her body—light yet stifling, as though it were thick wool in the height of summer. Even had she the presence of mind to kick it off, though, as she had a time or two already, the result was just a fit of shivers instead.

The faint buzzing of Olgun's touch, the burning at the edges of the wounds, the ointments Igraine had applied after washing off the worst of the grime and gore, the unfamiliar itch of the bandages and the bed, combined in Widdershins's feverish, semiconscious mind into a skintight covering of twitching, biting, dancing ants. She moaned, absently slapping at herself, and rolled over yet again, further twisting the sheet into a veritable rope of cloth.

Voices from the next room, voices from inside her head; she found it difficult to tell, between the bouts of oppressive silence, which were which. Still, a time or two, she'd caught snippets of conversation that were, she was *almost* sure, passing between the priestess and their rather grudging host.

". . . wasn't going to throw her out in the street in that condition," Evrard was snarling, or so she thought. "I'm not a savage! But you need to get her the hell *out* of here!"

"She's in no condition to be moved!" Igraine's voice lashed back. "And even if she were, I've nowhere to take her."

"Not my concern. Damn it, Vernadoe, you know what she did to me, to my fam—"

"Oh, don't even *start*. She's a thief. That's what she does. Your family hadn't even *seen* that stuff in years!"

"Not the point, and you—"

"And I rather clearly recall you fighting alongside her almost a year ago."

Soft thumps suggested pacing, followed by the much louder and quite distinctive *thud* of fist on wall. "That was an emergency! Just because I've decided I don't necessarily want her dead doesn't mean I've forgiven her, that she has any right to ask me for any sort of aid! The bloody *gall* of that little . . ."

At this point the voices were drowned out by a semi-waking dream in which Shins could only hear the horrid laughter of that ghostly chorus that had accompanied the creature Iruoch, except this time Robin's voice sounded clearly among them. Before she could even begin to contemplate *that*, she was out again.

And awake once more, to the sound of heated argument. And out again. Awake to the slam of a cupboard of some sort; for no reason she could articulate, she was quite certain it was a wine closet. Then out again.

Jolted away by the staccato, percussive clatter of a fist banging on the front door. The slow, soft patter of feet creeping across the carpeted foyer.

She pushed herself up on wildly trembling arms that felt less like flesh and bone, and more along the lines of a desperate effort to support her weight on two snakes doing headstands. The muscles in her back and her stomach seemed to be trying to switch sides. Nevertheless, no matter how difficult, she was determined not to lie here helpless, to go see who had arrived and what was happening in the rest of the suite.

It was a determination she kept all the way back down to the mattress, and once more into uneasy, hallucinatory slumber.

It was the cold—gentle, soothing—that finally woke her properly, hauling her slowly but steadily through the depths of fever and pain and exhaustion. A soft, cool touch, washing away some of the sting across her skin. She felt the shimmer of Olgun's power as the god worked his own magics, adding his influence to the herbs and clean water that Widdershins knew, without checking, were contained in the soft cloths caressing her.

Sheer bliss, in that peculiar way that pain can be a relief when it replaces a greater agony; Shins almost sighed aloud.

At which point, four semi-related thoughts sprinted across her mind in quick succession, chasing one another like maniacal weasels.

Gods, that's so much better on my back than that fig-flipping blanket was, even if the smell does *remind me of week-old tea! Dumb sheet felt like it was woven of hemp!*

*It would've been nice of everyone to keep their voices down, though. What
if they'd woken me up before the balm did? I'd have felt like—*

Wait, "everyone"? Why is this room suddenly so crowded?

And finally, if someone was tending to her back . . .

Oh, monkeys! I'm not wearing a shirt, am I?

Through sheer force of will, Shins broke through the last
remaining layers of fluff and cobweb draped across her mind, pried
her eyes open, and took stock. Her face was all but buried in an airy
pillow, so she still couldn't see much. She *was* still covered by the
sheet, she realized, now that she was paying attention. She could
still feel it; from her hips down. From there up, she could only give
thanks that Igraine—she assumed it was the priestess cleaning her
wounds and changing her bandages—was working on her back, not
her stomach.

Not that it would have mattered, had Igraine been the only one
present. But in the babble of voices—at *least* four—Shins could clearly
make out Evrard d'Arras, complaining almost petulantly about the
number of people who had invited themselves into his home.

And, too, the voice of Renard Lambert, arguing with him.

Only when Igraine snapped, "All of you, be *quiet*! She's awake,"
did Widdershins realize that she herself had been the source of that
sudden, mortified squeak.

"Is she going to be okay?" Another voice, familiar, quivering
with concern.

Robin. Robin's here, too?

Then that probably made the speaker she *hadn't* been able to
identify, that she had only barely recognized at all. . . . What was her
name? F-something . . .

Faustine.

Robin's lover.

Igraine was in the midst of telling Robin that if she wanted
to know how Shins was doing, she could very well ask her directly,

now that everyone's lack of consideration had woken her up, but the priestess didn't get to finish. For it was then that Shins finally redis-covered her *own* voice.

"*Renard!*"

She actually heard the impact of his skin on the inside of his clothing as he jumped. "What?!"

"If you've taken one tiny peek at anything you shouldn't have," she said, trying to squish herself more tightly against the mattress, "you're going to lose your eyeballs. And you'll be lucky if it's *just* the eye-kind!"

"My dear Widdershins!" The foppish thief sounded truly aghast, and perhaps just a bit defensive. "I would never even *think* of—"

"—admitting to such a thing," she finished for him.

"And why is it," he sniffed, "that I receive such suspicion and ill-treatment, and Monsieur d'Arras does not?"

"You leave me—!" Evrard began.

"Because I'm not yelling at *him*," she said, "until I either feel a lot better, or I know there are no sharp objects within reach."

"—out of this," he finished with a sigh.

"I think *everyone* needs to leave," Shins grumped. "I am too tired, too sore, and apparently too naked for this much company."

"All right, everyone," Robin announced firmly. "You heard her. *Out.*"

"This is *my* home—!" Evrard once more began without finishing.

Shins swore she could *hear* the scowl on Robin's face. "Then you should be quite well acquainted with the location of the doors."

Carrying a varied array of whispers, comments, and mutters with them, the ad hoc assembly trooped out into the next room. Robin whispered something to Igraine—Shins couldn't make out what, but even at so low a volume, she knew the younger woman's voice—and then the bed shifted as the priestess, who had been sitting at the edge of the mattress, stood up.

"All right," she said, in response to whatever Robin has asked. "But just cleaning them. Come get me for anything after that."

Steps sounded, the door shut, and the bed shifted again as someone took Igraine's spot. Shins suddenly found herself grateful that she lay on her stomach, face buried in the pillow, so she wouldn't have to meet her friend's gaze.

Although she still felt him tending her injuries, inspiring her flesh to knit far faster and more neatly than it ever should have, Olgun began to fade. Not completely, not ever, but enough so he remained only the slightest presence, a stray thought, all but forgotten.

It was, she knew, his way of offering Shins her privacy for what they both knew were the awkward moments to come. She loved him for it.

I should probably tell him that more often.

I should probably tell a lot of people that more often.

The soft slosh of heavy fabric, dipped in water; a renewed whiff of the herbal concoction; and then, once more, a gentle, cooling touch, feather-light across the worst of the welts and slashes.

And beyond that, and the muted susurrus of conversation leaking through the far wall, only silence. Only silence, until Shins couldn't stand it any longer.

"I can't believe Igraine let everyone in here with me like this," she observed, her tone so brittle a mistimed sneeze could shatter it.

"Well, there were some important things being discussed, and she *did* have you face-down. . . ."

"Hmph." Another pause, then, "Guess it's just like old times. I've been back two days, and I'm already a bloody mess, and you're in danger and hiding again."

Robin's chuckle was faint, but it sounded genuine. "I'm surprised it took *that* long, really."

"Well, I *am* out of practice."

Another soft laugh, from both this time. The atmosphere in the chamber remained thick as gruel, but Shins found herself breathing just a bit easier.

"So," Shins said again, a brief eternity later. "Faustine?"

"Yeah." Robin's ministrations halted for perhaps a second, then resumed. "Does that bother you?"

"I . . . no. No, Robs, it doesn't bother me. I just . . . never noticed some things, I guess."

"No." A tinge of bitterness, now, subtle enough that Shins would have missed it coming from anyone else. "You wouldn't have."

What the hopping hens is that *about?*

As this didn't seem quite the right time to ask for clarification, however, she chose a different tack. "Is she taking care of you?"

As Shins had practically heard her friend's scowl earlier, so she swore she heard the broad smile now. "When I need it. And the other way around. She's good for me, Shins, if that's what you're asking."

"I'm glad. You need good people in your life."

In the distant corner of her deepest thoughts, Olgun slapped a nonexistent hand to a nonexistent forehead. That had been, Shins realized when Robin's hands tensed, *exactly* the wrong thing to say.

"Oh, figs. Robin . . ."

"Faustine's been with me every second I needed her," Robin replied in a near monotone. "Renard's been by the Witch pretty regularly. Always somehow manages a free mug of something out of the deal, but it's nice to have him around. Also that guard, once or twice. Julien's friend; what was his name? Paschal, right?"

"Uh . . ."

"Never for very long, just sort of poking his head in. Even Evrard's been in a few times."

"Ev—he—what?"

Robin's shrug shifted the mattress a hair. "Well, he has."

"That's probably guilt, you know. From the whole 'kidnapping you' thing."

"Probably. But at least he was *here*."

"Robin, come on! I told you, I had to . . . had . . ."

Had to get away. Couldn't face losing Julien on top of everything else that'd happened, everyone else who's been taken from me.

She'd said it before, aloud. She'd said it a thousand times in her head. She'd believed it, wholeheartedly, when she left.

She had *not* believed it since Aubier, not since she'd nearly died in Castle Pauvril. Not really. She'd admitted as much at the time, to herself, even to Olgun. So why cling to it so stubbornly now?

And once she'd asked herself the question, the answer came as clearly as if Olgun had spelled it out for her in the stars.

She'd been wrong, selfish; and it meant she could no longer justify, even to herself, any of the hurt she'd caused.

Widdershins wasn't sure precisely when she'd begun weeping into the pillow. She knew only, now, that she couldn't stop. Her sobs were gasping, ugly, leaving splotches of tears all over the fabric. Her shoulders heaved, tugging, if only lightly, on wounds and bandages.

When she felt Robin's hands on those shoulders—gentle again, comforting, no trace of their earlier rigidity, no hint of anger—it only drove her into further, more copious tears.

"I'm sorry." Less than a whisper, less than a rasp, ground out between hiccoughs, gasping, and sobs. "Gods, Robin, I'm sorry."

"I know." Her voice, too, had grown unsteady. "I know you are, Shins. And I know you didn't *mean* to abandon me—any of your friends. That you weren't thinking clearly.

"I understand, but do *you*? Do you get why 'sorry' isn't enough? Why I can't forgive you yet?"

Something inside Widdershins crumpled into a tight mass at those last words. She wanted, literally, to pull the covers over her head, to break into a crying jag that would make the previous look downright celebratory.

She managed not to. Barely.

"Tell me. I want to make things right."

"Other than Genevieve, you were the only person I can even *remember* trusting—until Faustine, anyway. You were the one I counted on. Even when things were at their worst, when you were hurt and crying . . . I knew that, no matter what, you would be there when I needed you, and there was nothing you couldn't handle."

Shins felt something trying to reopen the wound in her gut, from the inside. "And then I left."

"And then you left."

"Robin, nobody could be what—"

"I know. I've figured that out. I'm not angry at you for being human, Shins. But that's where I was. That's who you were to me. And when I learned you could let me down . . ."

Shins nodded awkwardly into the cushion. "You felt betrayed," she hazarded.

The other woman's hair *swished* faintly, signaling her own nod. "By the person I trusted most, loved most, in the world."

Loved most . . .

Such an innocent turn of phrase, but the *click* as everything came together in Widdershins's head was so deafening, she was stunned it didn't bring the others running back into the room.

It explained so very, very much.

With infinite care—not only of her own physical wounds, but her friend's emotional ones—Shins turned and sat up, so she could meet Robin's eyes. She drew up the blanket, clutching it to her chest. Not out of any sense of modesty, not with Robin, but because doing otherwise would have felt as though she were making light of what she should have known years ago, but only just figured out.

"How long?" she asked softly.

Robin, to her credit, didn't even pretend not to understand. "The cliché would be to say since the day I met you. And I think that's partly true. But . . . for real, for certain? Since after Genevieve died."

One hand still holding the sheet to her, Shins reached out with the other to cup her friend's cheek. Robin's sigh was almost a sob as she leaned into the touch, her eyes shut.

"I *do* love you, Robin. You know I do. It's just, I don't . . . it's not . . ."

"Not like that." The younger woman's eyelids fluttered open, exposing brimming tears that she refused to shed. Taking Widdershins's hand in her own, she slowly removed it from her face. "I know."

Widdershins was crying again, this time—since Robin would or could not—for both of them. "But you *are* my family, Robin. Is that . . . is that enough?"

She took the other woman's fierce embrace—one that threatened to knock her back off the bed and would probably have been a lot more pleasant without the many wounds—as a yes.

They stayed there for a while, Shins gazing absently at the room beyond Robin's shoulder. Guest chamber, probably. Heavy oak furniture, polished to an almost golden gleam; basin of shining silver; heavy-framed mirror on the wall. She found herself idly planning different ways of sneaking said basin and mirror from the room—not because she actually planned to steal anything, but as an exercise to calm her racing mind, make her emotions lie placid again.

"Besides," Robin said mischievously, pulling back from the hug and rather shamefacedly wiping her nose on one sleeve, "I've drilled peepholes into all the bedrooms at the Witch, so wherever you end up staying will do for me."

Something in the way Widdershins's jaw so limply dropped, nearly bouncing off the mattress and quite possibly wobbling around the room, sent the girl into absolute hysterics. Shins herself joined her a moment later, the both of them laughing until even the uninjured one began to hurt.

She'd been to one of her flats; she'd been to the Flippant Witch; she'd been to the Guild. Here, now, for the first time since she'd returned to Davillon, Widdershins felt like she might be home.

CHAPTER TEN

Several more hours of sleep, a few more treatments of Igraine's balm, a large helping of Olgun's magic, and the emotional weight of almost losing her best friend finally lifted from her shoulders, Widdershins felt like a new woman.

A new woman who had been built with some defective parts, perhaps, but new nonetheless.

The fact that she was freshly bathed, no longer caked with dried sweat and blood, and once more dressed in clothes neither stiff nor well on their way to becoming confetti didn't hurt her mood any, either. Robin had brought along a portion of the wardrobe Shins had left behind, so long ago. They weren't her "working leathers," but the black trousers, forest-green vest, and deep-burgundy tunic were all dark enough, loose enough, and sturdy enough to make do.

Even if they did make her smell like the inside of a dusty drawer.

She stood, idly examining the portrait hanging above the (currently unused) fireplace, while the others drifted into the room behind her. Framed in gold filigree, it portrayed a somber, darkly dressed noblewoman in somber, darkly hued oils. She looked *just* similar enough to Evrard that she could have been of d'Arras blood—or she might have been an utter stranger, the painting provided as decoration by the Golden Sable itself. Who the steaming purple pits knew what sorts of luxuries the patrons of this place would expect? Even during the brief period of her life she'd spent with Alexandre Delacroix, when she'd truly been wealthy, she'd have avoided this sort of place like . . . well, if not like the plague, then at least a rash with open sores.

The mutter of conversation and the soft flops of people seating themselves on decadently overstuffed couch cushions or chairs grudgingly gave way to the clink of crystal and a faint sloshing. Evrard appeared beside her, a glass goblet in each hand. "A distant aunt," he said, indicating the portrait with one of the drinks before handing it over to her. "Sister of my great, great . . ." He stopped and thought a moment. "Great, great grandmother," he concluded.

"I figured something like that," she told him, nodding a brief thanks as she accepted the goblet. "She appears to have your sense of humor."

Evrard smiled at that, but it was a hollow expression at best—proving her point, in essence. "Why are you here, Widdershins?"

"Uh, did you not notice all the blood and desperation pooling on the floor when we first—"

"I know why you *came* here," he interrupted, his exasperation growing ever more evident by the syllable. "And I wasn't about to throw an injured woman out onto the street. You are, however, remarkably improved. I did *not* invite your entire social circle to join you. And I do believe I have exhausted even the most liberal definition of chivalrous obligation.

"So please, by all means, enjoy the brandy. Gather your belongings. And be so kind as to lead an exodus from my home."

"Why?"

Evrard, taking a dramatic sip after his pronouncement, nearly choked. "*Why?!*"

"I mean, we're not going to find a lot of other safe places where we can all sit and discuss this. And I figured *you'd* certainly be more comfortable here. But if there's someplace you'd rather be, lead the way."

The way he blinked at her, Shins had to wonder if he was trying to propel himself away by creating a strong enough gust. It took him a moment to stop, to fully comprehend precisely what she was implying.

"I am *not* a part of your little conspiracy!" he snapped at her.

Her smile was genuine, her tone sympathetic. "Of course you are, Evrard."

Shins had battled beside the man against a blatantly inhuman foe. She'd appeared unnoticed in his home once, when he had every reason to believe she wished him as dead as he'd wished her. She had even, on one occasion, sent him crumpling to the floor in a very crowded party with a very hard kick to a very sensitive spot.

She had still never seen him as boggled and speechless as he appeared now.

"You stayed," she said, placing her goblet carefully on the mantel. "From what I'm told, the city's been a mess for months. You have no family holdings here, no relatives. Nothing obvious to keep you. But you stayed.

"I don't know if you've just come to care for the city, or you have friends here now, or what. But for whatever reason, what happens here matters to you."

"Even if I were to grant all this," the aristocrat snarled, "not wanting to abandon colleagues isn't the same thing as volunteering to wage war against every last misfortune that afflicts Davillon. We have a Guard for that!"

"The Guard's as up to their necks as everyone else. You *have* actually left this place in the last few weeks, yes? There're more House soldiers on the street than guards."

"That doesn't—"

"You stood against Iruoch, Evrard. Because you realized you'd gone too far in your stupid vendetta with me, and because it was the honorable thing to do. For you and your family name."

"*Still* not the same—"

"It's partly our fault."

This time, his question wasn't a challenge but genuine wonder. And genuine worry. "What are you talking about?"

"The horrible witch of a woman responsible for these troubles? Lisette Suvagne? She has powers. Allies. They're not human. They're the ones that did . . ." She stuck a hand over her shoulder, pointing down with her thumb. "*This* to me. They're here because we killed *him*. Their—brother or cousin or creepy uncle or whatever he was."

"The Gloaming Court . . ." Evrard breathed.

Not a term she herself would have come up with, but hearing it spoken aloud, yes. From fairy tale and legend, the noble House of the worst the fae had to offer. Only a very few of the tales of Iruoch associated him with the Court, but a few was enough.

The nobleman made one last try, even if it was—transparently, almost ludicrously—for pride's sake. "And what makes you so sure you know me as well as you think you do?" he demanded. "We've spent a grand total of several *hours* in each other's company, in our *lives*. What makes you *so* certain I'm going to feel bound to help finish this?"

"You checked in on Robin while I was away."

Evrard snapped off a few words he *definitely* didn't learn from any of his proper tutors, shattered his goblet against the stone of the fireplace, and dropped into the nearest chair in a magnificent sulk.

Shins turned away until she could bring her expression under control and she was certain she wasn't about to burst out laughing at the sudden sensation of Olgun sticking out his (metaphorical) tongue and making various rude bodily sounds with his (metaphorical) lips.

Everyone else was already gathered—and, Shins realized, had probably heard every word of her conversation with their host. *Not my problem*, she decided. *I didn't say anything I'm ashamed of.* Renard and Igraine had taken a pair of matching chairs, on either side of a tiny, circular table. She couldn't say for sure, but Shins guessed that whatever whispers were passing between them, both leaning in toward the other, had something to do with the Guild. Frankly, she wasn't sure what secrets they'd be talking about that were worth keeping at this point, but old habits—and, if they were careful, old thieves—died hard.

The remaining pair had chosen the smaller of the room's two sofas, pressed tightly together, Faustine's arm protectively around Robin's shoulder, as though daring anyone to say anything. Robin twisted and fidgeted a bit, and Shins realized her leg must be bothering her. The young thief felt a sharp pang of guilt over her friend's injury, wondered how long it might be before that stopped happening.

And wondered if she *deserved* for it to ever stop happening.

Maybe there's one *thing I can do. . . .* Shins watched, waiting until Faustine happened to meet her gaze, and then inclined her head toward the table with the decanter of brandy. The courier's brow wrinkled in confusion, but she whispered a word in Robin's ear and stood. Shins met her, reaching out to refill her goblet while she was at it.

"Robin told me more or less everything," she began.

Faustine's expression didn't so much as twitch. "I know."

"Including how she feels about me . . ."

Definitely a twitch, this time. "I know."

". . . and how she feels about *you*. She's my best friend, Faustine. My sister. I want you two to be happy. I'm won't get in your way; I'm not competing with you."

The twitch became an avalanche, a score of different emotions, some fire and some ice, washing across the other woman's face faster than Shins could identify them. Faustine finally settled—though it appeared to take some effort—on a sad smile.

"Of course you are," she said softly. "You always will be. It's kind of amusing that you think it's even up to you. You have no say in the matter, Widdershins. Neither do I."

"Oh. I . . . oh."

Faustine's jaw marginally unclenched, her smile appearing more natural, if only slightly. "I do appreciate the sentiment, though. Thank you for trying."

As Shins couldn't for the life of her think of anything more to say to that, she simply watched as Faustine returned to the sofa, and her arm to Robin's shoulders. She felt strangely embarrassed, as though she'd just intruded into something in which she had no business.

"I meant for that to *help*," she sighed to Olgun. The surge of understanding, of sympathy she received in return only made her feel a little better. But even a little was good.

"All right, then," she said, abruptly pivoting to face the room at large. "We all know what sort of truly bizarre, horrible poop has happened in this city in the past."

"'Poop'?" Faustine and Evrard asked in unison. Shins ignored them.

"And we all know that some pretty bizarre, horrible . . . *stuff* is going on now. But does anyone know what the feathered, steaming horses is actually *happening*?"

Everyone glanced sidelong at everyone else, everyone shifted in his or her seat, and nobody said a thing.

"Yeah. Kind of what I thought. Time to compare heads and put our notes together, then."

Once more, a deafening array of no responses. They all agreed in theory—she could see that much on their faces—but nobody knew precisely where to start.

Evrard cleared his throat, and Shins pretended she hadn't nearly jumped from her skin. "*What?* Uh, that is, yes?"

"I'm not looking to reopen old wounds," the aristocrat said, and indeed, he sounded truly reluctant, even sympathetic. "Or new ones, I suppose. But . . . Widdershins, you seem to be near the center of this, if not actually *at* it . . ."

"As always," Igraine mumbled.

". . . and I'm still not entirely clear on just what *happened* to you."

"You didn't see those wounds!" Robin shouted, standing up despite the obvious discomfort. "Not up close! You can't ask her to relive—"

"It's okay, Robin." Shins could have hugged her about then, but

. . . "Everyone needs to know everything, if we're going to figure this out. It's okay. I—"

Except it wasn't. It *wasn't* okay. The thief's throat seemed to squeeze itself shut, a vise of fear and flesh. She tried to think back to that room, that pain, that *thing* that had caused her so much agony. Tried, and failed. Her mind fled, screaming, from the images; she felt her breath coming fast and weak, her heart pounding like a thousand hoofbeats.

Then . . . Olgun. Of course. *Always* Olgun, no matter what. As sure as sunrise.

It flowed from her heart, first, not her head. A cloud of peace and calm, ink spreading in clear water. He held her, took her arm as she turned to face those memories. Lay a veil across the images, so the finer details blurred. Whispered assurances in her ear.

Reminded her—promised her—she was safe.

Her breathing slowed, enough for her to murmur under it. "I don't know what I'd do without you."

One deliberately deep, languid breath, to steady herself; one deep gulp of brandy for a bit of *extra* steadiness. And it was time.

"What happened," she said to her tiny but rapt audience, "is I got cocky."

She paused, briefly, to allow for any of the expected gasps or comments of sarcastic surprise, but for a change, there were none.

"It's been a while since many people—human people—have been much of a threat to me, one on one. Not with the . . . help I have. And I'd already beaten Lisette once before. She knew exactly which nerves to strike to get me good and pissed and not remotely thinking. I . . . The things she did, before I was even back here . . ."

Again she'd have to omit Alexandre's name, much as it felt disrespectful to do so; most of the others didn't know Shins's history. But at least, once they'd learned the fae were involved (and had recovered from the various wounds they earned making that discovery), Olgun had been able to explain to her *how* Lisette knew. Creatures of spirit and passion, they'd probably managed to sniff out any number of people and places important to her; Lisette wouldn't have learned *why* the last patron of House Delacroix mattered to Widdershins, but she'd have easily learned that he did.

Digging her nails into her palms until she swore she was about to hit bone, Widdershins explained her gruesome discovery upon returning to her bolthole—and what she'd later discovered upon visiting the other graves, as well.

Robin wept openly by the time she was through, over this last indignity done to Genevieve, whom she'd loved as much as Shins had. Faustine held her, whispering, gently rocking her back and forth. Renard and Igraine had both paled, then adapted some new hues; he came over vaguely greenish-gray, as though struggling not be sick, while the priestess had flushed red with righteous indignation. And Evrard . . .

Well, one look at the twisted fury in his expression and the sheen of ice in his eyes, and Shins remembered why, even without a god or the fae at his side, he'd been a genuine threat when that wrath had been aimed *her* way.

And he was the only one, up to that moment, who *hadn't* already had a personal reason to despise Lisette Suvagne.

"I walked right into it," Shins admitted. "It was *so* frog-hopping clearly *exactly* what she wanted, and I just strolled on in. I was so angry, so sure she was nothing.

"And then she . . ." Widdershins only then realized she was clutching her stomach, one arm held protectively over her wound.

Robin had gently disengaged herself from Faustine's arms, limped to her friend's side, and taken her hand, before the thief even realized she was there.

"Only when you're ready, Shins."

Shins squeezed her fingers, forced a wan smile, and—still bolstered and protected by Olgun's own blanket-like embrace—recited the rest of what had occurred in Renard's former office.

"Embruchel," Robin breathed from beside her.

"What?"

"The one who did . . . who hurt you. There aren't as many tales about him as about Iruoch, but I recognize the description. Embruchel."

"I don't think I've heard of him." Shins looked to the others, but Faustine and the two men appeared just as puzzled.

Igraine, however, was slowly nodding. "He's referred to by title more often than name. You would probably remember him as the Prince of Orphan's Tears."

Widdershins shuddered. That name, she *did* remember from her childhood. She'd first heard the story from other children, not long after she had, herself, become an orphan.

"Does knowing that help us at all?" Evrard asked, his own fingers digging deep into the cushioned arms of the chair.

"We'd have to read up, see if any of the legends agree on much about him," Igraine said. "But it certainly can't hurt."

"And remember," Widdershins pointed out, "he's not the only one. I figure Lisette sought them out after she heard about Iruoch, though I don't even want to *guess* how she went about it. They had," she added bitterly, "an enemy in common."

"I'm not as familiar with fairytales as, apparently, I ought to be," Renard said. Although he spoke no differently than ever, Shins swore she heard something of the Shrouded Lord in his voice now. "But even I know that the fae are tricky and fickle. Would they do this *just* to seek revenge for Iruoch?"

"It's possible," Robin answered, taking Widdershins's goblet and refilling it without being asked. "They *are* pretty vindictive, in the stories."

Igraine started to gesture at Robin, then—perhaps remembering her limp—stood and fetched herself a drink as well. "At the same time," she said as she crossed the room, "they might very well want something more out of it. Widdershins, you said something about them not *really* being here?"

"Those wounds looked real enough," Renard growled.

"No, she's right," Shins told him. "They've granted Lisette some of their power, and that seems to let them manifest here for short periods of time, but . . . they come and go. Lisette said something about the Church . . . ?"

Again the priestess nodded. "You remember how Iruoch reacted to prayer and blessed objects. Normally, the faith of a community as large as Davillon is enough to keep them out entirely. He only came because of the . . . accidental invitation.

"If Lisette convinced them that she could offer them free reign here," she added thoughtfully, "that would surely be enough to buy their cooperation, revenge or no."

"What's she planning to do, murder the entire clergy?" Evrard asked—darkly enough that he very clearly was *not* being entirely sarcastic.

"I think I told you," Igraine sighed, "that I've been in pretty regular contact with His Eminence Sicard? Part of that is because of the panic and rumors. Stories are spreading, just like they did with Iruoch."

"And of course, if the Church can't do anything and people start to lose faith again . . ." Shins mused.

"It's more than that, though. The priests of some of the minor Houses have claimed to have found a way to protect their people from this 'unholy scourge.' And nobody from those houses has been hurt."

"It's not proof of anything, yet. There are still few enough attacks overall that those houses could have been spared by coincidence. But people are starting to listen."

Evrard, again, utterly incredulous. "The Church is letting them just splinter off like that?"

"The priesthood is completely overwhelmed," Igraine protested. "These 'hauntings,' all the political upheaval in Davillon. . . . And Davillon's not even a priority for the Church as a whole right now! The Archbishops are all still dealing with the fallout over Faranda's anointing! Lourveaux's dealing with open riots!"

Shins had learned the basics of that months ago, when she herself had been in the city of Lourveaux, heart of the Church of the Hallowed Pact. Nicolina Faranda, successor to the lamented Archbishop William de Laurent, was from Rannanti, not Galice. By the laws of the Church, there was nothing wrong with that; faith in the Pact wasn't limited to a single nation. After so many generations of rivalry and border skirmishes between the two states, however, quite a few Galicians had taken offense at the decision. The Church was swept up in controversy, the Galicien throne had dispatched much of the standing army to the border, to prevent the situation from escalating . . .

No. No, she couldn't. . . . This can't *be her doing, too! She can't have that much influence outside of Davillon?*

"Can she?" she asked, nearly begged, under her breath.

Except, as Olgun reluctantly pointed out, she could. She hadn't the pull to create the situation, no, but it would take only a few planted agitators, loud voices to stir up the simmering anger, to keep it all burning longer than it otherwise might.

And it would mean far, far fewer official eyes on Davillon.

"Gods . . ."

". . . tried to get word to Lourveaux of what's happening here," Igraine was saying, "but so far, they've been too busy to even send back more than an occasional perfunctory answer."

"Your messages may not even be reaching them," Shins said, jumping back in. She proceeded to explain to them the banditry and monster situation. "It's pretty obvious," she concluded, "that the two-in-one creature I fought on the way home was a fae trick, yes? I mean, now that we know they're involved."

"Just how powerful has the bitch *gotten?*" Renard demanded, rising from his own chair to pace the length of the far wall.

"You know," Igraine mused, "we've been wondering why she's been having the Guild behave more brutally. It hadn't occurred to me, since I didn't know she had plans beyond the Finders, until recently, but . . . it's everything the local priesthood can do to keep the Guard and the Guild from each other's throats. Open warfare between two institutions with patron gods of the Pact is forbidden, but the public outcry is close to forcing the Guards' hand. Dealing with the Finders' Guild is basically all they're doing, other than their increased presence at the walls of the city. What little energy and attention Sicard has remaining is tied up largely in keeping *that* situation from boiling over."

"Madame, um, Igraine?" Everyone stared at Faustine, apparently having forgotten she was there, so little had she spoken. "Which Houses are the ones whose priests are claiming to be able to protect people?"

"Um, I'm not sure I know the complete list, but . . ." The priestess pondered a moment, then rattled off some names, finally wrapping up with, "Why?"

"Which Houses," the other woman asked softly, "are the ones who have fielded private armsmen to keep the peace while the Guard is so busy?"

Renard halted in mid-pace, lost in thought. "There's . . . close to *zero* overlap," he marveled. "I mean, literally almost none."

Dead silence, as everyone struggled to absorb the implications.

"There's something else," the d'Arras scion said grimly.

"Oh, good," Shins crowed. "This was all starting to seem too simple."

"A number of the smaller Houses Igraine just named? Have had a change in leadership recently. Several House patrons have passed on in the last few months, leaving their heirs to take over. It would have been bigger news, I think, but with everything else going on, it's rather been pushed aside in favor of more pressing issues.

"The *major* Houses . . . they've closed up some of their businesses, the ones that are particularly vulnerable. There's a *lot* of calling in of old favors happening behind the scenes, as well as the establishment of some new ones. I've been approached a time or two myself. And *they're* the Houses with soldiers in the streets, ostensibly to help keep the peace, but . . . I think they're all jockeying for position to ride out the growing political upheaval. Maybe even to strike out at rivals in the process."

"Sicard *did* tell me," Igraine added, "that a lot of the major Houses are starting to take sides over the 'Should the Guard go to war with the Finders' Guild, despite the doctrinal prohibition' issue. And the various house leaders are all attending sermons far more often; he thinks they're just trying to shore up existing alliances with the Church, and to look good to the people around them."

"I'm actually starting to get a headache in *your* head from trying to follow all this," Widdershins complained.

Evrard shifted in his seat. "I'm finding it difficult to believe," he said, "that one person could manage all this. A lot of it could be her, sure, but *all* of it? Even with her powers and connections, and even assuming there's some half-sane plan behind it all—which I am *not* assuming, by the way—I'm having trouble swallowing it."

"It does seem rather labyrinthine," Renard added, "compared to the straightforward methods by which she used to operate. But of course, she's been gone a long time, and it's certainly *brutal* enough for her."

Shins paused, taking another sip as she gathered her thoughts, and only then stopped to wonder how much of the brandy she'd actually had, and why she wasn't feeling it.

Oh. Of course.

"You," she whispered, uncertain if she was grateful for his interference, irritated by it, or both.

Olgun smugly beamed at her, leaving no doubt at all as to how *he* felt about it.

"All right," she said to the others, "it's going to be a few days yet before I'm anywhere near my best." That "a few days" was still months sooner than any of *them* would have been okay was something every last person in the room knew, but nobody bothered to speak aloud. "Why don't we spend that time gathering what information we can? Between the lot of us, we have people in the aristocracy, the Guard, the underworld, the Church. . . . If we can't learn anything new, we can at least shore up suspicions and try to figure out what the *point* of this whole mess is, yes?"

When most of the others seemed to agree—or at least nobody *dis*agreed—she continued. "We'll meet back here at set times. Robin, Faustine, you'll stay—"

Three shouted protests at once severed the end of that sentence like an executioner's axe. Shins let them go on for a moment. But *only* a moment.

"Oh, for pastry's sake, *shut up!*

"You!" she began, two fingers pointing directly at the startled scowl on Evrard's face. "If you're in this, you're in it. This is some-place safe we can gather, where Lisette doesn't know to look for us. I think the rest of us really appreciate having somewhere like that, so if you object, feel free to leave.

"Besides, what do you care what happens here? You're just renting."

One hand dropped back to her side, the other rose in counterbal-ance, now aimed at the sofa. "The horse-plucking witch already came after you once! She *can't* . . . !" It was a gentle divine prod that made her realize she was starting to shout. "I need to be sure you're safe, Robin. And don't even start with the guilty 'I'm a burden' nonsense. I'd have said the same thing *before* your injury, and you hopping well know it."

Her friend frowned, turned her face away, but nodded.

"Faustine—"

"I'm a courier, Shins. I know all sorts of people, in the noble Houses, in merchant circles!"

"I know, but—"

"But you don't know me." Somehow bitter and understanding, both at once. "You don't trust me."

"Gods!" It was neither skill nor divine interference but sheer, dumb luck that Shins's goblet didn't go flying from her fingers to shatter against wall or ceiling as she dramatically threw her hands up in exasperation. "You're as stubborn as she is!" The thief stalked across the room—it was only a few steps, but she still managed to stalk them—to loom over the pair on the couch.

"Robin loves you. That's enough for me to trust you, until and unless you give me reason otherwise. Faustine, I need you to stay here because Robin's staying here." She went on, quickly, stampeding over the protest she could *see* rising in Robin's throat. "*I* need someone with her. Whether or not *she* thinks she does.

"Now, are there any questions or concerns that do *not* involve changing a plan that you all know isn't going to change?"

Renard had a fist raised to his mouth, openly grinning behind it. "No, General Widdershins, I don't believe so."

"Oh, be quiet."

"I have one," Evrard announced, far too calmly for Shins's taste. "Is there any chance of you finally returning my rapier any time soon? And please don't give me your line about how it can't be my missing sword because it doesn't have a ruby in the pommel."

"Uh, right. Well, that. . . . It sort of got left behind when Igraine and Renard hauled my rear out of the Finders' Guild. So, if I could just borrow another one? You know, only for the time being, until this is . . . all . . .

"Wow. I, um, I thought you had to be possessed to make that sort of expression. Doesn't that hurt? I'd think it . . . yeah, I'll just, uh . . . so, we'll meet back here tonight, okay everyone, right, bye."

She didn't *quite* break into a genuine run, but she *was* out on the street, the suite far behind, before she realized she was still gripping the wine goblet in one clenched fist.

CHAPTER ELEVEN

Paschal Sorelle, of the Davillon City Guard, leaned back in his plain, drab chair—which sat before his plain, drab desk in an office with dirty walls of plain, drab gray—and pressed the bridge of his nose between finger and thumb. Had anyone else been in the room, it wouldn't have required much detective work to determine what was causing the tension in his shoulders or the pounding in his head. The uneven and teetering stacks of paperwork, doubtless generated by Davillon's many ongoing troubles, probably outweighed the desk on which they sat.

Of course, there *was* nobody else in his office. Or rather, there shouldn't have been anyone, and he hadn't seen anyone.

"You're working too hard," Shins said from the corner nearest the doorway.

Paschal made a noise vaguely akin to a badger choking on a duck, and had his bash-bang out and aimed—albeit perhaps a bit inaccurately—before his chair ceased wobbling, or he ceased verging on falling out of it.

"You're not old enough to be going gray," the young—and, thanks to some cheap dyes, currently black-haired rather than brunette—woman continued, still utterly nonchalant. "Don't worry, though. It really doesn't stand out in the blond. You can barely see it."

"Gods above, Widdershins!" He plunked the flintlock down on the desk—or rather atop the papers on the desk—but still readily within reach. "How the hell did you get in here?!"

Her eyes narrowed to the teeniest of slits as she looked at him, idly tapping one foot on the threadbare carpet.

"Well, okay," he conceded. "Let's try *why* the hell are you here? By all rights, I should arrest you this instant!"

"Where does that expression even come from?" she asked him. "I mean, it's *not* by all rights. What you mean is, your *orders* would be to arrest me right now. But it's not *right*, and you know it's not right, or you'd be doing it."

Paschal required a moment, which he spent absently smoothing his goatee, to make sure he'd followed. "I guess I can't argue that." He smiled, then. "Not that I'd know how, if I wanted to. Julien warned me about talking to you before you and I even met."

Shins matched his smile with her own, though she knew the ache showed through it, no matter how she might prefer otherwise. It probably always would. "Paschal, you know about his . . . his . . . ?"

"Body. Yes." Several papers, probably important ones, crumpled under his fingers. "When I find out who did that—"

"Her name is Lisette Suvagne. She's currently running the Finders' Guild, after overthrowing the Shrouded Lord. I can also . . ." She took a deep breath, steadying herself. *There's no reason not to. Lisette and her people know where the flats are, so they're not safe no matter what. At least the Guard can bring everyone home.* "I can also give you some idea of where he might be. Also the body of Genevieve Marguilles. And, um, others."

Again she felt awful, not even saying Alexandre's name, but it had been during her life as Adrienne Satti that she'd known him. Trying to explain a connection between Widdershins and the Delacroix patron would be a challenge all its own, and she preferred to postpone that for as long as she possibly could.

Saying nothing, allowing his constantly wavering expressions to do all the talking, Paschal slid a quill and inkwell to the far side of the desk, apparently unconcerned that he knocked several forms to the floor in the process. He then retrieved some blank paper from a drawer and slid it over as well.

Shins retrieved both before returning to her seat and pulling up a second chair for use as a writing table. "The first address is where I know for sure you'll find one of them. The following five are where I think you should look for the others."

"This is about you," the guardsman ventured. "Julien and Mademoiselle Marguilles I comprehend, but what's your connection with this 'other'?"

"Private." Then, clearly intending to head off any further questions on that score and not caring how obvious it was, "By the way . . . congratulations on the promotion, Major."

She glanced up from her scribbling to see that his face had settled in a grief-concealing mask not *too* dissimilar from her own. "I'd rather the position hadn't needed to be filled," he said.

"I know. Me, too." A few final lines, their *scritching* the only sound in the chamber, and then she placed the paper on the floor beside her chair, using the inkwell to weigh it down. "The desecrated graves aren't the only reason I'm here."

"I figured as much."

"Paschal, you and I don't know each other that well, but we've worked together. I know Julien trusted you, and I know that you know Julien trusted me, no matter what I . . . what my life's made me. I really hope that means I can trust *you*, now."

"Assuming what you're about to ask of me doesn't give me reason otherwise."

"Heh. All right, that's honest enough. Paschal . . . why the happy hopping hens am I even *wanted* by the stupid Guard? I didn't kill anyone before I left—anyone human, anyway—and even if you had any jurisdiction over what happened in the Outer Hespelene, there are lots of important people who can explain it all, and I don't know why you're looking at me like that but you're making me *really* nervous."

"Widdershins . . ."

"I also recognize that 'I don't want to tell you this' tone of voice. I've heard it so often, I'm basically fluent in it as a separate language."

"It's just, you . . ." Again he seemed unable to continue. The mess on his desk suddenly seemed to require very close scrutiny.

For her own part, Shins was beginning to feel as though she had an equal amount of slowly uncrinkling paper in her stomach. "Spit it out, Paschal. Please."

The guardsman sighed, and when he finally did look up at her again, she was somehow frightened by the sympathy in his expression. "'In the name of Demas, justice, and the laws of Davillon,'" he said, clearly quoting, "'the street thief known as Widdershins—real name unknown—is to be apprehended on sight, with all due force, on suspicion of having murdered Major Julien Bouniard of the Davillon City Guard.'"

She couldn't breathe. Couldn't think. The room, the world, turned themselves over so completely that she might have fallen to the ceiling if she didn't keep a death grip on her chair.

"What?" When she finally squeaked it out, the voice wasn't her own. Only later did she realize it reminded her, more than anything else, of the girl she'd been ten years before.

"Widdershins—"

"How could you *think* that? How could anyone?"

"I *don't* think it!" he assured her. "But the order and the suspicion come from the top. Most of the Guard haven't heard the whole story of what happened in the graveyard that day, and it's not as if they'd likely believe it if they did."

"But you were there! You could tell people what happened!"

"I didn't actually see any of it, remember? Julien had me standing watch at the gate. I only know what happened because you and the others told me—and if I hadn't already seen Iruoch in action, I'm not sure that *I* would have entirely believed it."

Shins tucked her knees to her chest, her heels resting on the seat. "Gods. They think I. . . . Oh, gods . . ."

Paschal looked like he wanted to get up from behind the desk and do *something* to comfort her but hadn't the first idea what. It was so very like Julien that she almost broke into tears and a wide smile simultaneously.

"I'm not sure it would have mattered if I *had* been a witness," he explained. "Commandant Archibeque seems quite certain of your guilt. If I could show any sort of genuine, hard evidence, that might change things but . . ." Even his helpless shrug somehow jostled one of the stacks, the papers idly threatening to topple.

"Olgun?" she whispered. "Do we know him?"

Nothing but puzzlement. Okay, so either this Archibeque really, truly believed, to his toes, that Shins was guilty of a crime that was nothing akin to her prior record, or . . .

"How honest is he?" she asked bluntly.

Paschal's brow furrowed. "Major—and then Commandant—Archibeque has been a fixture since before I joined the Guard. There is no one in this organization more trustworthy!"

Shins waited for more, then, "But?"

"What? What 'but'? But what?"

"Wow. Everyone's starting to sound like me. Come on, Paschal, we both know what 'but.' It's the 'but' that you very, very loudly refrained from saying."

The guardsman's scowl survived a moment longer, then faded. "How do you do that?"

"It's easy. After a lifetime of trusting nobody, you can just sense a but coming from a mile away."

Other than the sound of Olgun nearly asphyxiating in hysterics somewhere in the back of her head, utter silence followed that pronouncement.

"I am going to pretend you found a better way to phrase that," Paschal said finally.

"Would you?" she asked through a blush that would have been visible in the dark. "I would *so* appreciate it."

"Commandant Archibeque," he reluctantly continued, "hasn't been quite the same since his promotion. It's almost certainly just stress and adjusting to his new authority, mind you. But, while he was always stern, he's become excessively strict. And he's making a lot of pronouncements—such as your guilt—where proper investigative procedure would allow for suspicions and theories at most.

"I do *not*," he added hastily, "believe it suggests any manner of corruption on the man's part."

"No, I'm sure you're right," Shins said, already running through various scenarios for finding out if he was wrong. "Thank you for talking to me, Paschal. I know you could get in real trouble."

She stood, and he rose as well. "Was the right thing to do, and it's what Julien would have wanted of me. I hope you find whatever it is you need to find before . . . well, soon."

"Yeah, me, too."

"Do you need an escort out? Someone to make your presence appear legitimate?"

"Thank you, again, but no. I've got it." She was already out the door, turning to shut it behind, when she paused. "Paschal? Things aren't *really* on the verge of open war on the city streets, right? Davillon hasn't gotten *that* out of control, has it?"

If the young major's expression hadn't been answer enough, his comment of "I'm not sure where you've been the past few seasons, but you might give some serious thought to returning there" certainly would have been.

❁

It would only be much later that evening, at the end of shift, that Paschal would notice. He couldn't begin to imagine when or how it had happened—he'd had his eyes on her for the entire conversation, and she'd never left the chair—but when he reached to collect the

Guard-issued rapier he'd leaned upright in the corner nearest his desk, it was simply gone.

At which point, after a long moment gawping like a fish who'd just discovered fire, he was—despite his best efforts—too busy laughing, and recalling some of Julien's less believable but more exasperated stories, to be angry.

※

Leaving Paschal's office did *not* translate directly into leaving the Guard headquarters. Widdershins had someone else to see.

Or, well, to look into.

She wasn't especially concerned about being recognized. The changes in hair color and wardrobe, her skill with adjusting her posture and pace to blend in, the inaccuracies and vagaries of her "wanted" portrait, and of course the fact that the Guard headquarters boasted all sorts of visitors and messengers at this time of day. . . . Frankly, Shins was all but guaranteed to go unnoticed even before Olgun began subtly encouraging people to look the other way.

Assuming she didn't run into anyone who actually *knew* her. A guard who'd arrested her in the past, perhaps, a fellow Finder being brought in for interrogation, or possibly Archibeque himself, since she still had no idea why he had it in for her, could all ruin her efforts, her day, and quite possibly the rest of her natural life.

So, easy it might be, but no point in dawdling.

It didn't take long, just a few moments of loitering and wandering the building—its walls stained an oily charcoal by years of exposure to cheap oil lamps—to learn which room she wanted. Given the quantity of traffic in the main halls, it was *far* more difficult to find a moment of privacy long enough to slip the lock and get *into* said room. Ultimately, it required Olgun providing a distraction— the poor courier wouldn't suffer anything worse from his stumble than a bruised knee, but he'd be ages reordering the stack of papers he'd scattered—and funneling as much assistance and luck as he could into her efforts at the latch, before she finally managed to crack the door open long enough to duck inside.

Dim, but not dark; the sun's smallest fingers felt around the edges of the shutters, providing enough light to see. The shelves and desk were bigger, the stacks of paper neater, and the back wall had that aforementioned window, but still and all, it wasn't all that different from Paschal's.

Or rather, it didn't *appear* all that different.

It smelled off, for one, though Shins found it impossible to put her finger—or her nose, to be more accurate—on what it was. Only later would she realize it was the *absence* of scent that had nagged at her. That lingering combination of sweat and ink and food and drink and a dozen other little things, the scent of *work*, was faint, *too* faint, far more so than even the presence of the window could justify.

Then, of course, was the fact that Paschal's office hadn't made Olgun scream.

Shins's plan *had* been to carefully scour the room, sift through the papers, hunt for the slightest sign of any connection between Commandant Archibeque and Lisette or the Guild. That, if one were to judge by the divine conniption she'd just experienced, would no longer be necessary.

"Holy horsebubbles, Olgun! Calm down!" Then, after a frozen moment spent waiting to see if her own outburst had drawn any attention from beyond the office door, she continued. "Are you sure?"

The god's response to that question was so blasphemously profane, Shins wasn't entirely certain he hadn't just mortally insulted *himself*.

"All right, yes, you'd be in a position to know! I wasn't thinking. Don't say it." She pondered, mind spinning, while casually rifling a random drawer without really paying any heed to what lay inside.

If the fae had been here—and often enough to leave an aura Olgun could sense even in their absence—what did that mean, exactly?

"So, what, the commandant's been meeting with them?"

Her head swam with sensations and images of various mixtures, liquid concoctions of color swirling around and within one another. One of the pair was disturbingly akin to blood.

It only took her a moment. "It's *mixed* with the commandant's aura?!"

No, not quite. Another few flashes of uncertainty were enough to explain that Olgun couldn't swear it was Commandant Archibeque. But *some* human-fae combination had been present within, and frequently.

"Lisette?"

Again, no. *That* sensation, he'd recognize.

"Then I don't unders—can the fae possess people, like a ghost or demon? Do we need, I don't know, special medicine, or an exorcism? Does the Church of the Hallowed Pact even *do* exorcisms anymore?"

And then, "You know, that's starting to get really aggravating. If you're going to keep shrugging at me, you can hopping well grow some shoulders already, yes? I—"

The deity's power surged, making her ears crackle, and then she could clearly hear the sound of steps out in the hallway. Steps that grew louder, nearer, with deliberate purpose.

"Right, we'll discuss shoulders later. Don't forget to remind me! Make a note of it. 'Shoulders.'"

And speaking of shoulders, she had hers (along with the rest of her) through the window, and the shutters tugged closed behind her, before whoever was approaching—be it Archibeque or some lower functionary—could crack the door to the office.

Not, in and of itself, the most inconspicuous exit, but luck— perhaps with a nudge from Olgun; she never did ask—was with her. The commandant's window opened up on a smaller street, to one side of the building, rather than on the main thoroughfare out front. Between that and the thick, soaking mist that threatened to coalesce into yet another heavy rain any minute now, only a smattering of passersby witnessed her unorthodox exit. And while Shins drew more than a few peculiar looks and puzzled mutters, she'd be long gone before anyone—even should they decide to do so—had flagged down and returned with an actual guard.

Arms wrapped tightly about herself, save for those moments when she needed to wipe water or strands of hair from her face, Widdershins made her way back toward more comfortable environs. Her cold clothes pasted themselves to her skin, making her shiver, and the moisture in the air was so think it didn't merely smell but *tasted* of society's many odors. She was almost sure, were she dropped blindfolded anywhere in the city, she could instantly guess her rough location by the specific combination of flavors.

Which is why she noticed almost immediately when the harsh grating of fire and smoke crept in to season the bouquet. The sting of fumes, the grit of ash, the sharp tang of what had once been wood . . . all scarcely hinted at in the tiny whiffs that reached her, but imprinted so heavily on her memories that she gagged; her eyes began to water for reasons other than the weather. Something about a burning building . . .

Fire had ended her childhood, changed her life into something unrecognizable for the first of what would become many, many times. It was not a scent, especially when it snagged her unawares, that she would ever be comfortable with. She couldn't imagine how such a blaze had gotten started in this weather; it must have been *intense.*

Something else to do with the ongoing chaos and upheaval, no doubt. Still, it was far enough away that Shins couldn't see any billowing smoke amidst the lighter haze, and while the wind wasn't precisely steady, she could tell that the fumes came from nowhere near the direction she was headed. No matter how severe the blaze, the weather would keep it from spreading too terribly far before the locals got it under control.

She felt a pang of sympathy for whoever owned the burning place (or places), and another surge of fury at Lisette, for causing so much widespread hurt and chaos with her insane machinations. Still, deepest and darkest truth be told, what Shins felt more than anything else was *relief*.

It was good to be reminded, on occasion, that not *everything* that went wrong in Davillon was her problem.

CHAPTER TWELVE

How in the name of every damn god of the damn Pact did I get roped into this?!

Evrard d'Arras strode—more "stomped," really, though he'd have rejected the description as undignified—across cobblestones made dark by evening and slick with the ever-present humidity. The wind whipped his long coat about his ankles, where it also collected dirty runoff and occasional speckles of mud from his feet; not-quite-rain dripped from the corners of his tricorne hat. (Popular in all the most fashionable Galicien circles, the damn things never *had* caught on in Davillon. Of course.) At roughly every third streetlight, he forced his hand to unclench from the hilt of his sword, to hang casually at his side, only to find before long that it had wrapped itself about the weapon once more, seemingly of its own accord.

Oh, he recognized *this* mood when it came over him. He *wanted* trouble to find him, wanted someone to give him an excuse to burn off some aggression. Enough self-awareness to identify the feeling, not remotely enough to dismiss it. The *scrunch* of his leather gauntlet was accompanied by a soft, unintended growl of his own.

He didn't even *like* the bloody woman! Oh, he'd developed a grudging respect for her during the Iruoch affair, and he no longer nursed the sizzling coals of hatred he'd once felt, but that was about the kindest he could say. He didn't like her attitude, he didn't like her presence, he didn't much care for her friends—though he still harbored more than a bit of guilt toward the girl, Robin—and he sure as *hell* hadn't wholly forgiven her for burgling his family's ancestral tower during the years the d'Arras clan were "political guests"

in Rannanti. He wanted nothing from her but to never see her again
(and perhaps the return of the rapier she'd stolen).

So how does she keep talking me into these things?!

He was fortunate enough to come across a discarded bottle at
that point, a rare occurrence in this nicer district, and kicked it across
the road with a vicious, childish glee. It shattered against someone's
doorstep; the clatter set some nearby dog to furious barking.

He knew how it felt.

Everything the damn thief had said was true. He *did* care deeply
for his family's name and honor; he didn't care to let people suffer
when he was in a position to stop it; and he did, indeed, feel that
these new fae meant last year's task remained undone.

He would even admit to himself, if no one else, that fear drove
him as well. If he *did* have to face more monsters like the nightmarish
Iruoch, he wanted it to happen according to *his* plan, not theirs.

But none of that explained it, not really. Wanting to preserve the
d'Arras name, to help people—a far distance indeed separated that
from "volunteer to hunt monsters and criminals." Evrard was neither
guardsman nor professional soldier, for all that he was a better duelist than
most who *did* practice those professions. Refusing to get involved in this
mess would have left no blemish at all on his honor, personal or familial.

Then why the ravenous burning hell, he began again, *am I—?*

At which point an abortive scream and a dull crunch sounded
from behind. With barely time for a quick flicker of *Careful what
you wish for, Evrard*, he pivoted, dropping into a defensive stance, his
rapier flying free of its scabbard . . .

In time to see that his skills weren't precisely required.

❋

Jogging and leaping along the rooftops—only the easiest gaps and
smoothest roofs; she still hadn't fully recovered, even with Olgun's

aid—Widdershins had followed Evrard for blocks. Or, rather, she'd followed the two men, dressed in shabby coats more than large enough for hidden blades, lingering a short ways behind him.

She'd been almost certain they were tailing him, and she lost the "almost" when they halted in their tracks the instant he'd stopped to kick that bottle. They clearly didn't want to be noticed.

"Let us," she breathed at Olgun, reveling in the feel of his magic as it began to surge through muscle and flesh and bone, "notice them."

Shins landed on the first one's shoulders, felt a few disturbing crunches beneath her feet as he just folded under her. He managed maybe one quarter of a scream. She felt a brief pang of sympathy, but . . . well, it was better than if she'd just up and stabbed him.

Wasn't it?

A crumpled human, especially one now capable of bending in a few spots that nature had not intended, makes for very unstable footing, and even Widdershins's enhanced reflexes weren't perfect. She stumbled a step toward the squishy fellow's companion.

As he appeared locked in place, however, his senses and his brain arguing over what had just happened, she decided to turn it to her advantage.

(Mostly so the whole wobbly landing would appear—to her enemy and Evrard both—planned and deliberate. But she wouldn't have admitted it under torture, and neither of the witnesses could hear Olgun snickering about it.)

The stagger transformed into a forward roll, her palms slapping wetly on the cobblestone, and the thug had just enough time for the strangest expression to cross his face before both of Widdershins's boot heels did likewise. When all was said and done, and the dust—or rather, spray—had settled, he lay sprawled on his back in the street, Widdershins sitting comfortably atop him. The initial impact might or might not have been enough to render him unconscious, but the fact that Shins currently had one foot resting heavily on his throat removed all doubt.

"Evening," she said as Evrard stalked closer, fists and jaw quivering.

"Showing off?" he spat.

"Uh, no." *Not exactly, anyway.* "Nobody here worth bothering to impress."

"I could have taken them!"

"Sure. If you'd noticed them. And if they were normal robbers." She rose, stretched hard until something in her back popped, and then began wandering in the same direction Evrard had been heading. Given no other option—especially since that remained the way he had to go—the aristocrat joined her.

"'Normal robbers'?" he demanded.

"Yeah. As in, robbers who plan to rob you. Like normal."

"And what else *would* they have been?"

"Spies for Lisette, who knows you were involved in the fight against Iruoch and might have noticed you asking questions. In which case, sure, you could still have taken them—unless their job was just to follow you and confirm where we were, and that you were working with us, in which case you'd never have known they were here. Well, until the Finders showed up to stab us in our sleep. Probably with fire."

"Stab us with . . . ?"

"This way, they don't see where you're going, and they didn't really see who or what hit them."

"So which are you?" Evrard asked.

"Huh?"

"A *who* or a *what*?"

"Cute," Widdershins said. "A few years of practice, just like that, and you could really be marginally less unfunny."

"I . . ." He glanced abruptly downward, something having snagged his attention. "You're wearing a rapier."

"So are you," she pointed out.

"Yes, but you did not *have* a rapier when you left. In fact, you asked me to lend you one of mine."

She shrugged. "And you said no. So I borrowed from someone else."

"I see. And does this someone else *know* you 'borrowed' his sword?"

"Well, by *now* he probably does . . ."

Footsteps, the very sporadic murmur of other pedestrians, the faint sizzle as the occasional bead of water worked its way inside the burning streetlamps. Otherwise, silence.

"I'm afraid I wasted my day," Evrard began. "I didn't learn any—"

Two raised fingers and a quick "Shh!" stopped him cold.

"Not now," Shins told him. "Wait until everyone's gathered. Then we can all report to each other at once."

"But I just told you I don't *have* anything to—"

"So wait until we're all together and *then* don't report anything."

Evrard actually swayed, appearing almost drunk. "You want me to wait," he said, slowly and clearly, perhaps making sure they were both speaking the same language. "And tell the group I've got nothing. Without telling you, alone, right now, that I've got nothing."

"Precisely."

"For the love of the gods, *why*?!"

Shins stared at the man as though he'd gone mad for even asking. "I don't want to lose track of all the details."

Once again, footsteps, the very sporadic murmur of other pedestrians, the faint sizzle as the occasional bead of water worked its way inside the burning streetlamps. Otherwise, more silence.

"How did I let myself get talked into this?"

He hadn't really been asking Shins, hadn't even meant to mutter it aloud; it was just another repetition of what had become the evening's anthem. Yet, without even looking his way, Widdershins answered.

"Because you and your family spent almost a decade doing nothing but playing at manners and propriety as 'guests' in another country, yes? Followed almost immediately by your silly obsession with getting revenge on me."

"Silly—?! You stole dozens of our family heirlooms! Gods' sakes, Lisette only hates you because you beat her to robbing *my*—!"

"Now that that's all behind you, you haven't the faintest wiggling idea what to do with yourself or your life. You're bored, you're completely aimless, and you're looking for something to do that actually matters."

Evrard rocked, raising fingertips to his cheek as though he'd been slapped. "You have no idea what you're talking about!"

"Oh." Another of Widdershins's shrugs. "Okay."

"You *don't*!" he insisted.

"Okay. And Lisette's a few strands short of a mop, anyway. She'd have found some other reason to hate me. No reason to blame yourself."

The aristocrat roared something that, at closest, was related to genuine words solely by marriage, and stormed ahead, his rapier an angry and twitching tail, with nearly enough force to leave an Evrard-shaped hole in the fog. Shins stood, blinking, in his wake.

"What'd I say?"

Olgun could only sigh.

❁

"I'm worried," Robin conceded, doe-eyed and imploring, from her spot at the end of the sofa. Around the room, the various conspirators took this seat or that, while Evrard—fulfilling his duties as host, for all that he constantly grumbled about it—passed around brimming goblets and morsels of those fruits available in this peculiar season.

To everyone other than Faustine, who was nowhere to be seen.

"I told her to stay here!" Shins fumed, not merely pacing but stomping as though the carpet were made of spiders. "I didn't want you alone!"

"Calm down, Shins. I wasn't. She didn't leave until Renard got back."

"I'm not sure that's any safer," she growled.

"I daresay, I can hear you," the older thief protested from across the chamber, idly studying a crystalline vessel of a rich wine.

"I'm not surprised; it really isn't much of a dare." Shins cast about the room, sort of idly flailed her hands a bit, and then resumed her previous spot beside the hearth. "Gah!"

"Widdershinsian catastrophe or not," Robin insisted, "I still have responsibilities."

"'Widdershinsian'. . . ?"

"I have to make decisions about the Witch, and for that I need to know how business is running. You're lucky I just asked her to go, but I knew I'd slow everything down too much if I went along."

"Oh, all right. Point made. Let's start with the basics. Broad strokes. If Faustine's not back after that, we'll go look for her before we get down to details. Okay, Robs?"

Robin appeared rather less than okay, but she nodded agreement.

"Good. Evrard hasn't learned anything, so let's start with you, Igraine."

"Certainly," the priestess began. "I've been . . . uh, Widdershins?"

"Yeah?"

"Is Evrard *supposed* to be turning that color? Because that doesn't look entirely natural to me."

"I'm sure he's fine. You were saying?"

"O . . . kay. . . . Since I wasn't trying to drag a bloody, collapsing companion with me, I had no difficulty in reaching the Basilica. I spent the day speaking with his Eminence Sicard's people. No new information, but I *can* confirm that there's almost perfect overlap between the Houses whose priests are claiming to be able to ward off this latest supernatural threat, and those that have refused to put soldiers on the street to help keep the peace. And also that not a single one of them has suffered any sort of attack by the fae, at least not that's become public knowledge."

Shins chewed the ends of her hair a moment. Then, "All right, Renard?"

"Ah, my dear lady, I am sorry to say I discovered nothing from my Guild and underworld contacts we had not already known. I fear I'm in the same spot as Monsieur d'Arras. Albeit apparently less crimson about it."

More unintelligible grumbling from Evrard.

"What of you?" Renard asked, after sparing the aristocrat no more than a passing glance.

"Oh," Shins replied, "right. Well, I'm wanted for the murder of . . ." She swallowed, hard; it was still so difficult to say. "Major Julien Bouniard."

It proved impossible to make out Robin's, Renard's, or Evrard's responses beneath Igraine's strenuous and rather unpriestly "Horse shit!" but Widdershins was pretty sure they all amounted to that same general sentiment.

"Kind of what I said, only with less, uh, feces. And not everyone believes it. Julien's friend Paschal knows better. But the order came from the top."

"Commandant Archibeque?" Renard asked.

"Yep. *Oh!* Also, he's possessed by Lisette's fae."

That, of course, required more than a bit of elaboration. Shins had just gotten everyone to stop shouting questions at once and had begun to explain what had occurred at the headquarters of the Guard, when a faint, even timid, rap on the front door halted her in mid-word.

They all knew who it probably was, yet hands dropped to weapons and muscles went tense until Evrard, after a careful peek through a tiny sliding window, hauled the door open and stepped aside for Faustine to enter the suite.

Her hair and skirts hung limp, weighted down and fatigued by the damp, and all of that made perfect sense. Shins's gaze flew almost instantly to the woman's face, though. The redness, puffiness . . . that wasn't rainwater glistening on her cheeks. Faustine had been crying, and hard.

Shins felt a faint tingle in her nose, almost like a building sneeze, except spiritual. She knew what it meant, knew Olgun had sensed something she couldn't, and needed her to smell it, too.

He guided her, softly, gently, and there it was. Clinging to the courier's clothes.

The faintest, lingering whiff of smoke.

And Shins knew. As thoroughly as if Faustine had already spoken, as if she herself had witnessed it, Shins knew. She slumped hard against the stone of the hearth, and only that kept her from the floor.

"A problem in Davillon that's not my responsibility," I thought. *I'm so stupid . . .*

Olgun's comforting touch warmed her from within, and she was grateful, but she could barely even feel it.

"Faustine?" Robin was on her feet, hand clasped unconsciously to her throat. "Shins? I don't. . . . What's going on?"

"It's . . . Robin, it's . . ." Faustine's voice cracked. She took a single step, arms raised, then froze, blatantly uncertain what to do, knowing only that these would be among the hardest words—for herself and the woman she loved—that she would ever, *could* ever say.

"It's gone. Oh, Robin, I'm *so* sorry. The Flippant Witch is gone."

CHAPTER THIRTEEN

Candles flickered, a few of them guttering, adding more of a waxy scent to the room than any great degree of illumination. Oil lanterns and the chandelier sat cool and dark; nobody had felt it proper to wander around lighting them.

The gloom seemed more appropriate to the mood.

"Everyone got out," Shins said softly to the weeping girl beside her. Robin, completely limp, still hiccoughing now that her body could no longer handle the sobs, huddled near one end of the sofa. She shook inside the circle of Faustine's arms, wrapped around her, while Widdershins lay what she meant to be a comforting hand on Robin's shoulder. She *hoped* it was comforting; she knew it wasn't.

A quick flicker, and she found herself catching Faustine's eye. The courier offered a wan smile through her own tears, and Shins returned it. The both of them struggled to hold back their own grief, to be strong for the woman they both loved, each in their own way, and both barely managed. For that moment, at least, Shins and Faustine completely understood one another.

"The property's still mine," the thief continued, growing desperate. "We can—we *will*—rebuild. It'll be just like new . . ."

Robin sniffled, and Shins could think of nothing more to say. In fact, this was far from the first time she'd said precisely that, since Faustine's revelation, in the hopes that repetition might penetrate Robin's grief.

Except that Robin didn't *want* the Flippant Witch "like new." Neither did Shins.

Something *else* Lisette had taken from her. One more mark on an ever-growing list.

"Why is she doing this?" Renard muttered. For a long time, everyone else had remained silent, out of shared grief or at least respect, but the night wouldn't wait indefinitely.

"Are you kidding?" Igraine snapped, less angry than incredulous. "She didn't need any better reason than to hurt—"

"No, no, I get that." Renard reached upward to idly stroke the feather he was accustomed to wearing in his hat, apparently only recalling when his fingers came together that he currently wore no such thing. "I mean . . . all of this. Everything she's doing, everything we talked about last night, I'm still not seeing how it's all connected."

"I think I am," Widdershins said. Then, "Did you guys practice that? Even your blinking's synchronized."

When the staring and blinking continued to happen, and further speech continued to not happen, Shins squeezed Robin's shoulder one last time and stood, idly meandering from sofa to hearth and back. "I ran into some, uh, political maneuvering when I was away, so I've sort of been thinking along those lines. It came together when I found out the snake had her talons in the Guard, too."

"A snake with talons?" Renard gibed, for all that his voice remained strained.

"A very dishonest snake. I'm sure she stole the talons from something that needed them more than she did.

"Look at it all together. Davillon's on the edge of panic and a collapse of law and order. The city's been pretty well isolated from outside help. The Church is paralyzed trying to deal with about a thousand crises at once. The major Houses are on the edge of open conflict—at least political, if not actual violence.

"The fae are responsible for the weakening of the Church and appear to be cooperating to bolster the claim that the priests of these minor Houses can protect people. Those same minor Houses have *not* put soldiers on the street, so they're in a good position to hunker down and ride out what's coming, without taking the kind of damage their bigger rivals will. And some of those Houses have new leadership—almost as if the old patrons were in the way of something, yes?"

Nods all around.

"And the Guard, too," Faustine interjected in growing understanding. "We never did get a really good reason why they've suddenly devoted so much manpower to guarding the walls, and it's partly the lack of those soldiers on patrol that's forced the Houses to step in."

"Precisely!" Shins spun so quickly her hair made a hail-like *pitter-patter* across the wall beside the hearth. "So in other words, Lisette—who already runs the criminal underworld in Davillon—is poised to see Houses and priests, who are presumably loyal to her, rise to become the predominant legal powers in the city. And she has enough influence to keep the Guard too busy to do anything about it, if not actually make them assist.

"Government. Commerce. Church. Law. Underworld. She *told* me the whole city would be hers, but . . . I thought she was just taunting me. I don't think so anymore."

"Gods," Igraine marveled. "It's absolutely insane, and it's enough of a twisted web to make a spider dizzy, but . . . she really just might do it. Lisette may be on the verge of ruling Davillon!"

Faustine, however, was shaking her head. "For how long, though? A city in that much chaos, and possibly with the fae running free? How long could she possibly maintain that?"

"I don't think she cares about anything that far ahead," Shins said. "I think as long as she gets her reign as queen of the heap, nothing else matters."

"There is no way," Evrard declared, leaning so far forward in his seat that his grip on the armrests was all that kept him in it, "that either the Church or the Galicien throne would allow someone to just step in and take over a major city!"

"What would they do about it?" Renard countered. "The military and the Church are both occupied at the border. All they know is that there's some social chaos happening here, and that's no different than half a dozen other cities. Lisette could have the situation stabilized, with nobody the wiser, long before any official eyes turn this way."

"And even if the throne *did* find out," Igraine added, "if Lisette's smart enough to play along, pay taxes, do everything the nation expects a city government to do . . . the cost in money and lives to take Davillon by force might not even seem worth it."

"Politics," Robin all but spat.

"Could we maybe tell people?" Shins asked without much confidence. "Stir up the rest of the city against her? Her control's nowhere near absolute, yet."

"How would we prove any of it, dear Shins?" Renard asked. "We certainly won't get the Guard to turn against the orders of their commandant without overwhelming evidence, and trying to get all the major Houses to do anything together is rather akin to neatly stacking live eels."

"No!" Robin sat bolt upright, fists clenched, visibly startling the hell out of Faustine. "None of this crap! No negotiations, no schemes, just kill the bitch!"

Shins shuddered. Her dear friend was the last person in the world from whom she wanted to hear that level of vitriol. Even Olgun blanched. "Robin," she began, "we can't. She's too—"

"What about Bishop Sicard's ritual?" Evrard interrupted. Then, at Faustine's puzzled expression, "His Eminence dabbles a bit in magics beyond the priesthood's norm. Last year, when we battled Iruoch, he was able to link us, in pairs, allowing us each to draw on the other's strength and skill."

"And potentially killing both if one were badly injured," Igraine reminded him.

"It's not a bad idea," Shins said, "except . . . I don't think it'll work. I saw how fast Lisette moved, how unnaturally—worse than Iruoch, in some ways. And her allies can manifest around her. I don't think we could take her even with the ritual, and that's assuming the Gloaming Court couldn't just sever the hopping link."

"That's very possible," Renard confirmed. "We had protective wards on the Shrouded Lord's office. They never even triggered; she just walked right through them." He smiled, then, at Widdershins's double-take. "What, you thought you knew everything there was to know about the Guild?"

"It does make sense," she whispered at Olgun's protest. "They'd be very well hidden. Even you might have missed them."

The tiny god managed to convey the distinct impression of crossing his arms and slumping to his seat in a huff.

"You're both right, though," Shins said thoughtfully. "We need to be stronger, and we need to be more direct. Igraine?"

"Hmm?"

"You said something the other night about the heads of the major Houses still attending Church services, yes? In order to keep up appearances during this whole mess?"

"I did. And I already hate this plan."

"You don't even know what it is yet!"

"I've heard enough to know I hate it."

"You haven't," Shins insisted. "Wait until I've gone through the whole thing," she added with a wry smile. "*Then* I promise you'll have heard enough to hate it."

❋

Shift change at the various station houses, and the buildings all but bled the black and silver: tabards and hats and medallions of Demas, patron deity of the Davillon Guard. This flowing into streets already

crowded with workers and crafters, vendors and patrons, racing
against the setting sun to see who could reach home first. Men and
women came, men and women went, and the result was somewhere
between a spinning tornado and a cresting tide.

"There should be a term for that," Shins whispered to Olgun,
crouching at the very edge of a nearby rooftop, precisely midway
between an old and worn waterspout gargoyle and a disturbingly
broad speckling of old bird droppings. "Something to combine
filling up and mixing up at once. Fixing! Wait, that's already a word.
Milling? Oh, goose muffins! I think my language is full."

She might have had more to say on the topic—no, she *doubtless*
had more to say on the topic—but her deity shouted and pointed, or
performed his equivalent thereof.

Shins peered down, dubious. "Are you sure? From here, all the
guards just look like big floppy hats. All right! I'm sure you *can* sense
it. Excuse the feathers out of me!

"What? No, I don't *have* feathers in me! You excused them out!
Weren't you listening?"

She was already moving, jogging along the rooftop, leaping a
narrow side street, keeping their quarry in sight. Widdershins still
couldn't actually see anything to mark this one guardsman as different from any of the others, but she recognized him all the same;
when Olgun had singled him out, her own senses had latched onto
him as well.

Unfortunately, there was precious little even Olgun could do
about the growing width of the roads, and thus the widening gaps
between buildings. Shins still wasn't at her best, though it wasn't far,
now; but even if she had been, some of those jumps were beyond her.
Far sooner than she'd have liked, she had to trade in the soaked rooftops for the slightly less soaked cobblestones. The throng of travelers
offered plenty of cover, so she wasn't too worried about being spotted.
Losing the target, on the other hand . . .

After a trek that Shins swore should have taken them to the far end of Davillon and back again, the roads began to thin—in terms of width and traffic both—and she decided the man wasn't going to offer a better opportunity than this. Breaking again into a run, she turned down a side street and then another a block ahead, paralleling the main road. With Olgun's assistance, the ground flew by, her feet spraying lingering puddles of rainwater in a wake behind her.

More than fast enough for her to be waiting a few paces down the next side street, when the man she'd been following passed it by.

"Hey! Commandant Archibeque! You dropped your . . . uh . . . mustache!"

Said mustache, a thing of iron gray to match the beard, of course still clung to the leathery and leather-hued face that turned her way.

"Yes," she murmured at Olgun's protest, "I'd rather have jumped him by surprise, too. Main avenue's still too crowded."

"Is this meant to be a jest?" He took two steps from the intersection, confident but wary. "Because I'm not laughing."

"Aww, you're not? I thought you were just hiding it really well."

"Young lady—"

"Oh, stuff the 'young lady' nonsense." Although fairly certain it wasn't necessary, Shins moved half a pace from the wall, ensuring that her face was visible in the light of the setting sun. "You know exactly who I am.

"And more importantly, 'Commandant,' I know exactly *what* you are."

Fast, *so* fast! Even with Olgun's magics infusing her vision, she scarcely registered that his hand was in motion before it was already aiming a bash-bang pistol at her chest.

Well, at least he didn't waste our time with the "I don't know what you're talking about" routine . . .

The partners, one mortal and one otherwise, made no attempt to execute their usual trick for facing a flintlock, not without knowing precisely what the possessing spirit could do. If it was able to ward off Olgun's own power, however briefly, she'd simply be killing herself by forcing the weapon to discharge.

Instead, a second's heartbeat before the *bang*, she leapt.

No. She *soared*.

She was sure it must appear impressive, even melodramatic. Her body rising up and back, higher than any human could jump; arms outspread, legs tucked up under her, well above the path of the hurtling ball.

But then, the posture wasn't *meant* to be melodramatic; that was merely a fringe benefit.

Aiming at the rough lumber that was the nearest wall, Widdershins kicked. And not only with her own strength.

The air around her all but crackled with Olgun's magics, slipping her through a narrow gap in the laws of physics. Many a time before, she had taken a step on nothing, her god's power catching and boosting her. Now that power coursed through her legs, propelling her from the building at impossible speed—but also at an impossible *angle*. Without the slightest concern for minor details such as inertia, Shins's kick transformed her leap up and back into a forward dive.

Caught completely by surprise, even the fae-ridden guardsman couldn't react. Widdershins plowed into him, a human ballista bolt, slamming him to the hard ground. A quick handspring from his chest, even as he fell, and she was on her feet behind him.

Her heel rose and fell like a headsman's axe, intended to put him good and out, but the unnatural creature wasn't so easily felled, not even by a blow that should have left him too battered to stand. As though his own heels were hinged to the earth, his entire body sprung upward and straightened; a narrow tendril of shadow trailed from his back, propelling him off the ground.

Archibeque spun, rapier whipping free of its scabbard, and Shins drew as well. No pause, no threats. Steel screamed against steel, a chorus of death thwarted and frustrated as each parried the other, only to have every riposte parried in turn.

Back and forth along the street, occasionally swapping places as one flipped or wall-kicked over the other. She thrust at the man's arm, trying to catch his strike on flesh rather than blade, hopefully rendering the limb useless. It should have worked; he'd need a second elbow to bend out of the path of her rapier, and he had yet to display any of the inhuman flexibility that Lisette had revealed days before.

The commandant's arm broke from within as muscles flexed where they shouldn't, bending at a near right angle between elbow and wrist. The second her blade had passed by and withdrawn, the limb snapped itself back together, the audible crunch of bone fitting back into bone somehow worse than the crack of the break itself.

"Ow!" Shins backed up a pace, initiating the first pause the duel had seen. "Doesn't that *hurt*?!"

Archibeque grinned so widely the corners of his mouth began to bleed. "Of course it does. But not *me*."

Shadows lashed from his fingertips, dancing before her like drunken serpents, and abruptly the entire world went black.

For all of half a second, before Olgun's magic surged once more and cleared the unnatural veil from her sight.

The possessed guardsman had already committed—even over-committed—to his lunge before he realized that his "victim" wasn't remotely as blind or helpless as she was supposed to be. Had Shins wanted him dead, she could easily have run him through as she sidestepped.

But killing Archibeque was never the plan.

Widdershins's fist, protected by Olgun to keep it from breaking, met the man's jaw at the apex of his lunge. Even *that* didn't put him out, but it wasn't a blow he—or the creature riding him—could just shrug off, either.

"See," Shins told him, circling around his sprawled form to stand by his head, "I know that you guys are only kind of here, in Davillon. And I figured you were spending more than a bit of your concentration keeping this poor fellow compliant, yes?

"I bet your jaw hurts, so feel free not to answer. Oh, and sorry about that, Commandant. If you're in there."

Carefully, watchfully, she knelt beside him, reached into a pouch at her belt, and shoved a handful of dried and powdered leaves in his face. Startled, he inhaled. His entire body spasmed, choking, thrashing, but only briefly. The drug worked fast, and he started to go limp almost immediately.

"I'm thinking you can't drive an unconscious body," she said. "So either you get to leave—if you even can—and poof on out of here, because you're not even supposed to be *in* Davillon, and you won't have Archibeque as an anchor. Or you get to come along with me. I'm good either—"

"You! Stay right where . . . Commandant? Commandant Archibeque's down!"

Shins whimpered something unintelligible. The patrol—and it looked, silhouetted against the light at the end of the street, to be about six of them—must have been near enough to hear the gunshot. The thing behind Archibeque's face began to laugh before unconsciousness finally claimed him.

Slowly standing to face the charging squad of guardsmen, Shins made the only commentary on the situation she possibly could.

"Figs."

CHAPTER FOURTEEN

"My friends . . ." Ancel Sicard, Bishop of Davillon, used those words a lot these days. *My friends.* And for the most part, he meant it. He cared, truly, for the city he'd been assigned to shepherd.

The city had not, if one were to judge by the clergyman's mien or carriage, showed him the same care in return.

His frame, thin and bent, bore precious little resemblance to the robust barrel of a man who'd assumed the office. The last tiny flecks of pepper had faded from what had formerly been a salt-and-pepper beard, leaving only a snow-white expanse. The same was technically true of the hair atop his head, but it hardly mattered, since most of it was gone, now, leaving only a rough, age-spotted scalp.

But his voice still boomed, when he wished it to, as though the Pact truly spoke through him, and he still wore his determination as a second set of vestments.

As he prepared to wrap up this afternoon's mass, he couldn't help but sneer internally, just a bit, at the vast array of bright hues on display, or at the aroma of uncountable colognes and perfumes. It seemed his audience strove to outshine the stained glass, out-sweeten the ceremonial incense. The aristocracy were Davillon's life, and he well understood the need to maintain appearances, but the knowledge that the most powerful people in his congregation were there for reasons that had little to do with faith left a bad taste in his mouth.

And they *were* powerful, today especially. Beatrice Luchene, the Duchess Davillon, Voice of Vercoule, and the nearest thing the city's Houses had to a true ruler, had put in an appearance. The rich reds and purples of her finest gown, the intricately coiffed ropes of gray and black that were her hair, probably drew more eyes to the front row of pews than his sermon had drawn to the dais.

Good thing, too, that she was so impossible to miss. Her presence was precisely what Sicard had been awaiting, why he personally led the afternoon mass for the first time in weeks.

"My friends," he said again, "you do not need me to tell you that Davillon has seen some truly hard times over the past two years. And I assure you, you've no need to remind me that no small part of those troubles were, in part, the fault of our Mother Church."

More, I fear, than you will ever actually know.

"But today, the Houses, the Church, and the people of this city stand together, in the face of tribulations that, it would appear, are not all entirely of a natural sort. I know you have heard much but confirmed little. I know that fear rides among you on a saddle of whisper and hooves of rumor. And I have been unable to reassure you as well as I would like."

He stepped forward, to the very edge of the platform. "I make you no promises, but tonight *may* be the night that changes!" Gasps and hushed murmurs filled the chamber at that, just as he'd intended. He had *everyone's* attention now.

Attention that would also be directed toward anyone he now addressed.

"I see that we have a great many of Davillon's lords and ladies among us tonight. I invite all of you to come join me at the conclusion of this service, so that we may speak, and I may suggest to you a new plan that might see our city rid of its various tribulations!"

The murmurs were no longer hushed. A cresting wave of sound crashed through the cathedral as congregants wondered amongst themselves. Many gazed at Sicard in unabashed adoration, hopeful for the first time in months. A few others, however—a selection of the matrons and patrons of the noble Houses, specifically—could not entirely disguise their angry glares.

Sicard had trapped them, wholly and utterly. To leave now, to refuse his invitation, would antagonize the common folk. It would appear that the house of whomever declined was uninterested in a possible solution to Davillon's woes.

Some more enthusiastically than others, the highest of the high rose from their seats, leaning over to whisper instructions to assistants or bodyguards.

"I realize, in these troubled times," the bishop announced, "that some of you might be nervous, considering the impropriety of bringing personal servants or armsmen to accompany you. So please, let me assure you, I have gathered a sizable squad of Church soldiers, who will be present to ensure that no threat can reach you from within or without! Not," he added, "that I envision any sort of danger appearing within our own ranks."

Glares turned to outright snarls. Had Sicard openly commanded them not to bring anyone, they might have had room to object. By casting it as a matter of propriety and trust in the Church, he had again made the eyes of the common folk his own enforcers. And surely they understood, as well, that his comment about "threats from within" meant that no political infighting or such misbehavior would be tolerated, either.

Sicard smiled beatifically over his flock, but he couldn't quite suppress a nervous twitch at one corner of his lips. If this *didn't* work—and it could go wrong in so very many ways—he might well have just made himself more than one enemy among the aristocracy.

Then again, if the situation is as dire as has been described, it's entirely possible that failure on our part will render any *such political rivalries a moot point.*

With a wave toward one of his under-priests to lead his "guests" to their gathering, Sicard descended the dais and vanished into the rear hallways as rapidly as propriety would permit.

✳

"I trust I need not point out," the duchess intoned in a voice that even career soldiers found intimidating, "that this is not your office."

From his position at the head of the massive room, beneath a graven image of the Eternal Eye, symbol of all 147 gods of the Hallowed Pact, the bishop dipped his head. "No, Your Grace, I am quite well aware. My own chambers, roomy as they may be, seemed insufficient to host a group this size. I decided that the private chapel was more appropriate."

Intended for familial rites or other exclusive religious gatherings, the smaller sanctuary bore only scant resemblance to the greater one from which they'd come. A small podium stood beneath the Eternal Eye, as did a table holding all the ceremonial basics: a few holy texts, a bronze censer, some incense and candles, and so forth. An array of pews, rather more comfortably cushioned than those in the main hall, faced the podium in tidy rows. No stained glass here; just a pair of oil-burning chandeliers, only one of which was currently alight.

Intended to seat as many as a hundred, if need be, the chapel was more than roomy enough for the dozen or so guests now occupying it.

Well, a dozen or so guests, plus Sicard. And his allies, though they had yet to make their entrance. And a small contingent of Church soldiers.

Anyone unfamiliar with the traditional garb might well have laughed at those guards, in their brightly colored pantaloons and puff-sleeved tunics, their mirror-polished breastplates and overly elaborate helms, the old-fashioned halberds too large even to effectively swing in the smaller rooms or narrower halls of the Basilica.

Anyone who had seen them in action—either with those bladed pikes or with the pistols and dueling swords they also carried—would absolutely *not* have laughed.

That they had very carefully positioned themselves so that some were always beside the exits, others always within a few running paces of the gathered aristocrats, made them even less funny.

"So, out with it!" This from Charles Doumerge, the Baron d'Orreille, a limp-postured and limper-haired dishrag of a nobleman, who, it was commonly accepted, must have had a weasel, or some form of large rodent, in his ancestry. "Now that you've blackmailed us all into coming here, you could at least be prompt."

"Blackmail?" Sicard asked innocently. "I merely made a request of you all, as the civic leaders of our fair city."

"Laying it on a bit thick, Your Eminence," Beatrice Luchene warned, not without a touch of humor.

"Ah. Apologies, Your Grace. If you'll permit me just one more moment's unpleasant business. . . . Guards?"

Backs and halberds snapped to attention, and most of the nobles couldn't help but flinch.

The bishop glanced down at a small scrap of paper, mumbling to himself, then nodded. "Him," he said, pointing to one of the guests, who had now gone far more than fashionably pale. "Him. Her. Her. And . . ." His finger ended its ragged course aimed directly at Doumerge. "Him."

"Now just a minute—!" the baron began.

"Would you kindly escort these five madames and monsieurs to my office? And keep them there until I instruct otherwise?"

Multiple voices shouted protests, Doumerge's only one among them. Even several of the House worthies who had not been named decried this bizarre treatment of their own.

"We can hardly discuss how to deal with conspiracy," Sicard boomed, cutting everyone off short, "with conspirators actually *present*, can we?"

Everyone but the select five went silent, and amidst those five, protests and expressions had gone wan indeed. Surely, when Sicard had singled out everyone present who represented a House that had refused to put armsmen on the streets, they must have known he was on to them. Nonetheless, they were unprepared for the direct accusation—no, not even accusation, *announcement*, for it contained no trace of doubt.

A bit more shouting and other chaos ensued, but when all was said and done, the gathering was smaller by five participants, and the Church soldiers' intimidating reputation remained fully intact.

"The gentlefolk I've just had removed," Sicard told those who remained, "represent only a portion of a larger plot. Quite a few of the smaller Houses are engaged in all manner of illicit activities. It's important that you—"

"I cannot help but notice," observed one Baron Merchand, a slightly rotund but imposingly tall fellow who always seemed quite jovial—until his temper flared, "that our five absent colleagues all represent Houses whose priests claim to be able to protect their people, and the citizens of Davillon, from unnatural threats that the Church cannot. If, as I suspect, you are about to name the *other* such houses as collaborators in this conspiracy of yours, Your Eminence, I should warn you that you may find the rest of us a dubious audience."

"Do you truly believe, Monsieur, that I would concoct a charge against any of the city's nobles, in the midst of the present crises, purely to remove political rivals?"

Merchand's heavy-lidded expression was more than answer enough.

The bishop sighed, wandered over to the icon of the Eternal Eye, kissed his fingertips, and then lightly brushed them against the holy symbol. "We thought you might feel that way," he admitted. "Which is why I will not be the one telling you of this."

He waved broadly at one of the doorways. The nearest soldier responded to the obvious signal, hauling open the door and admitting three newcomers, only one of whom was garbed quite as nicely as the attending aristocrats.

"Igraine Vernadoe," Sicard announced, "is a priestess in good standing with the Mother Church. Monsieur Lambert is . . . a concerned citizen with certain useful contacts. And I believe many of you already know Evrard d'Arras."

The first two inclined their heads in respectful greeting; the third swept his hat from his head and offered a full bow from the waist.

The trio quickly delved into a basic (and heavily edited) summary of Lisette's schemes. Unfortunately, even with Evrard doing most of the talking, his fellow aristocrats weren't buying a word of it.

They didn't trust the source; the d'Arras scion could have political ambitions, the priestess answered to Sicard, and they knew absolutely nothing about Renard.

They didn't believe anyone could have the power or influence to do what they claimed Lisette had done, certainly not without them becoming aware of it. It was too far-fetched, too crazy.

And they scoffed overtly at tales of the Gloaming Court or monsters on the roads beyond Davillon. Many still refused to believe that anything supernatural had happened during last year's so-called Iruoch affair, and even those who did dismissed the possibility of such a thing happening *again*. It went against all odds.

It was this environment that Shins casually walked into, the bruised and unconscious commandant of the Guard slung over her shoulder like a sack of bearded, possessed, and mildly drooling potatoes.

CHAPTER FIFTEEN

The sudden rumble of shock and anger from the assembly only grew louder still when she dumped the guardsman in a heap on the floor at Sicard's feet.

"Yeah, yeah, I know," she forced out between heaving breaths. "But in my defense, he's *really* heavy!"

"What in the gods' names have you done to him?!" demanded one of the nobles, a stooped old man whose name and House Widdershins didn't know.

"Jumped up and down on him, punched him in the face, and shoved herbs down his throat. Why, what did you *think* I'd done to him?"

In the stunned silence that followed, Shins turned to face the bishop. "We were . . . interrupted," she said softly. "Six of his guardsmen. They thought . . . well, you can imagine."

Sicard's face went paler than his ecclesiastical robe. "You didn't—!"

"Nobody's dead, Sicard. But I had to . . ." Her shoulders slumped. "I did my best, I really did. But I don't think a few of them are going to be able to work in the Guard anymore. You'll make sure . . . ?"

"The Church will see that they and their families don't go wanting, yes. I know you did all you could."

"Yeah. Be nice if it was enough one of these days."

"Widdershins . . . *they* made this necessary. Suvagne and her unholy allies are responsible for this. Not you."

"Great. Maybe they can come help clean the blood off *their* sword. This man," she said more loudly, turning from the bishop before he could speak again, "is not who you think he is. Or rather, he is who you think he is, but he's *also* not who you think he is."

Dead silence. Narrowed glares.

"Well, how would *you* have phrased it?" she whispered to Olgun, before speaking aloud again. "Commandant Archibeque hasn't been in control of his own actions for some time. He's been possessed, by a creature of the Gloaming Court."

"Your Eminence . . ." Duchess Luchene rose from her seat, carrying what appeared to be all two or three hundred yards of fancy gown and train with her. "I've no idea what you think you're doing, but I believe I've had just about enough—"

"Your Grace," Shins interrupted, "with every last ounce of due respect, I think you need to lose some of that mountain of hair. Your brain's suffocating."

The gasps from before her were insufficient to drown out the slap of several hands against several foreheads behind her.

"Am I the only one," she continued while the noblewoman's outrage was still more rage but less out, "who remembers what happened to this city last year? Iruoch wasn't exactly *likeable*, but I thought he was pretty boiling well *memorable*."

"Mademoiselle," Luchene intoned, quite clearly using the term as a synonym for *lowborn ill-mannered little bitch*, "this is my city. The duchy of Davillon has been my family's to oversee since before there *was* a city by that name. Don't you *dare* insinuate that I might simply forget something as awful as the events of last year!

"But the notion that it was truly some supernatural creature, despite what many of the witnesses believe they saw—"

"I lost someone I cared about very deeply to Iruoch. I watched him die. Through the magics we used to try to kill that creature, I *felt* him die. And less than a week ago, I was tortured almost to death by one of Iruoch's lovely cousins. Not so much of a family resemblance, really, but they share certain hobbies.

"So don't *you* dare tell me these things aren't real!"

"As it happens," Sicard cut in before Shins could talk herself out of a potential ally (or into a potential noose), "we have both a means of proving to you that these creatures have come to Davillon and a weapon against them. Faith and divinity are anathema to the entities of the Gloaming Court."

"Commandant Archibeque," Luchene said stiffly, "appears to be lying in a sanctuary of the Hallowed Pact without bursting into flame."

"Because, as with anything to do with faith," the bishop explained, "a symbol is only as powerful as the belief behind it." So saying, he knelt at Archibeque's side, drawing an amulet from around his neck. Gleaming in the light of the lone chandelier, it was a smaller version of the Eternal Eye on the wall—only this one was pure silver.

He cast a single glance at Shins, one she interpreted as *You better be right about this*, and then pressed the icon to the commandant's chest. His head bowed, his lips began shaping themselves around muttered prayers.

"I think," Baron Merchand began, "that we've all had just about enough of—"

Archibeque screamed. Or rather, something inside him did.

This was no human voice, for all that it issued from a human throat. No, not it, *them*. Two separate voices, coiling and sliding around one another. One was high, piercing, enough to make everyone in the room clasp hands over ears; the other deep enough to feel through the floor.

An awful stench, some foul combination of peppermint, rotting oranges, and bile, seared nostrils and lungs. Dull black sludge welled up from within the commandant's mouth, bubbling and oozing before it began to drip down the side of his face—and then trailed away into a wisp of smoky shadow.

"I'll need rather more time," Sicard said, breathing heavily, "as well as the assistance of other priests, to drive the intruding spirit from him. But I trust you've seen enough?"

When nobody claimed otherwise—although that could just as easily have been because they still stared in fascinated horror at the sprawled guardsmen as because they agreed with him—he continued, "I've taken the liberty of summoning the most senior of your House priests. I had messengers waiting; they departed the moment mass adjourned. They can confirm for you that what you've just seen was no trickery.

"I also require them because my under-priests and I aren't sufficient to make up a formal quorum, but we'll discuss that later."

The duchess, and her portable house made of dress, returned to her seat, beckoning the others to follow. "Perhaps you had better tell us your story and your theories again. I'm sure that Mademoiselle . . . ?"

The cue was an obvious one. "Widdershins. My name is Widdershins."

"Ah."

Ah? What does she mean "Ah"? This is not a good "Ah." I don't like it.

"Your, um, Your Grace, about before . . ."

"If what you said is true, you've been through a great deal. I'm willing to dismiss it as heat of the moment."

Oh, are you? You're so kind . . .

"As I was saying," Luchene continued, "I'm sure Mademoiselle Widdershins can add all manner of fascinating details to what the others have already told us."

Oh, you have no idea . . .

Widdershins took a deep breath and launched into the nightmare that the past week had become.

❁

To say the aristocrats appeared skeptical when her recitation wound to a close would have been rather an understatement. Narrowed glares, furtive whispers, and furrowed brows all suggested a rather distinct lack of credulity. At the same time, they hadn't dismissed her outright. Partly because she had the backing of the bishop and Evrard d'Arras, of course, and partly due to what they'd seen moments before. Still, Widdershins found herself more nervous than if they'd simply declared her crazy, a liar, or a crazy liar.

"I'm not liking this, Olgun . . ."

The duchess raised one imperious hand, and the muttered conversations ceased as though neatly beheaded. "You understand why we might have some difficulty with this tale?" she asked.

Shins nodded. "I only believe me because I was there to see me go through it."

A faint quirk of the lips was the nearest thing to a smile Luchene appeared willing to part with. "I think," she said—and though she hadn't turned, everyone present knew she was addressing the lot of them, not the thief alone—"that many of us have heard some of the whispers and rumors. Gossip among the servants and the guards, both, about the mysterious Widdershins and her unusual skills."

And while several of the nobles looked nothing but puzzled, a good half of them nodded in agreement.

If she had stumbled out of bed and, two-thirds asleep, planted herself on a chamber pot sculpted entirely of snow, Widdershins might have been as shocked, as chilled, as she was now. She actually fought with her own body, her own nerves and instincts, to keep from fleeing the room. Olgun assisted as much as he could, but the bulk of his willpower was devoted toward keeping *himself* from the edge of panic.

It . . . made sense, though, as much as she hated the idea. People were bound to notice, especially once she'd gotten caught up in (or hurled herself into) city-wide incidents such as the Apostle's schemes or the Iruoch affair. It had just never so much as crossed her mind that said rumors would make their way any higher than the street.

Of course, it's not like I haven't robbed most of the people sitting here, at one time or another . . .

"Well," she told Olgun, voice shaking until it almost crumbled, "that explains her earlier 'Ah.'"

Her divine companion did not appear to take much solace in that.

"I'm . . . flattered?" she squeaked out, some ten or eleven years later.

"Don't be flattered. Show me."

"I . . . what?!"

"Show us," Luchene commanded. "Let us see that these vaunted abilities aren't just some trick. That you know what you speak of, where the supernatural is concerned."

"You want me to put on a performance for you? Do I get to keep my clothes on?"

"Widdershins!" Sicard, Igraine, Evrard, and Renard barked in unison.

"Someday, Your Grace, I'm going to ask you to order them to tell me when they find the time to practice that." Widdershins sighed melodramatically. "Fine. Sica—uh, Your Eminence?"

"Hmm?" Sicard asked in response.

Shins moved to stand beside him beneath the Eternal Eye, at the center of everyone's attention. "You have soldiers standing guard elsewhere in the Basilica than just this room, yes?"

"Indeed."

"Would you please send someone to tell them that what they're about to hear is a demonstration, and there's no need to come running? And *especially* no need to come shooting or stabbing?"

The bishop's suspicious glower was not the only one to fall upon her, then, but he waved one of the guards to go deliver the message. The few minutes it took him to make the rounds and return were spent largely in silence, with everyone smiling awkwardly at everyone else.

Well, *almost* in silence. Shins did take the opportunity to fill Olgun in on what she had in mind.

The moment the soldier returned, the door shutting behind him with a dull click, Shins said, "All right." She twisted, pointed a finger toward one of the other soldiers, a man stationed near the rear of the sanctuary—and who, she'd made a point to note, was wearing his flintlock in such a way that a misfire would strike the carpet, as opposed to his foot or perhaps a neighbor. "Him!"

Olgun's power flowed, a single spark sizzled, and the weapon fired.

Those in the assembly who hadn't already begun to turn that way when Widdershins pointed certainly did so now, jumping in their seats or at their posts. Guards and more than a few of the aristocrats reached for weapons, while the lone soldier whose gun Olgun had triggered could only gawk, at it and at them, in almost puppy-like confusion.

As the burnt sulfur scent wafted through the room, Luchene turned back around in her seat. "All right, Widdershins, that's a . . ."

More whispers and mutters, then, as everyone intently studied the spot next to Sicard where Shins had stood an instant before.

"Up here!"

Crouched atop the chandelier, Shins gave them all a jaunty wave.

"Assuming it's not too much trouble, Your Eminence," she continued, "if you would just pass my compliments on to the architect and craftsmen? I don't think this chain—" and here she flicked said chain, a great brass monstrosity that held the fixture in place, "— even noticed my weight."

"Uh . . . the Basilica's almost a hundred years old. The folks who built it are rather long dead."

"Oh. Well, then, you should know where to find them."

"How did you get up there?!" one of the aristocrats squawked. "There's nothing to climb!"

"Noticed that, did you? That's why I didn't climb. I jumped."

"Preposterous!"

"I'm here, aren't I?"

"Yes, but . . . you, but . . . I . . ."

Baron Merchand rubbed at his chin. "You didn't even disturb any of the lanterns."

"Well, I don't know about *that*. This one here seemed right annoyed at me."

Luchene shook her head, creating an odd ripple effect when the upper coils of her hair seemed to hesitate for an instant before following. "If you'd come down, now?"

Shins stepped between two branches of the chandelier and dropped. She was once again at Sicard's side, clearly none the worse for wear, before the various gasps had entirely ceased.

"So," she said, "will that do? Can we get on with this, or do I need to jump through hoops and fetch a stick?"

"Widdershins . . ." The duchess stood and trundled her heavily swaddled way to the front of the chamber. "We've all seen that there's something—unnatural—in the body of Commandant Archibeque. We've seen your abilities, or a hint of them. Our House priests are apparently on their way—and you've still to explain that little breach in decorum, Your Eminence," she added with a sharp look at Sicard. "—and I'm fairly certain, at this point, that they will confirm what he has to say, about Archibeque and about you."

So why does this sound like a bad thing . . . ?

"I believe, too, that—your status and profession notwithstanding—you truly do seek to do right by Davillon."

"Your Grace, if the forthcoming 'but' gets any larger, we're going to need to move to a bigger room."

Another polite quirk of the lips. "Indeed. *But* . . . you are asking us to believe in a conspiracy amongst multiple noble Houses. And their priests. *And* the guard. *And* the criminal underground."

"Well, yes, but—"

"And unless I'm very much mistaken, your plan to deal with this conspiracy, when you finally deign to reveal it to us, will involve our own Houses, and the city government proper, moving *against* these forces? Why else bring this to us, when you must have known even getting us to believe was an uphill battle?"

When Shins just sort of scuffed her feet, oddly reluctant to answer, it was Evrard who jumped in. "More or less correct, Your Grace."

"So. I cannot make such decisions—none of us can—based on 'believe' and 'fairly certain.' We must *know*, Widdershins. We—I—must know that you can be trusted."

Had the snow-sculpted chamber pot returned at that moment, Shins would have been too numb to feel it. "What do you mean?" she asked, despite knowing full well, *too* well, what answer she'd receive.

"How do you do what you do, Widdershins? How do you know what you know? *Who are you?*"

Years. That was it, the one question that for *years* she had never, ever answered. It remained fresh in her gut, more recent than the wound left by Lisette's blade, more recent than yesterday; the hot stench of blood, the mutilated bodies of friends and brethren.

The world-ending realization, horror, despair, that everyone thought *her* responsible.

No amount of travel, no god-granted speed or agility, had ever allowed her to outrun *that*.

And yet . . . it never even occurred to her to refuse to answer. Not with so much at stake.

Not with so much at stake, and . . . maybe it was just time. For good or ill, right or wrong, life or death, maybe it was just time to lay that burden down.

"You won't remember."

Her voice, hoarse, feather-soft, still sliced through the rising tide of conflict throughout the chamber. Her friends had been arguing with the duchess; not a one of them knew the truth, and yet each of them had struggled to protect her, to allow her to keep her secrets. She wouldn't forget it, no matter what.

But yes. It was time.

"You won't remember," she said again, more firmly, "but I've actually met most of you before. When I was younger."

"Where, child?" Luchene asked, not unkindly.

One last deep breath, one intense image of kissing Olgun affectionately on a cheek he didn't actually have. "Mostly, Your Grace, at the fetes and affairs of House Delacroix."

"Oh, my gods . . ." The duchess got it, then and there. The others? They others didn't yet understand.

"My name," Widdershins acknowledged for the first time in what felt like a dozen distinct lives, "was Adrienne Satti."

CHAPTER SIXTEEN

I should tell her.

Ignoring the conversational cacophony rumbling about him, Renard Lambert leaned back to peer over one nobleman's shoulder and gaze intently at the thief he'd always known—and still thought of, no matter what other names he'd now heard—as Widdershins. She lounged in the farthest pew, ankles propped on the next bench over, idly staring at the ceiling. Either she truly wasn't bothered by the fact that one of the topics under consideration was her potential trial and execution, or she was putting on a damn good show of pretending. Either way, the attitude was just one of the many things he loved about her. And had, for quite some time, now.

I should tell her. With the kind of power Lisette has, plus the Guild. . . . Even if the plan goes off without a hitch, there's no guarantee she and I will both still be here when this is all over. I should tell her . . .

Except . . . to what end? What good would it do? She didn't think of him in that manner, never had; this he knew, without doubt. Was that suddenly going to change? Did he expect her to just throw herself into his arms?

Right. And then we'll appoint Bishop Sicard as the new Shrouded Lord.

It would just be one more thing for her to carry, one more complication to deal with. And for what? So *he'd* feel better? Because he couldn't live with it if she died without knowing?

She'd be dead. How much worse than that could it be?

No, it was selfish. Better to leave it. He'd decided long ago not to tell her, and nothing had changed. Maybe, if they both made it. . . .

Renard halted, glanced around, and wondered when he'd risen

from his seat, walked halfway toward the rear of the chamber. *Gods dammit, no! I'm not going to—*

But what if I'm wrong? What if there's even a chance?

He'd already come so very close to losing his last opportunity. He still felt hollow, heart in his throat and stomach sinking, any time he thought back to how she'd looked days earlier. How the sight of her, bloodied and broken, had nearly sent him screaming. How, once she'd begun to recover, he would have suggested the group split up for a time, if she hadn't done so for him—for fear of what he might say to her, otherwise . . .

Even now, just at the memory, Renard had to blink hard, set his jaw, to keep from weeping.

Shouldn't I find out? For both our sakes? Shouldn't—

"Your pardon, Monsieur Lambert."

"Oh." Renard stepped aside and bowed extravagantly, clearing the aisle between the pews and allowing the bishop to pass him by. "Of course, Your Eminence."

Sicard smiled his thanks and continued on his way—straight toward the spot where Widdershins sat.

Well, that was a sign, wasn't it? With a soft sigh, Renard returned to the front and reclaimed his seat.

Later. If we both make it through all of this, maybe I'll tell her later. . . .

❀

Gods only knew how long it had been—no, really, they probably did, but she hadn't bothered to ask the one she knew personally—since Widdershins had concluded her recitation.

Since she'd spilled her life story, in its entirety, for the first time ever. Not to a mentor, not to a lover, not to a trusted companion, but to an audience of bloody hopping aristocrats!

Even in my own little corner of the world, blue bloods just can't help but claim special privileges, can they?

She had tried, at first, to make herself part of the conversation that followed—the conversation, the debate, the argument, the demands, the threats—but swiftly tired of it. That was when she'd retreated to this distant corner of the chapel, pretending not to notice that any number of mistrusting eyes now followed her every move, to let the others sort it all out.

Judging by the constant ebb and flow of speech, echoing just around the edges in the vaulted chamber, they still had a ways to go.

The wood creaked as it shifted beneath her, taking on someone else's weight. Shins continued to stare upward, not bothering to look.

"It's quite a different perspective than I'm accustomed to," the bishop told her, "looking up at the Eternal Eye from the congregation. I ought to remember to do this more often."

"You should see how it looks from the chandelier," she said. "So, have they decided who has to buy the rope to hang me with?"

Sicard snorted. "I'm fairly certain a few of them would be happy to use whatever belts or cords might happen to be handy." Then, more seriously, "Her Grace has decided that, for the duration of the current crisis, your guilt or innocence is a moot point. Assuming their House priests confirm what I've told them regarding the current threat, she and many of the others have chosen to take you at your word for the time being."

"That," Shins observed, vaguely pointing the toe of one boot toward the assembly, "doesn't sound a lot like agreement. Unless I've been doing it wrong all this time."

"No, you're hearing the malcontents raising the same objections they've *been* spouting. You can't be trusted, and your story of a demon slaughtering Olgun's old worshippers is ludicrous. This despite the fact that you didn't have to admit to being Adrienne Satti at all, if you were lying. I believe that's part of what convinced the duchess."

"So this is still all about me? They haven't even gotten to—"

"Oh, no, I've filled them in on the rest of the plan, as well. More or less the same, ahem, *nobles* who object to *you* are objecting to *it*. Not proper. Not legal. Bad precedent. Need more time. And so on and so forth.

"But it's all over save the prideful lingerers. With Her Grace and many of the others convinced, plus my own support behind you, it's largely a done deal."

Shins uncrossed and recrossed her ankles, one over the other. "They're not necessarily wrong," she pointed out. "You said even you didn't know for sure that this *is* legal."

"There's some uncertainty, yes. My authority as bishop is substantial—and I was granted more leeway than I otherwise might, given the circumstances between Davillon and the Mother Church when I was initially assigned here—but this sort of thing, to my knowledge, has never been attempted. Still, once the other priests have arrived and I've a full quorum, it should be . . . ah, legal enough."

"Heh. Now you sound like one of us, Your Eminence."

"Oh, dear. I'll have to do penance."

Shins finally dropped her feet to the floor and turned, facing her companion for the first time since he'd joined her. "Was that sarcasm, Sicard? I didn't think you had that in you."

"I don't. It must be a miracle."

She couldn't help but giggle, even as her suspicions grew. And grew further still, when she observed that the clergyman, despite the banter—or what passed for it, with him—stared straight ahead, seemingly unwilling to look her way. His fingers even plucked idly at the fabric of his frock. "All right, spill it."

"Beg your pardon?"

"You didn't come over here to fill me in on the status of a conversation that's not even finished yet."

"Ah. No, in truth, I did not."

"And you're fretting like a nervous schoolboy. Or a cat in a lightning storm."

"I—"

"Maybe like a nervous schoolboy who's fretting like a cat in a lightning storm."

"Widdershins—"

"A cat with a copper tail, even."

Now Sicard *was* willing to look directly at her. "Did you want me to actually answer your question? Or were you just going to keep talking?"

"You know me. These aren't mutually exclusive."

"I want you to consider allowing the Church to formally incorporate Olgun into the Hallowed Pact."

Only the fact that, in their panic, neither Shins nor her god could figure out which way to run, or where to go, kept her in her seat at all. "Wh-what?"

"My dear, we both know that it's only by sheer luck and the grace of the gods that you've survived this long. If you should die as his only worshipper—"

"I *know*!" The pew was tugging at her with its own gravity; she found herself curling up tight in the corner of the bench, knees pressed to her chest and arms wrapped around them. The sanctuary, which had seemed so vast, closed in on her, a clenching fist of stone and terror.

She'd known for years they'd have to deal with this eventually, had talked about it more than once, but it had always been so easy to put it off. Of course she *should* go along with it; that she was Olgun's only worshipper left him vulnerable, meant if she died, so did he.

It was also the only reason they had the bond, the relationship, they did.

Sicard saw her turmoil and reached a comforting hand toward her. She stared at it, unrecognizing, and otherwise made no acknowledgment at all.

"I understand," he said gently, "what I'm asking you to give up."

"Understand? *Understand?!*" She only realized she was screaming when the conversation elsewhere in the chamber ceased, and even then, she couldn't find it in her to care. "You have *no idea!* We can't—I can't . . . No!"

"It's the right thing to do. I believe you know that."

"*No!*"

Sicard finally withdrew his hand, perhaps realizing how foolish it appeared just hanging there. "I will, of course, respect your decision." His old shoulders stiffened as he began to stand, then stopped. "But Widdershins, it may not always be up to me."

She was rocking, now, staring at the toes of her boots. "What do you mean?"

"I didn't know what it was at the time," he said gently, "but I do, now, after having heard your story. When you were. . . . When Suvagne was . . ."

"Torturing me."

"Yes. That. You see, I felt it. In my dreams. As though it were a sign, an omen."

"No. No, that's not possible!"

"Over the past few years, more than a few people—including some, like me, in positions of influence—have become aware of Olgun. You know that."

"Yes, but . . ." She was crying; when had she started crying again? It seemed to be happening a lot, and she was royally sick of it. Almost angrily, she wiped a cheek dry with the back of her hand.

"But knowledge isn't the same as worship," he finished for her.

"No, you're right, it's not. Not to begin with.

"You must realize, though, that when people know of Olgun, and when they begin to realize how much he has watched over them, as he did when he assisted you in freeing the city of Iruoch . . . well, this whole situation is unprecedented, but one has to assume that their knowledge is going to mature into reverence. Perhaps not to the point of genuine worship, but then again . . ."

Shaking her head, still rocking, it was a wonder Shins hadn't grown dizzy enough to fall off the pew. "I can't. No. Sicard, I can't deal with this now. There's too much. Maybe . . . Maybe talk to me after, if we're all still here to discuss it." *Or better yet, don't. Ever.* "Not now. Not right now."

"Of course. I'm sorry to have disturbed you."

She was up before he'd gotten more than four steps away. Hands clenched tight—and toes, too, inside her boots—to keep herself from trembling, she stalked at an almost predatory pace toward the gathering at the far end of the sanctuary. Like it or not, they *were* going to let her in on the conversation, in on the planning. Anyone who objected was more than welcome to try to *make* her leave. In that moment, she and Olgun both greatly preferred the idea of hurling themselves headlong into danger, of planning to fight and kill and perhaps even die, to any further contemplation of the bishop's words.

In part because, deep down where they could never admit it to themselves or each other, Shins and Olgun both knew that Sicard was right.

CHAPTER SEVENTEEN

The heavy mists and constant drizzle had finally made good on their threats. Rooftops and cobblestones reverberated with what seemed a million tiny hoofbeats; the rain was thick, drenching, a blanket of wetness trying to stifle the whole world within its folds.

Standing at the roof's edge, water running from the edges of her hood, Widdershins could barely even see the building across the street; it was little more than a darker shape, etched in falling droplets. Between the dark of night and the inclement weather, it might as well have been miles away.

She stared anyway.

How many times am I going to have to do this, anyway? How many—?

"You realize," Major Paschal Sorelle said from behind her, "that I'm going to need that sword back."

"Of course. That was the understanding when you lent me one of your Guard-issued blades for the duration of this operation, wasn't it?"

The peculiar sound he made in response to that might have been a stifled laugh or simply an accidental mouthful of rainwater. "Something like that."

"I mean, it's not as though someone could just take a weapon from under a trained guardsman's nose."

"Don't push it."

She finally turned his way, then struggled to repress a laugh of her own. "You're wilting."

Paschal glared at her from beneath the brim of his hat, which was now heavy enough with rain to fold down around his ears. The normally erect plume dangled and wobbled, a sad, wet rodent's tail.

"I hope you guys are better at keeping your powder dry," she noted.

"We *have* dealt with weather in the past, believe it or not."

"Paschal," she said, suddenly serious, "I can't stress this enough. The idol—"

"I know, I know. You told us. The priestess told us. Over and over."

"You need to take it seriously. All your people do. It's easy to scoff at the idea of a curse, but—"

"You mean it. I know. You and the others just get us there, let us worry about keeping ourselves alive and, um, un-cursed. If the place is as much of a maze as you've described it—"

"More. And thank you for giving me my turn to interrupt; you went twice in a row."

"How unchivalrous of me. Widdershins, I'm more concerned about you. Are *you* up to this? Are Lambert and Vernadoe? There are those who would call what you're doing traitorous."

"Lisette's the traitor. Lisette and anyone who's loyal to her. They can all rot, the seams of breeches."

"'Seams of . . .'?"

Thump-splash-squish announced the approach of a Guard messenger, sprinting across the rooftop. He skidded to a halt at Paschal's side, spit out a mouthful of rain, then said, "Last team's in position, sir."

Shins smirked, wondering idly if the rain made her teeth glisten, said, "Try to keep up," and stepped off the edge.

❁

Nearly blinding, nearly deafening, but even the downpour could not wash away the reek of the alley. Old garbage had soaked into the earth; its stench was baked into the bricks. Burning down the entire block might, *might* have been enough to cleanse the odor.

This was hardly Shins's first time in this specific alley, let alone the many just like it, so she knew she could deal with it. Nevertheless, she gave some very serious thought to asking Olgun to turn off her nose for a bit. She decided, however reluctantly, that he was probably busy enough enhancing her sight and hearing, and didn't need the extra distraction.

Besides, she wouldn't be here long.

She found the sentry more or less where she expected. He appeared to be a beggar, sheltering in a shallow doorway in a futile attempt to escape the elements. Most passersby, if they noticed him at all, would dismiss him just as readily.

Which, Shins knew, was the entire point.

Come to think of it, she wondered, as she studied the man far more intently than the ambient light and visibility should have permitted, *don't I know him?*

"Say," she said over the rain, stepping out of the shadows, "didn't I once drug you and force you to guide me through the Guild?"

The rather comical, tangled-marionette thrashing as the thief tried to leap to his feet, draw his weapon, and reach for his signal whistle all at once granted Shins more than enough time to act. With an almost casual openhanded shove, she bounced the man's head off the brick wall behind him. Not too hard—she wasn't looking to kill the guy—but definitely more than enough to daze him, at which point she spun him around by the shoulders, wrapped an arm around his neck in a brutal choke hold, and made sure he was down for a good long while.

"You'd probably have preferred the drugs again," she observed as she carefully lowered him back to the stoop on which he'd sat, watching as the rain swiftly diluted the blood dribbling from his scalp. "Maybe if we ever have to do this a third time, yes?"

From neighboring streets, her god-enhanced hearing detecting the muffled thumps and stifled grunts of other sentries receiving more or less the same treatment from Paschal's men.

The sounds of fellow Finders being silenced, beaten, maybe worse by the City Guard.

I should feel weird about this. I should be at least a little conflicted. Shouldn't I?

And yet, nothing. The thought of battling against her former brethren with her former foes, even the possibility of remaining an enemy of the Guild *after* Lisette was gone, scarcely registered. This was what she had to do. For herself, for the people she loved.

This was what Lisette had *made* her do.

She was still lost in thought when the five-hundred count Paschal had allowed for silencing the sentries came to an end. Still lost in thought when something enormously heavy clanked and clattered over the haphazard cobblestones, moving into position directly across the main entrance to the Finders' Guild.

The canon roared. The fortified door disintegrated in a cloud of fire and splinters and smoke. From every visible alley, every street corner, every doorway, soldiers—heavily armed and clad in the black and silver of the Guard—charged their longtime enemy.

Shins charged with them, and there was no more time for thought at all.

❀

Major Sorelle's cannon was not the only one fired within Davillon's borders that night.

Across town, in a district where not only cannon fire but violence of any sort was nigh mythical, one of the walls of the Ducarte estate had come tumbling down at the first shot. Louis Rittier—son of the late and lamented Clarence Rittier, newly risen to the office of the Marquis de Ducarte, had shot from his bed, screaming, at the sudden blast. Sheets and carpet grew thick with rainwater; shreds of silk, all that remained of the bed's canopy, flopped and writhed like dying worms. He huddled now behind a heavy table, frantically scrambling to don his trousers and sword-belt, while the captain of his House soldiers struggled to report over the twin percussions of rain and gunfire.

". . . not just any soldiers, either!" the captain was shouting as he, too, crouched behind the makeshift shelter. "My people are reporting the ensigns of multiple families, including Luchene's!"

"Gods damn it!" She knew. The duchess somehow knew about Suvagne's planned coup and just as clearly knew that he was to have been a part of it. What he could *not* imagine is what could possibly have possessed her to move against them with open violence rather than politically. "Get a messenger to the Guard! Tell Archibeque to get his people over here and restore some semblance of bloody order!"

"My lord, I. . . . There are guardsmen among the attacking force as well."

Rittier felt the blood run from his cheeks. "How did this. . . . How have we heard nothing of this?!"

"It's only possible if they put this together *fast*, my lord. And if we're the first of the Houses they moved against. . . . If we're to be the example . . ."

The young aristocrat was nodding, slowly pulling himself together. All right, so . . . his own House soldiers were gathered in their full numbers on the estate. They'd been intended to *initiate* open action, not defend against it, but they were well armed, well rested, well equipped. Whatever maneuvering Luchene had done to unite the larger houses and the guard, to engage in something of this sort, had to be borderline legal at best. His allies would almost certainly mount a magisterial challenge, and even if they did not, most of the soldiers outside had to be harboring doubts about opening fire on an aristocrat's property.

This wasn't a battle House Rittier could win, but they didn't *have* to win, just endure.

"Captain," he ordered, finally snapping shut the buckle on his belt, "send a messenger under a flag of parlay. Tell whatever bastard's leading this farce that I do not recognize his legal authority to attack me or mine. Tell him I challenge him to a duel of honor for staining my own, and point out that he'll be saving lives on both sides if he accepts. That should buy us enough time for you to slip other messengers out into the street to inform our allies what's happening."

"Sir!" The soldier snapped off a salute and scurried out the door at an awkward, crouching shuffle.

Some few minutes later, the firing stopped.

Slowly, suspiciously, the marquis stood, abandoning the safety of cover, and moved to the window to see what he might see. His captain joined him once more just as he twitched the curtain aside.

"Louis Rittier!" The voice echoed from beyond the wall, more solid than the rain, doubtless audible to every man, woman, and child on the street. "Come forth and address me!" A pause, then, "My word that you will not be harmed or touched."

"Do we trust him?" the soldier whispered.

Rittier grunted. "He gave his word openly, publicly. He'll have issues in his own ranks if he breaks it." He wiped the last of the crust from his eyes, wished he had the opportunity for a shave, and stood upon the window pane.

"I am Louis Rittier, Marquis de Ducarte!" he shouted back. "By what possible right have you attacked my home? Ordered your soldiers to fire on their fellow citizens?"

"By right of legal writ, authored by Her Grace, declaring House Rittier—among others—traitors to the city and duchy of Davillon!"

"Even if this were true, which I wholeheartedly deny, this is hardly due process! The duchess hasn't the legal standing to make such a declaration without trial!"

"Oh, but she does! In the presence of, and ratified by, a tribunal of House patriarchs, Beatrice Luchene, the Duchess Davillon, has claimed emergency powers and temporarily reinstated her right to absolute rule by virtue of lands and titles!"

The young aristocrat only realized his mouth hung open when the wind tossed a gulp of rain between his lips. "That authority hasn't existed in generations!"

"That authority hasn't been *exercised* in generations!" the voice shouted back. "It was never legally abrogated! And Her Grace has decided that the conspirators in her domain need to be sent a message.

"That's you, in case there was any confusion."

Rittier felt himself held aloft on equal parts rage and mounting terror.

The distant noble continued, making Rittier wonder how he kept from shouting himself hoarse. "If you wish to challenge the legality of all this before a magistrate, I'm sure you'll have that opportunity. *If* you surrender. If you insist on making this personal, on dueling me gentleman to gentleman, I accept—but I have no choice but to demand our duel be to the death! As part of Her Grace's . . . message."

"My lord . . ." the captain began. Rittier brushed him off. He was hardly the world's greatest duelist, but he was better than most casual swordsmen. And the fellow shouting at him definitely had the superior tone of the aristocracy, not the gruffer mien of a military man. Killing him wouldn't get House Rittier out of this mess, but it would give their allies time to act. Legally or . . . otherwise.

"And what," he called back, drawing his rapier and taking a few muscle-loosening swings, "is the name of the miscreant I'll be punishing for this assault upon my property and person?"

"Evrard d'Arras!"

Rittier's rapier halted in mid *swoosh*, and if his face had paled before, the blood must surely now be pooling in his toes.

"Captain?" Rittier was fairly proud of how steady his voice was.

"Yes, my lord?"

"Please send our messenger back out and inform Monsieur

d'Arras that, while we intend to protest this atrocity most strenu-ously in a court of law, for the time being House Rittier surrenders to city custody."

"Yes, my lord."

CHAPTER EIGHTEEN

Thick with smoke, with dust, with powdered stone, the air in the Finders' Guild's upper hallways seemed more solid than the walls crumbling around them. Coughing, choking, hacking, and spitting were as prevalent as shouting and screaming—questions, orders, demands, and cries of far less coherent meaning. Guns fired, crossbows twanged, and projectiles of every sort gouged furrows into flesh and brick alike.

The cannonballs, along with the first fusillade of flintlocks and blunderbusses, had opened the building like a jar of preserves, cleared those halls of any initial lines of defense, thrown the thieves into absolute, panicked chaos. Now the guards moved in, creeping through the haze, firing at any sign of movement, any sound of resistance. Still, they knew that beyond those clouds, the Finders were also regrouping; that both sides were now equally blind, until the battle moved farther into the complex. That once the element of surprise wore off, no matter how well orchestrated the assault, the guards were going to start taking casualties. It was just the cost of this sort of raid.

"This sort of raid," however, didn't normally include Widdershins —and Olgun had no eyes for the smoke and particulate to blind.

"Hold your fire!" She hoped the shout, coming from the ranks behind, would carry enough weight for the front-line soldiers; guess she'd soon find out.

Olgun's power wrapped around her as she broke into a sprint, flowing through her like a waterfall washing over her soul. She ran, leapt, kicked off the wall to one side, braced both hands on a startled guardsman's shoulders as she arced overhead. Her feet struck the floor between the massed soldiers at one end of the hallway, the clumped thieves at the other, and went airborne again just as rapidly. Tucked into a tight ball, one flip over—then a trio of rolls below—either side's line of fire. She shot upright from the final tumble, one last dive over the heads of the first of the Finders, landing on her hands in the midst of the group until she finally sprung into a standing crouch once more, rapier in hand.

Pity nobody actually saw *any of that.*

"Here, boys," she taunted—and then spun.

Twisting, lunging, sidestepping, ducking, never because she saw the danger coming, but because Olgun guided her every move, a faint but unmistakable pressure on her limbs to which she reacted faster than thought. She leaned back at the waist and knees, almost horizontal, as a pair of blades flashed through the space she'd just occupied, and then struck out with two lightning-quick ripostes of her own. Cries of pain, the clatter of metal on the floor, followed by the thump of bodies. *Moaning* bodies; Olgun knew that she'd prefer to avoid killing if she could help it.

Just as he knew she'd not hesitate if she *couldn't* help it.

The shouts from all around were wild, panicked. The Finders had no idea who, even what, had plummeted into their midst; they knew only that it wasn't hindered as they were. Through the haze, dancing this way and that with the currents in the hall, they must have caught a flash of steel here, a blur of gray there, always gone before stinging, tearing eyes could make sense of it.

The click of hammers punctuated Olgun's warning, and Shins only smiled. Sparks snapped and sizzled before those hammers fell, a trio of flintlocks spat balls of lead, and three of the Finders fell screaming in pain, shot by their own confused and horrified allies.

Step, pivot, parry across, parry high. The clash of steel was swift as the patter of rain, as though the storm outside had elected to join the assault. Shins lunged, felt her rapier punch through something soft and whimpering; dropped into a low crouch beneath another thief's thrust and spun, kicking the ankles out from beneath the woman who'd just tried to stab her. The heavy *thunk* against the floor suggested this particular enemy wouldn't be getting up again anytime soon, but Shins stabbed her through one leg, just to be sure.

Finally, dispersed as much by the wind of Shins's own movements as anything else, the haze began to clear. Small patches of stone wall grew visible to either side. The blood oozing across the floor glistened in the lanternlight, and only then did Shins become aware of the faint and rather disturbing *squelch* of every step.

Still, she thought with a shudder, *at least I'm not lying in it.*

The seven Finders scattered around her, sprawled across the floor and all sporting various holes that neither nature nor the gods had granted them, weren't so lucky.

Well, maybe one *of the gods granted them, sort of . . .*

The eighth thief, still standing only by virtue of the fact that he'd been farthest to the back when all hell broke loose, hung limp as an under-stuffed scarecrow. His lip quivered, tears actually ran down his face, and the trembling that was only faint in his arms had, by the time it traversed the length of his sword, become violent enough to make the tip little more than a metallic blur.

Shins smiled. He squeaked, dropped his rapier, and sank to his knees, hands clasped on his head.

"Good call," she told him. "You're going to grow to be a wise old man." And just like that she was sprinting down the corridor, heading ever deeper into the complex and leaving the cleanup to the guards who followed.

❀

Face drenched in sweat, Renard plunged into a chamber in the lower passages of the Guild, sliding to a halt behind a small cadre of Finders. Most were clad in casual clothes, even sleepwear, but the guns and blades they carried were well kept and ready to go.

They'd been, the lot of them, watching the room's *other* entrance, having piled up tables and chairs to form makeshift cover. All of which made sense, since the direction they faced led out into the halls, from where any invader would surely approach, while Renard had appeared from below.

"Coming up . . . from behind!" he gasped at them, doubling over with hands on knees. "Don't know how, but . . . they found one of the secret entrances! They're just minutes behind me!"

Immediately, swearing up a storm, the gathered Finders shoved furniture a few paces over, slipping around to the other side. They'd show the damn Guard, though! Bloody lawmen expected to take them by surprise; well, they were going to walk right into a wall of lead instead.

Renard made his way to the opposite side of the room, taking up position beside the door they *had* been watching.

The door from which, of course, the Guard would *actually* be coming. Yes, Renard had led them in through one of the hidden passages; just not the one he'd implied.

Rapier loose in its scabbard, a flintlock in each hand, Renard stared at the backs of men and women who really should not have thrown their lot in with Lisette, and waited for the firing to start.

❀

"We're going to have to go room by room," Paschal ordered, however reluctantly. He bitterly begrudged the time it would take, but this had to be done right.

He just hadn't expected the hallway to have this bloody many doors! They mocked him in the flickering lanternlight, teeth in an insufferably smug grin.

"Teams of four. Two in, clearing the room, two in the hall as backup. Nobody does anything alone, and no enemy contact is too minor; you run into someone or find something important, you call out. *Immediately*."

All standard procedure for an operation of this sort, but the major wasn't about to let his people get sloppy. Not with *this*.

"Colliers! D'Ilse! Reno! You're with me!" He didn't bother to check as he began his march down the long corridor. He knew they'd fall in.

The entire passage echoed with the clatter of heavy boots kicking open doors, of orders shouted, of desks turned out and papers examined. Only on occasion did those sounds include any hint of violence, and when they did, it appeared little more than a few quick shots. The bulk of these rooms, clearly, were empty, and the inhabitants of those that weren't had, more often than not, wisely chosen surrender over resistance.

For all that it was going well, Paschal frowned. The problem with being this methodical was that it would take forever just to reach the far end of the hall. If anyone waited farther on, they'd have plenty of time to set up a proper ambush or escape in the chaos.

"We're starting at the other end," he announced to the trio on his heels. "We'll move back this way and meet up with everyone in the middle."

From there, for a brief while, it become routine. Kick in the door; dash inside, eyes and bash-bangs tracking quickly across every corner, digging through every shadow; a minute of more intense searching, to ensure nobody hid behind the furniture and no blatant dangers or evidence lay scattered openly; and on to the next room. Paschal and d'Ilse inside now; Colliers and Reno inside the next, while they waited in the hall; then Paschal and d'Ilse again. Familiar, efficient as clockwork.

And with the familiarity of repetition, even the most professional of guards could grow, however slightly, inattentive.

Paschal was already sweeping into the darkened room, slipping aside to clear the doorway, when the room flickered and barked with the sound of a single shot. Constable d'Ilse cried out from behind him; no way to tell how bad it was, though the fact that she kept up a string of muttered expletives was proof enough, at least, that the wound hadn't been lethal. The others should come bursting in, drawn by the sound of trouble, but the major had no attention for them, either.

No, his focus fixed entirely on the brass barrel of his flintlock, and the enemy—crouching low by a door in the far wall—at the end of it.

He returned fire, the thunder even more deafening than before, and then the enemy was *lying* by the door in the far wall. Except for small bits of his shoulder, which were splattered across it.

The injured man screamed; the injured woman cursed a bit more before subsiding into the raspy breathing of suppressed agony. Colliers knelt beside her, treating the wound as best he could, while Reno moved quickly to secure the prisoner—not that he was apt to go anywhere any time soon.

Which left Paschal to check that far door. None of the *other* offices he'd seen in this hall had a second door. . . .

Narrower than the exit to the hallway, it was otherwise functionally identical. The major slammed it open, charging in with rapier in hand . . .

A massive shape loomed from the shadows, a tall and barrel-thick figure wielding an equally massive pistol.

Idiot. Gods damned bloody idiot! "Nobody by themselves!" *I'd have a constable on latrine duty for pulling something like this!*

Paschal crossed the distance between them in a desperate lunge, blade outstretched—a blade the colossal thief sidestepped with ease—his other hand grabbing for the gun even as it fired . . .

"*Ow!* Gods bloody dammit!"

The pain was sharp, biting, sending tingles of aggravation throughout his entire arm. Still, it was preferable to having been shot. He and the large-framed Finder both stared for an instant at the flintlock—and the flint clasped in the hammer, which had come down not on the striker but on the web of flesh between Paschal's thumb and forefinger.

Laremy Privott, Taskmaster of the Finders' Guild—now, up close, Paschal recognized the snake-bald head and apish body from prior encounters—grunted something vaguely disbelieving but otherwise unintelligible, then said, "You have *got* to be shitting me."

"I am as shat as you are," Paschal said, even as he grabbed desperately for a weapon with his free hand. Not his rapier; this close in, it'd be awkward to the point of useless. No, the guardsman dropped his longer blade and went for his dagger, a heavy-basketed main gauche. Went for it and got nowhere near it, as a vise pretending to be a fist clamped down hard enough to grind the bones of his wrist together. He couldn't help but gasp between his teeth in pain.

They staggered about the inner office, slamming one another into walls and furniture, locked in this peculiar duel. Paschal could not risk releasing his grip on the flintlock, agonizing as it was; Privott couldn't relax his own hold without being stabbed.

In better shape than most, Paschal still had no doubt that this was a contest in which he could only come out second best. Privott, judging by his mocking grin, knew it, too.

"Anything you want to say before I tie a pretty little bow in your spine?"

"Actually . . . yes," he answered between grunts. "You're . . . under arrest."

The taskmaster chortled.

"You can surrender . . . to me now," Paschal croaked on, "or you can . . . kill me and then . . . be shot dead by my people . . . in the next room."

Privott froze. "You're bluffing."

"No," d'Ilse rasped from the doorway, voice firm despite the obvious pain it carried. "He's not."

She and the other two soldiers stood or crouched, leaning around the doorjamb to aim bash-bangs at the struggling pair.

"Were you waiting . . . for an invitation?" Paschal asked them, still bent halfway backward.

"Didn't seem desperate enough to try shooting *through* you, yet, sir."

"The consideration is appreciated." The major looked up into the Finder's eyes, which were now darting side to side, seeking an escape that didn't exist. "You could try taking me hostage, of course," he said, his breath slowing. "That might get you past those three. But there are a lot more of us in the hall. Nowhere you can turn where you won't be exposing your back to someone.

"How loyal *are* you to Suvagne, Privott? Are you ready to martyr yourself for her?"

The hefty fellow slowly straightened, releasing his grip on both his opponent's wrist and the flintlock (the latter of which Paschal gingerly detached from his throbbing and already bruising skin). "I believe, officer" he said, "I'd like to turn myself in.

❀

"You don't want to do that."

Muskets and flintlocks hung on the walls and in racks throughout the chamber. Crossbows sat, unstrung but otherwise ready to go, on the shelves of massive cases. Swords and daggers, some on those self-same shelves, some standing upright in stands, smelled heavily of oil. And from behind an iron-shod door, currently standing ajar, drifted the pungent and sulfuric scent of black powder.

Nearly a score of Finders occupied the Guild armory, gathering up weapons and equipment, and all of them stopped to stare as Igraine Vernadoe stepped calmly through the chamber's outer door.

"It's not too late," she continued. The priestess paused, ensuring all attention was on her, before she resumed her casual stroll through the armory. "You can still return to the Shrouded God's grace."

"Like you?" one of the men spat "By siding with the fucking Guard?! You're a traitor! You're—"

"The Shrouded God utilizes what tools he needs, Pierre. The Finders' Guild is currently under the thumb of an apostate, who has dismantled our priesthood and banished our most senior members. Do you truly believe that our god will let such an affront stand?"

"We're not a church!" the other—Pierre—snapped back. "Suvagne's made us more profitable than we ever were under the Shrouded Lord or your god!"

Rumbles of agreement from more than a few of those present, but Igraine could see, as well, the doubt and hesitation in the faces of many.

"Lay down your weapons," she commanded. "Merely being present here isn't a crime. Most of those arrested by the Guard will be free in a matter of days and can assist in rebuilding the Guild into what it should be.

"Or you can fight, and possibly die, on behalf of the true traitor among us. Even if, by some stroke of fortune, you were to prove victorious, how long do you believe you can survive this life without the Shrouded God's approval?"

By now, she had crossed the armory, wending her way between the racks and the shelves and the indecisive thieves, so that she stood near the door to the powder chamber. Even those who seemed unmoved by her words hadn't yet made any move against her, as she'd known they wouldn't. Perhaps they'd turned their backs on the Shrouded God, but they would still hesitate to murder one of his priestesses within the walls of the Finders' Guild.

Hesitate, but not necessarily refuse. Pierre and several of the others raised their weapons.

"You're standing with the Guard, against Finders. In my book, that's a lot more treasonous than anything you're blathering about."

"Then we shall prove it. All of you willing to hear me out, please seat yourselves upon the floor."

Confused glances and worried murmurs followed, but a small number of the thieves did, indeed, sit down.

"So few? A shame."

Pierre grinned nastily. "I think you're done here, Vernadoe."

"Yes. Yes, I suppose I am."

She ducked suddenly behind the armored door as the Guards in the hall, who'd crept up on the armory while she'd held the Finders' attentions, opened fire.

Opened fire *over* the heads of those few thieves who had been wise enough to heed the warnings of their priestess.

❁

"You realize you just wasted your time and shed blood for nothing, right?" Although manacled and on his knees, the presence of so many of his brethren—equally restrained—had apparently reignited some of Laremy Privott's defiant streak. "Even if all this shit was legal without Commandant Archibeque's orders—"

And how did he know that, I wonder? Paschal mused, not really wondering at all.

"—the Church is going to crawl all the way up your asses and kick them from inside, for violating the laws of the Hallowed—"

Paschal cleared his throat and held out an open palm. One of his constables immediately slapped a coiled scroll into it. The major examined it, turned it around so Privott could see the seals of both House Luchene and the Church of the Hallowed Pact. Snapping them both with one thumb, Paschal flipped the scroll open—with, he would admit, a totally unnecessary flourish—and began to read.

"Whereas Beatrice Luchene, the Duchess Davillon, has executed her legal right under emergency powers and claimed full ducal jurisdiction over Davillon and its official entities, *including the City Guard. . . .*" That last bit wasn't actually written; the major just wanted to make sure it was quite clear.

Ignoring the low muttering, he continued, "And whereas, in response to its actions in expelling its senior priesthood and turning from communal worship of the Shrouded God, His Eminence Sicard—in concert with a legal quorum of fourteen ordained priests—has declared the establishment known as the Finders' Guild to no longer fall under the protections granted religious institutions of the Hallowed Pact—"

He didn't bother to read any further; nobody could have heard him over the roar of protesting disbelief, anyway.

"You can't do that!" Privott finally shouted when the noise level had subsided to only *almost* bone-breaking. "Not even the bishop has the authority to make that sort of declaration."

It was not Paschal who answered, but Igraine Vernadoe, slipping out from behind the front rank to crouch before the flushed and sweating taskmaster. "It's a gray area," she admitted. Then, with a broad smile, she added, "I'm quite certain you can appeal to the Church, just as soon as you're capable of getting a message to anyone in the upper echelons. It's even possible they'll agree with you, though I rather doubt it.

"But in any case, as the most senior clergyman currently accessible and a bishop in the ranks of the Mother Church, His Eminence's declaration stands as legitimate until and unless overturned."

"You treasonous bitch!" he hissed, yanking futilely at his chains.

"Me? You're the one who chose to follow the usurper, Remy. You should thank her, by the way. It was only because of the threat she

posed that we were able to get the Church and the Houses on board
with something this massive."

She leaned even closer, until she could whisper almost intimately
in the taskmaster's ear. "The protection of the Shrouded God was
never just silly superstition, you ridiculous fool. Such a pity you had
to learn that the hard way."

Then she was up and back amongst the guards, leaving her former
friend and ally cursing and spitting in a frustrated, fearful rage.

❋

Riding the momentum of another humanly impossible sprint, Shins
dropped to her knees, leaned back, and slid the length of the hall,
passing beneath the fusillade fired by the gathered Finders. Beneath
the fusillade, and beneath the outstretched arms of the first rank,
slashing a calf here or a hamstring there as she swept by.

Then she was up in the midst of them. She snatched one of the
Finders by the belt and collar as she shot upright, driving his head—
with a bit of Olgun-boosted strength, of course—into the ceiling.

Those still standing in the front spun to face her; the bulk from
the back pressed forward, eager to see her bleed.

Which, of course, had been the point. Clumped, focused on her,
facing in multiple directions, this last gaggle of sentries were *not*
watching down the hall whence she'd come.

Widdershins smiled, dropped her rapier, and leapt. Her right
hand and foot slapped hard against the wall, her left against the
ceiling. Even with her god's assistance, it was a position far too
awkward, far too lacking in any real support, for her to hold more
than a few seconds.

But a few seconds was long enough for Renard and the guards
accompanying him to fire down the hall, unimpeded by any return
shots.

Those thieves who survived wisely raised their hands.

Shins dropped to the floor, landing—for no reason other than showing off, at this point—on the pommel of her sword with the toe of her boot. Pivoting on the basket hilt, the weapon flipped into the air inches from her chest, where she caught it as smoothly as though it'd been handed to her.

"I can't help but wonder," Renard mused as he strode up beside her, "if that last bit was truly necessary."

"It'll just have to remain one of life's great mysteries." She indicated the door with a tilt of her head, looking first to her friend, then to the squad of soldiers with whom she'd met up moments before. "Everyone ready?"

Gruff nods and the hefting of very large weapons were her answer.

She hurled open the door to the Shrouded Lord's chamber.

So accustomed was Widdershins to seeing the room choked with smoke, she needed a moment to realize that it wasn't supposed to be anymore. That, and the fumes were far darker, and far more redolent of singed flesh than the incense-laden stuff the Shrouded Lord had used.

It billowed from the hidden trapdoor, the exit Renard had used to escape Lisette some months before. An entire contingent of the Guard had waited down there, armed with blunderbusses, and the area directly beneath the trap had been soaked in oil. Their orders, if anything were to come through that portal without shouting the proper pass phrase, had been to ignite the oil and then fill the passage with enough shot to stretch wall to wall, floor to ceiling. It should have been more than even Lisette, with all her unnatural gifts, could penetrate.

It wouldn't be until later, after much careful examination and questioning of the survivors, that Shins and the others would learn what happened: that the madwoman had used the bodies of her own people to smother a portion of the flames and to shield herself from the wide-barreled guns. Once she'd closed to within the range of blades, the soldiers never stood a chance.

But that, again, Shins would find out later. For now, she knew only that after all they'd just been through, Lisette had still managed to escape them.

CHAPTER NINETEEN

Twice the sun had risen and set again, since the raid on the Finders' Guild, and it did so over a city fallen into a strangely controlled and formal chaos.

Courts across Davillon swelled with thieves who argued that their arrest had been blatantly illegal, Guard and city officials who swore otherwise, and a woefully undersized population of magistrates who were coming to regret the choices they'd made in life to bring them here.

The smaller Houses, particularly those who'd been involved in Lisette's schemes, huddled in tight and waited to see what fate might befall them. Oh, they made their own legal cases, challenging the laws and traditions by which Beatrice Luchene had seized power, but they made those cases quietly. Their House soldiers remained on the estates, guarding against attack but taking no other action; the patriarchs and matriarchs kept inside, never so much as appearing at an un-curtained window. With the Guard *and* the larger Houses arrayed against them—and the example of House Rittier fresh in their minds—none were willing to stick their heads up and risk being hammered back down.

Those larger Houses? They weren't precisely glorying in the tension or legal limbo, either. That their interests and Luchene's currently aligned was no guarantee they would still do so next week, next month. The aristocrats of these more potent bloodlines cemented alliances, reinforced their businesses, and otherwise worked to ensure they remained stable and powerful enough to survive whatever might come.

What they knew—what occupied the minds of every citizen of Davillon who paid attention—was that the next move belonged to the duchess. Any course of action the Houses might choose, indeed the entire future of the city, hinged on a single question.

Now that the immediate crisis was over, would she return shared power to the noble Houses of Davillon? Or did she intend to make the regional return to the proper feudalism on which Galice was founded a permanent one?

It was a good question, one that might have led to the establishment of any number of legal precedents.

Too bad it would never be answered.

❀

In her simple nightclothes—without the added bulk of her formal gowns, the armor of her corsetry, the looming height of her fancy wigs—Beatrice Luchene was beginning to look old. Still imperious, with a spine of iron and a glare sharper than any rapier, but old. And she knew it, though she'd never admit it aloud.

She reclined on a fat sofa, lined in red velvet, its cushions so over-stuffed it probably represented the end of entire dynasties of geese. On her lap lay a heavy tome, a book of laws and history, one of many she'd consulted over the course of the last few days. And like all the others, the answers it offered were muddled and inconsistent at best. Too tired to rise and restore the book to its proper resting place on one of the dozen bookshelves that made up her massive library, she instead rested her hands atop it, tapping it with one finger as she stared into nothing. Greedily sucking up the last of the oil, the lantern she'd placed on the small table beside the sofa began to gutter and fade, filling the chamber with gauzy shadow and a vaguely sour aroma.

Lower. Smaller. Dimmer. Until it was no more than a glowing ember at the end of a wick, and the duchess had dozed off on her sofa.

And then it was a conflagration, blinding in its intensity, the sun made manifest. Luchene rolled from the sofa, screaming, one arm thrown over her face—and only then did she realize that she felt no heat. That the room was not, in fact, engulfed in flame.

No, it remained lit by that lonely lantern. Indeed, squinting as she waited for her tearing eyes to adjust, the duchess realized that it was still only a tiny, lingering ember! An ember that, against all reason, now illuminated the chamber in sharp contrasts, casting razor-edged shadows over the walls and shelves.

And along with that light came the sharp tang of sugar candies and cinnamon.

Luchene forced herself upright on shaking legs. Still squinting, she felt around blindly until her fingers came across the stiletto and small flintlock that lay atop the table beside the impossibly gleaming lantern.

Every room of the estate was similarly equipped; the duchess had survived too many assassination attempts in her youth to live otherwise.

"Not the most friendly welcome I've ever received." Twin voices, speaking in unison, a young boy and an old man. Luchene spun toward the sound; the creature she recognized from Widdershins's description as Embruchel, the Prince of Orphan's Tears, gazed back at her through mirrored eyes.

She felt as though a jagged hailstone had formed in her throat. Simply speaking was a heroic effort.

"How . . . how did you do that with the lamp?"

The gleam of the fae's inhuman gaze flickered as he blinked. Apparently, whatever he'd expected her to say, that wasn't it.

"I stripped away the shadows around it," he said finally. "So the light had more room to expand."

"I don't . . . ." She took a shuffling, sideways step toward the door. "That doesn't make any sense!"

"It makes perfect sense," Embruchel insisted, almost petulantly. "Your definition of 'sense' is too narrow."

In the distance, a chorus of children cooed and chortled.

Another slow, careful step, edging closer to escape. "Don't you—" she began.

"Slow, stupid mortal thinks we're all slow, stupid mortals! That's no door, not for you. Wrap your sweaty fingers around the latch, and I could still pull your bones out through your flesh, slick and dripping, and suck them dry before you could squeak the hinges!"

Luchene shot him.

It was difficult to tell, given the lack of pupils in his glassy eyes, but she thought they might have crossed as he tried, in vain, to examine the large hole in his forehead. "What was the point of *that?*" He sounded honestly puzzled.

The duchess softly gurgled something in reply.

He strode toward her, that impossible creature. She couldn't help but note that he left bloody footprints on the lush carpet, a trait that Widdershins had *not* described. "Weren't you asking me something?" he inquired.

"What? I . . . ?" She'd just been trying to distract him, then. Still, keep him talking, maybe she could buy herself some time . . . "Just, I thought you always traveled with an entourage."

Embruchel looked at her as though she were the crazy one. "They're busy," he explained, his words slow and precise, as a parent might speak to a particularly dim child. "What did you expect, that I would take the time to murder your entire household by *myself?*"

Beatrice's soul shriveled. Her dagger fell from a suddenly limp grip.

"I don't normally take a personal hand with someone old and childless, like you." He raised one arm, allowing the hideous lashes that served as digits to unfurl dramatically in the bright light. "But I'm doing a favor for a friend, you see."

Screaming—in rage far more than fear—the duchess lunged at him, determined at least to go down fighting, not as some helpless, sniveling victim. She had only her bare hands now, since she'd dropped her blade, but really, it would have made no difference.

❀

". . . determine what exactly falls into our purview," Bishop Sicard was saying as he addressed an assembly of priests, gathered in that same private chapel. Some were his own people, clergy of the Basilica of the Sacred Choir; others were loyal to various Houses. For days, now, they had remained in counsel, taking time only for sleep, for meals, and for prayer. What they had done regarding the Finders' Guild would rock High Church law. What Sicard had told them he *wished* to do was absolutely and utterly unprecedented.

"Again, we may not even have the opportunity. In the end, it's not our decision whether or not even to try." Several members of the assembly muttered at that, as it was something like the eighty-third time he'd made the point. "But if we do, I want us all to be certain that we are moving forward with only the greatest reverence for—"

He couldn't breathe. The air in the chapel seemed to have frozen into a thick paste. His whole body shivered, his skin reddened. With an effort that pained him from head to stomach, he forced himself to inhale. It was like trying to suck wet soil through a straw.

After that first breath, it grew easier, but the room still felt deathly chill. Yet he saw no other signs of cold; his breath didn't steam, nothing around him was frozen to the touch.

The priests had stood, or fallen, or knelt to pray. Clearly they felt it, too, whatever it was. The two Church soldiers—present mostly as a formality, since nobody expected the assembly to turn violent— dashed forward, struggling to find some means of helping. They, obviously, were *not* experiencing the same effect.

Then what . . . ?

Tarnish crept over the Eternal Eye, symbol of all 147 gods of the Hallowed Pact. The chandelier strobed, darkening and brightening to impossible extremes. The air thickened further still—no harder to breathe, but an oppressive weight, a building pressure.

That pressure, and the rightmost door to the sanctuary, both burst.

The thing on the threshold was only somewhat human. Back-bending, batrachian legs supported a torso that seemed normal enough, but its head . . . utterly hairless, it gaped open as if the jaw were hinged at the ears, revealing a writhing mass of barbed and grasping tongues.

Although their faces blanched, the soldiers advanced with halberds raised. Sicard waved them back, his mind racing. This creature of the Gloaming Court, as with most fae, would be undaunted by normal weapons. He might hold it at bay for a time, with prayer and his own icon of the Eternal Eye, as he had with Iruoch, but only for . . .

Even as the monstrous creature stepped into the chapel—leaving, for some reason, a trail of bloody footprints behind—a smile split Sicard's beard.

"Iruoch stood inside this church," he announced, retreating toward his fellow priests. "And his presence felt nothing like yours. Nothing so heavy. And having met him, seen him, I feel safe in saying that he was no more holy, no less profane, than you."

The fae halted, eyes rotating obscenely to peer over the edge of its own distended jaw and meet the bishop's gaze. A wet, burbling sound popped from its throat, a sound that *might* have been, "So?"

"So perhaps it's the excess of devotion in this room. You appear darker, against a brighter light. And while I, alone, might prove unable to stop you—"

The thing hurled itself forward, tongues lashing out, stretching yards from its maw. At the same moment Sicard raised his amulet and began to pray. First one of the priests, then a few more joined him, until their voices filled the chamber in a deafening paean.

The thing froze, leaning forward as though battling against a mighty wind. It pushed, and the holy men and women of the Hallowed Pact pushed back. Both sides strained, both refused to yield.

And both began to tire . . .

❧

The corridors of the Guild were strangely, even disturbingly quiet.

No surprise, there, not with so many dead or incarcerated. Still, as Igraine knelt in the darkened chapel, before the hood-blinded idol of the Shrouded God, it nagged at her. A sense of wrongness, nibbling at the edges of her focus as she prayed for guidance.

The place wasn't *entirely* silent, of course. Not every Finder had been present for the raid, and the Guard was too busy dealing with the masses of criminals they *had* arrested, as well as the tension on the streets, to pay much attention to the headquarters of what they knew to be a broken Guild. Slowly, then, in dribs and drabs, a tiny population of remaining thieves had returned to their halls.

Some were Finders who fled when they learned of Lisette's take-over, either loyal to the Shrouded Lord and the priests or simply unwilling to follow a woman they clearly remembered as unstable. Others were members of the Guild who'd simply happened to be out that night, and who, though they'd been willing to follow Lisette while she was here, were wise enough keep their heads down and ride out this new change in regime as they had the last. A few had even been present during the raid but managed to remain hidden from even the most meticulous searches.

So, disturbingly quiet, yes, but it meant that when the nearest hall went *completely* silent, when sound ceased trickling around the partly open door to the chapel, Igraine noticed swiftly enough.

I suppose I should have expected this.

The priestess concluded her prayer, then stood from vaguely aching knees and turned, facing the door and placing her back to the effigy of the Shrouded God. Idly wishing that she had a pistol or a larger blade on her person, she slid a thick-bladed dagger from its sheath.

"I know you're here!" she called.

It obliged her by appearing in the doorway, and for all her bravado, Igraine couldn't repress a shudder as she pressed herself tight against the cold stone of her god. It was gaunt, painfully so, and taller even than the idol, which was itself slightly larger than a big man. Shadow clung to it in rags, ignoring the efforts of the chapel's lanterns. She could make out little, save that its limbs were gangly, diaphanous wings buzzed at its back, and its facial features consisted solely of a pair of glinting, faceted eyes.

And given that shudder, she could never be certain, but she'd have sworn the statue at her back also quivered a bit at the thing's approach.

Not one of the creatures that made its presence known at Widdershins's capture, according to the story as she'd told it, but "Gloaming Court" wasn't precisely a difficult conclusion to reach.

Clicking and chittering, it advanced on her, though she noted on two separate occasions that it hesitated in mid-step. Only for a fraction of a second, almost unobservable, but definite.

"You don't like being in here with the idol, do you?" she asked, just a hint of taunting peppering her words. It buzzed something in reply and came on once more. Only a few steps away, now.

"I *live* by my faith," she continued, struggling to meet its terrible, cracked gaze. "I have faith, for instance, that he will guide me, prevent me from looking where I must not."

A narrow, serrated limb stretched toward her. Still she hadn't so much as raised her dagger in defense.

"And that his curse, though meant for mortals, isn't something you can just ignore. Shall we see?"

Inches from the fae creature's grasp, Igraine reached up and yanked the hood from the idol of the Shrouded Lord.

❀

Evrard d'Arras fell backward, tumbling awkwardly over the carpet. The ragged gashes in his cheek and his shoulder left a smeared trail of blood across the weave. It looked like a child's art project, compared to the delicate footprints, also a wet crimson, that had stained that carpet moments before.

He coughed, wincing as a ripping pain ran across his face. One hand on the wall, the other using a rapier as a cane, he forced himself to his feet. Not good for the blade, that, but given how horribly marred and scratched up it had become over the past few minutes, it hardly mattered.

Heralded by a gust of floral-scented air, she emerged from the hallway. Lithe, graceful, with hair of autumn, wardrobe of leaves, eyes of bark, and fingers of thorns. She laughed, and it was the airy rustling of wind through the branches.

Through the windows, thunder roared its deep counterpoint.

"At least tell me," Evrard gasped, "that I get the most beautiful of you because I'm particularly worth it."

Those rose-stem digits struck, wrapped around the sword he'd barely raised in time to parry, digging more creases into the steel. Skilled duelist as he was, he didn't even try to riposte; he knew from personal and painful experience that a normal blade would barely even inconvenience the creature.

Time for other options.

When those tendrils withdrew again, preparing for a new attack, he hurled the rapier along with them. By no means harmful, of course, but it startled her into retreating half a step. That extra instant was enough time for Evrard to reach the rack of swords he'd been steering them toward with every fall, every backstep.

The weapon he drew from it was too thick to qualify as a rapier; perhaps a particularly long and slender arming sword.

Even stranger, however, was the dull hue of the blade—very much *not* the glint of steel.

"Had this custom forged," he told her, pausing to wipe blood from his lips, "after our little spat with Iruoch last year."

The creature's hiss at the mention of that name was a cracking branch, slowed to a drawn-out breath.

"So yes, that *is* holy scripture etched down the blood groove. And yes, it's iron. Pure."

He swung through a few muscle-loosening arcs, then dropped into an expert defensive stance. "Now . . . shall we try this again?"

❀

The soaking rain transformed cinder and charred wood into thick paste, clinging to shoes or mixing with the mud in a distasteful slurry. Choked with soot, the rivulets running over the wooden skeleton— the portions of it still standing—came over black in the light of the overcast moon and streetlamps.

So thickly had they permeated the property over the years, the aromas of roasting meats and pungent alcohols remained detectable even over the much stronger, crisper stench of the more recent fire.

"We'll rebuild?" Robin asked for the hundredth time, forcing the words out between sniffles and slow, erratic steps.

Faustine, her arm already around her lover's waist, supporting her as she limped through the ruin of the Flippant Witch, squeezed Robin more closely to her. "Of course. You heard what Shins said. It'll be better than it was!"

"But it won't be the *same*!"

"No." Faustine turned Robin so she could hug her with both arms, now. They gazed at one another, bedraggled, shivering, drenched to the bone and hair plastered flat by the rain, until they pulled themselves tightly together. "No, love, it won't. But nothing ever really is."

Robin sniffled again in response but nodded against the other woman's shoulder.

At the far edge of the seared property, Shins waited, arms wrapped around herself, staring intently at nothing. It seemed awfully considerate of her, giving the young couple a few moments of privacy, but the truth was she'd almost forgotten they were there, forgotten where she herself was.

As much of her heart as the Witch occupied, she was currently deep in discussion about something far more important. Unlike her two friends nearby, when she shivered, it had nothing to do with the temperature.

". . . course I don't want to!" It shouldn't have been possible for her to shout under her breath, but she'd been talking that way long enough to learn the tricks. "Gods, Olgun, you're a *part* of me! It's like asking me to give up my sense of humor, or my lungs, or . . . I don't know, any knowledge or memory of anything that starts with a vowel.

"But you . . ." She welcomed the rain, not so that it would hide any tears from Robin, or even Olgun, but because it provided an excuse for her to deny them herself. "We've been lucky these last few years, and we both know it. If something happens to me. . . . Oh, stop that! It's *absolutely* possible! Just last week, if Renard and Igraine hadn't shown up . . ." She squeezed herself tighter, until her ribs creaked.

"I don't want anything to happen to *you*. I'm *supposed* to die eventually. I mean, not for a while or anything, yes? Eventually, though.

But you? You're supposed to go on. You're supposed to have forever. I don't . . . you can't lose that. I can't . . ." So much for pretending she retained any composure whatsoever; her sobs nearly doubled her over. "I can't be the reason you lose that.

"We've been talking about this since it all started. We knew it had to happen." Each syllable was an effort, one she could barely stand. Her throat was so tight she'd almost have wondered if Olgun were doing something to her, trying to keep her from speaking, if she didn't know him so much better than that. "I need to do this. For you! I need to go to Sicard and—"

It all replayed before her, as clear and clean as when it happened. In a span of seconds, she relived every good moment of her life with Olgun. Every triumph, every joy. Every comfort.

All followed by an aching loneliness such as she'd never known, vaster than the gulfs between the stars of the night sky.

He was willing to risk death itself—an immortal willing to relinquish at least one hand from his grip on eternity—to stay with her.

It was too much, too overwhelming. Something inside her melted. "Of course you'd feel that way now," she sobbed, "but in ten years? A hundred? A thousand?"

If anything, his grip grew tighter. She felt him entwined with her memories and dreams, wrapped around her soul. And despite her tears and her certainty, she couldn't help but shake her head and smile.

"All right, all right! No decisions for now. We'll take our time. I won't break up the team just yet."

Her grin widened at the surge of joy that bubbled up inside her. "Or maybe I should say I won't kick you out of the nest yet. Big baby." She laughed aloud—something she had wondered, mere moments ago, if she would ever do again—at the expression she felt him make.

Behind her, two feminine voices cleared their throats in unison, barely audible over the rain.

"How long have you two been there?" she demanded, blushing faintly.

Robin stepped forward and offered her friend a short hug from behind. "Long enough to know you're upset. What's wrong?"

"Nothing." Widdershins turned, making this a proper embrace—and then, after only a moment's hesitation, held out one hand for Faustine to join them. "Nothing's wrong." They stood, the three of them, by the grave of the old Flippant Witch and, they swore, the cradle of the new, each drawing support from the other.

"Okay, enough of that!" Shins finally declared, stepping back from the others with an obviously false scowl. "We don't need to spend all night here. I'm pretty sure if I get any wetter I'm going to sprout gills. Tomorrow, or whenever the rain stops, we'll come back and start trying to figure out—"

On a rooftop across the street, obscured by curtains of night and storm, something howled in a voice just barely human.

The second cry was heard by Widdershins alone, as Olgun screamed in terror at what he felt was coming.

CHAPTER TWENTY

"It means so very much to see all of you here tonight."

No empty words, those; he absolutely meant it. His head pounded, his stomach still rose and fell in burning waves, but Bishop Sicard would have chosen to be nowhere else than standing at the pulpit of the basilica's main sanctuary. Every lamp, chandelier, and candelabra glowed warm and bright, glinting in deep colors off the stained glass and a clear, almost blinding white everywhere else.

It wasn't the light, however, lifting Sicard's spirit after what had, thus far, been a difficult and terrifying night.

Word had spread quickly, faster even than rumor's normally swift wings, of the unnatural entity that had invaded the church, and the assembly of clergy who stood against it. By the time Sicard and the House priests had emerged from seclusion, their combined faith having finally banished their fae attacker back to the shadows whence it came, the Basilica of the Sacred Choir was already packed with enough people to raise a deafening cheer.

The crowd grew further still when the other priests sent word back to the noble Houses of what had just occurred. When midnight mass rolled around, the normally sparsely attended service was packed, so much so that the temperature in the great chapel had grown uncomfortably warm, and the sound of prayer and paean utterly dwarfed the thunder shaking the building from outside. Despite the deathly late hour and the pounding storm, the people had come to hear the word of, and lend support to, the voice of the Hallowed Pact in Davillon.

Had Sicard not been so drained, so exhausted, he might have realized—either through the faint intuitions that often came from the 147 gods to their most devout clergy, or simply via educated guesswork and deduction—that other such attacks must have occurred throughout the city. He might have attempted to do something; even though there seemed precious little he *could* have done, he would have wanted to try.

But exhausted he was, and what energy he could muster was devoted to delivering service and sermon at an hour to which he was unaccustomed even on normal days.

So, with the equally exhausted, aching, and worn House priests fanned out on the dais behind him, Sicard launched into the tale of what had occurred—and, to an extent, had been occurring recently throughout Davillon—assuring his flock that the situation was gradually coming under control, that the Church was with them, that there would soon be no more reason to fear . . .

She was afraid, terribly afraid, before she even knew why.

Although she could certainly guess.

For Olgun to panic that completely, that loudly, whatever was coming had to be something *bad*. Really bad, demon-bad, Iruoch-bad.

Lisette-bad.

So when she felt her god's power pulling her vision through the darkness, winding around the raindrops to the distant rooftop, she wasn't remotely surprised to spot the thick red hair or the bestial snarl on the otherwise shadow-veiled figure.

The world narrowed, so there was nothing but the rain, the cobblestones, the buildings before her and the burnt-out ruin behind. And Widdershins—brash, confident, defiant to a fault; thief and duelist and, no matter how she tried to avoid it, how she never would have accepted it, hero—had, for one instant, a single despairing thought. Foreign, even alien, and cold as the oldest glacier, but as absolutely certain as if it were written on the bedrock of creation.

I'm going to die tonight.

It wasn't fair. It wasn't right. After everything she'd been through, everything she'd done, she deserved better than this. She wanted to shriek at the injustice of it, kick the mud and spit in the rain, curse the world and the fates and the gods who would do this to her.

She did nothing of the sort, of course. She kept herself, on the surface, calm. Collected. She knew what Lisette could do, knew that no help of any significance would arrive, could *possibly* arrive, in time to do any good. She couldn't win. She couldn't escape. Not even Olgun could save her. Simple fact.

Even as her gut twisted like a dying snake, though, and her heart began to pound faster than the falling rain, Widdershins realized that *that* wasn't what scared her.

I'm going to die tonight.

But I'll be baked and breaded if anyone else *is!*

She continued to scan the street, as though still searching for the source of that horrid cry, as were Robin and Faustine—hand clasped in hand, until the skin went white as bone and not a trickle of the rain could squeeze between. In the process, Shins took a step back, nearly bumping into her confused and frightened friends.

"You need to run!" she hissed between her teeth.

"What? We're not leaving you alone!" Shins could hear the steel coalescing in Robin's voice, the stubbornness that she absolutely, positively couldn't afford to indulge right now. "There's no way we—!"

"Robin! There's no time for this. I need you to go. I *need* you to go!" The idea of lying to her best friend almost made her throw up in mid-sentence, but she managed to force it out anyway. "If you stay, if I have to worry about you, you're going to get me killed."

A second howl shook the night, closer. Even knowing it was Lisette, now, Shins could barely hear her voice in the horrid sound, a roar of murderous fury soaked through with a burgeoning pain.

"Faustine, get her out of here!"

Robin still protested, growing ever more frantic, but Faustine clearly heard the urgency in Widdershins's tone. She nodded once, began gathering the younger woman to her, leading her away, when Shins called after her.

"Faustine! As soon as Robin's safe, I need you to get to the bishop as fast as you can. Tell him I said yes, but it has to be *now* or it'll be too late! He'll understand."

Olgun was screaming again, this time at *her*. It buffeted her, harsher than the storm. Had the earth vanished beneath her feet or she found herself slammed into one of the nearby walls, it wouldn't have come as the faintest surprise.

She ignored it. It wrenched at her, like dismissing the pleas of a drowning loved one, but she remained steadfast, refusing to take back her demand.

Maybe she had been willing to *risk* Olgun's life along with her own, but she wouldn't throw it hopelessly away.

Widdershins held herself rigid, a statue in the rain, unwilling to take the chance that Olgun might yet manage, mystically or emotionally, to influence her actions or her words. Only when her friends were off—Faustine helping Robin to shuffle along as fast as her bad leg would permit, Robin staring back with wide eyes glinting in the glow of the streetlamps—did Shins force her shoulders to relax. She stepped into the road, drawing the rapier she'd thus far "neglected" to return to Paschal.

"Stop yelling at me!" she snapped as she reached the center of the road. Then, as she looked up at the roofs, blinking against the rain that seemed like it would never stop, "So much was awful, but I wouldn't have missed it. I love you, Olgun."

She actually smiled, then, trying to remember the last time she'd felt him so utterly stunned. Lips tight to filter out the water, she took a single deep breath.

Her shout, when unleashed, seemed to stomp along the street, knocking on doors and windows as it passed. "You just going to stand around all night screeching, Lisette? And what's with that, anyway? Got to be murder on your throat, and even you can't have a singing voice *that* bad. Is it a mating call? Is this deranged homicidal lunatic season already?"

A vaguely human-like blot, dark even against the gloom, shot from the roof down the street. It sailed in a sharp arc, an impossible leap, landing atop the building directly in front of Shins. A juddering *thump* announced her landing, but for the moment she remained too far from the edge for Shins to see.

"You'll have to excuse the screaming." It sounded more like Lisette's voice, now, calling over the rain, though there remained something raspy, bestial within. "I'm still getting accustomed to controlling foreign emotions. And they are so *very* angry with you, little scab! Not as much as I am, but close!"

Foreign emotions? Shins could come up with three or four ways to interpret that, and not a one of them were pleasant.

"It's almost funny, in a way," the madwoman continued from above, her tone suggesting absolutely nothing at all in the way of amusement. "Such an intricate, interlocking plan, and all you had to do to bring it down was *open your fucking mouth!*"

"Well, it wasn't *that* easy. They took some convincing."

"The godsdamned Houses haven't worked smoothly together in *decades*! It should never have happened. But that's what Widdershins does, isn't it? Find new and unexpected ways to bugger everything up! I should have killed you years ago, when I had the chance!"

"Uh, you never actually had—"

Something moved at the roof's edge. Shins tensed, waiting for whatever came next.

"Those friends you just oh so gallantly sent away?" Lisette purred from above. "I'm not chasing them down because you might use the opportunity to hide for a few more days, and I really want you to die tonight. But I want you to know that, once you're dead, I'm going to hunt them down. We're going to make them suffer, body and soul, until they beg with their last sane thoughts for me to kill them, and then they're going to suffer more.

"And only because you care about them!"

Shins's breath came quick, now. Her clenched fingers left divots in the wet wrapping of the rapier's hilt. She felt it roaring up inside her, not merely her own anger but Olgun's, too.

"Then I guess," she spat, "I'll just have to not die tonight!"

Lisette jumped, laughing, from the roof.

She landed hard in a crouch on the building's stoop, the impact spraying puddles in every direction. Although the nearest street-light shone clear upon the doorway, she remained partially obscured. Shadows rolled and dripped from her arms, her legs, her shoulders, as though she were ridden by a variety of dark and fidgeting serpents.

Still, they were not so thick, those shadows, as to obscure her from Widdershins's sight, not with divine power augmenting the young thief's vision.

"Gods! You look terrible!"

A statement that was rather akin to telling a vampire he appeared "a tad pale."

That crimson hair seemed straw-like, brittle, noticeable even matted and wet as it was. Her lips were cracked and broken, her gums—as Shins saw when she snarled—shrunken and retreating from her teeth. But worse, far worse, were her eyes.

Or what had been her eyes.

Sunken sockets held pools of a lumpy, viscous black, like ink mixed with the congealed fats scraped from atop an old stew. It sluiced down her face, leaving tarry streaks on her skin that the rain seemed powerless to touch. Water dribbled away from it, polluted and dark, but failing to dilute the stuff even slightly.

"You should see it from my side," Lisette sneered. "I'm going to need months to recover. Maybe I never will."

"Oh, but it's worth it! They're here with me, you see—*and* they're painting the walls with my other enemies, at the same time!" Her face twisted into an almost conspiratorial smirk. "That's people you care about, dying horribly as we speak, in case you weren't sure. If a part of me is the price they need to manifest like that, I'm *thrilled* to pay!"

Oh, gods! No, no, no, who else has she—

A steadying hand and whispered emotions stopped her before her thoughts drove her to hysterics. *Don't think about that. Can't be distracted; that's what she wants. Focus on her, worry about the rest later . . .*

As if there would *be* a later.

Instead, hoping the sounds of the storm would hide any of the tremor she couldn't quite banish from her voice, Widdershins said, "You may feel different when you're too shriveled up and pathetic to use a chamber pot without a pulley, three assistants, and a mule."

Honestly, she barely knew what she was saying. It didn't matter. Lisette was arrogant, a talker, always had been. *So keep her talking and taunting! Every extra second Faustine and Sicard have . . .*

Either the Gloaming Court had added mind-reading to the powers they'd granted her, however, or—more likely—Lisette had simply grown tired of trying to get a rise out of her enemy. Perhaps, even in the midst of her overconfidence, she'd recalled what happened the last time she'd taken the opportunity to gloat, to draw things out.

The shadows about her swirled faster, sliding over her skin, a dancer's train of dark silk, as she took her first step from the stoop. "I may awaken feeling like the floor of a stable," she sneered as she approached. "But for tonight, I—*we*—are as strong as ever. How does that make you feel, little scab?"

"Like I'm still waiting for you to actually come here and prove it," Shins snapped. At which point, despite her defiant words, she did the only sane thing she could.

Olgun's power pumping through her body, augmenting muscle and blood and bone as never before, Widdershins *ran*.

Every extra second . . .

CHAPTER TWENTY-ONE

The first time she had nearly fallen, her bad leg scooting out from beneath her against the treacherously slick cobbles—the first time she'd been saved from a short, painful stumble only by the sudden tightening of Faustine's grip around her waist—Robin had only yelped aloud, startled and a bit embarrassed.

The second and third times, she'd cursed a blue streak, profanities that would make the average longshoreman sound more like Widdershins.

This, in the lee of an old gothic building, its gargoyles huddled miserably against the storm and cringing from the lightning that made them visible, was the fourth.

"Go on without me."

Faustine turned her head, dragging a snake of wet hair across her neck, to gawp. At first Robin assumed it was disbelief, until she realized that her words had been swallowed by the latest crash of thunder.

"Go without me!" she shouted.

Now it was disbelief. Then the older woman's face hardened and she continued on, Robin clasped to her, apparently not even planning to acknowledge the request.

Until Robin locked both her feet, and Faustine could either stop or drag her over to fall against the cobblestones.

"I don't know why you think there's a chance in hell—!" Faustine began.

Robin brushed her fingertips over her lover's sodden cheek, halting her in mid-sentence. "You run all over town every night. You could be at the Basilica in minutes. It's going to take an hour or more, if you stay with me."

"I don't care! I'm not leaving you alone!"

"If Lisette comes after me, there's nothing you can do. If anyone else does? Even robbers are at home on a night like this. But Gerard's place is only a quarter-mile from here. Even I can walk *that*." Much as she tried, much as she had other concerns at the moment, she couldn't quite silence the bitterness. "I'll be safe there."

Faustine actually stomped her foot, which would have soaked Robin's shoes if they hadn't already absorbed all the water they could possibly hold. "No!"

Robin smiled, even as her gaze hardened. "This is important. You know it is. Shins is out there, fighting, maybe . . ." She swallowed once, moved past it. "I know you worry about me. Want to help me. What you can do for me right now, tonight, is to help *her*. Please."

A taut, almost violent shaking came over Faustine's shoulders—and then they slumped in resignation. "Swear to me you're going straight to Gerard's," she pleaded. "That you're not going to try to go back and do something stupid."

"I promise. I know I can't do anything—and I'm not leaving you." Robin stretched up on her toes for a kiss—brief, all too brief—and then stepped back. "Now run, damn it!"

One more second of reluctance, and then she was gone, gracefully slipping away as though racing between the torrents.

Robin sighed, and then, before she could stop herself, called out as loud as her lungs could manage. "I love you!"

In the moment, Robin realized with some dismay that she couldn't remember if she'd ever said that to her before. She hoped Faustine had still been near enough to hear.

Then, for just a few heartbeats, she looked back the way they'd come. *Maybe, just maybe I could . . .*

No. I can't. And we all know it. Besides, she'd promised.

With a second, deeper sigh, Robin shuffled across the street and set her feet toward Gerard's tiny flat.

※

Another cry of warning, a surge of panic from Olgun. They came so fast and frequent now that Shins was having trouble distinguishing one from the next. She dove, rolling painfully over the road thanks to her inhuman speed. Mud splattered up even as the blades swept down, not merely ringing loudly against the cobblestones but actually carving divots into them.

Lisette was keeping up, *and* her arms were again somehow warping, winding, slashing, and stabbing at Shins from a good fifteen feet away, or even more. It just seemed unfair, perhaps even *rude*, for her to do both.

The swords spun and whipped around each other, swirling in circles that no human arms—even bizarrely lengthened and disjointed as Lisette's now seemed to be—could have managed. On the rare occasions Shins had felt it safe even to glance over her shoulder, she'd seen the woman coming after her and the steel flashing, but she'd been utterly unable to make out the movement of the limbs between, or even how they connected to the shoulders anymore.

Not even Olgun's help could allow her to see through the rain, the blurred steel, the writhing shadows.

The *height*.

Fae-ridden, leaking dark magics, Lisette didn't follow Widdershins from directly behind. She hung suspended, above the level of the streetlights, from wavering limbs of shadow. They skittered silently, unevenly, the horrible offspring of spiders and the very specific darkness found only under the bed; stepping across ground or the walls of surrounding buildings with equal facility. The awkward gait flopped Lisette around at the apex of those shadowy, segmented legs, until she looked as boneless and yielding as a corpse in a waterfall.

Despite that, her inhuman arms remained steady. The blades grew closer with every slash, and Lisette herself with every step.

Widdershins could hear the expected and despised giggling chorus of children, the tang of herbs and sweets beneath the olfactory weight of the storm.

How can she be this hopping fast*?!*

"I have decided," she gasped to Olgun as she rolled back to her feet and made a sharp turn down a narrower street to her left, "that I prefer . . . the kinds of spirits . . . that don't have bodies and . . . just possess people. Do those really exist, too? Can we get one . . . instead of fae next time?"

The little god was too busy projecting another warning to answer.

Lisette had come to the intersection and simply thrown herself sideways, the limbs of shadow changing direction inhumanly fast, pushing off the opposite building to absorb momentum. Shins's desperate turn had only resulted in her pursuer *gaining* ground.

"Got anything more?"

She'd guessed Olgun's answer before she'd even asked.

Blades sliced over one another like murderous scissors, coming together mere inches behind her. She ducked forward, stumbled, barely regaining enough balance to keep from toppling face-first to the road. Fast as she was sprinting, she wondered idly if a fall like that would've saved Lisette the trouble of killing her.

Her chest burned, her side was splitting. The aches were coming faster than Olgun could quell them. She'd never asked this sort of speed or strength from him for longer than a few seconds. Neither knew how long she could endure it; both knew the answer had to include a "not very."

Again the end of the block loomed, a wall of void and water. Again Shins broke left, but this time, as Lisette began to pivot, she jumped at the nearest corner wall. Spinning her body up and back, she struck the building feet first, with enough momentum from her impossible run to take a good three or four steps *up* the sheer side. Another leap, entirely horizontal, and Shins shot past her opponent, breaking again into a mad dash the instant she hit the street.

That, even the fae couldn't react to immediately. For the first time since the chase began, Shins gained a few yards.

It wouldn't last, she knew it wouldn't last, but maybe she could—

"*Enough of this!*" It was Lisette's voice, rattled by the uneven motion, but it wasn't *just* her voice. Beneath it, Shins heard Embruchel's horrible twin tones.

The lower half of the former Taskmaster's face was pitch-black, now, and looked as though she'd been drinking tar. Without any apparent movement, without "retracting" or shrinking in any way, her arms were human again, holding their twin blades crossed over her chest.

But where limbs of flesh had returned to their natural state, one of the limbs of shade lengthened.

Lisette had chosen her spot deliberately, no doubt: directly beside one of the flickering streetlamps. At that angle, the leg—had it been real, had the light not been diffused by the rain—would have cast its own shadow halfway down the block.

As the leg *was* shadow, it *stretched* that far.

Shins felt a crushing pain in her side as she was hurled into a tangled heap on the street's far side. She throbbed from a hundred different bruises, probably bled from a hundred different cuts, though any blood washed away before she could be sure. And she knew it was only Olgun, desperately yanking the threads of luck and chance, which had saved her from far worse injury.

"I guess we're done running," Widdershins whispered. "I'm sorry. I hope it's long enough."

Wincing, she stood, drew her rapier, and turned to face her enemy.

✳

It began with the faint thump of the doors to the grand chapel. Unusual and perhaps more than a bit gauche for anyone to enter while the bishop himself was speaking, sermonizing, but hardly unheard of. Sicard only remembered later than he'd even noticed; at the time, the sound failed to register.

Then the low mutters and whispers started, sprouting at the rearmost pews and swiftly blossoming through the congregation, echoing along the vaulted ceiling. A few attendees stood, trying to see over their neighbors, curiosity about the disruption temporarily overwhelming piety or politeness.

Only then did Sicard trail off, going silent in the midst of praising Vercoule—of all 147 gods of the Hallowed Pact, the one most venerated in Davillon itself—as the newcomer revealed herself to him.

A young woman, blonde, in skirts more rain than they were fabric. They slapped audibly against her legs with every step, spattering congregants with cold water. She ignored it all; the weight, the discomfort, the propriety. Although staggered and gasping, she struggled up the aisle with a pace and intent that suggested she was still trying to run.

And several of the Church soldiers, weapons raised, were converging on her.

"No!" Sicard stepped to the edge of the dais, a hand raised. "Let her pass."

It might have been a foolish call. Given what had occurred recently, she could have been some trick, an agent of the fae or of Lisette. It didn't feel right, though. Everything he saw shouted that this was an exhausted, desperate woman.

Even as he ordered she be allowed to approach, however, his brow furrowed as much in anger as curiosity. The sheer impropriety. . . . That frown deepened further still as she stumbled up to the dais, leaving fat puddles to soak into the carpet of every single step.

"Young lady, if this is not absolutely the most urgent—"

Struggling to breathe, she wheezed something at him. Though

he hadn't been able to make it out, a frisson of alarm ran through him all the same. "I'm sorry, what was that?"

Again she rasped at him, carefully forming each word between ragged breaths.

Sicard, suddenly dizzy, had to grab tight to the pulpit to avoid falling. He could only guess how pale he must appear, but he'd lost enough blood from his face that it had actually gone chilly.

"Why?" he whispered.

The messenger looked up, seemed to regain control of herself in an instant. "She thinks she's about to die." Then, more softly, "If she hasn't already, I think she's right."

He reeled, struggling to comprehend, overwhelmed even as seconds ticked by that he knew he couldn't spare. His eyes, somehow empty, cast about every which way, perhaps seeking help. Though what form help could even take at this point was a question he couldn't answer.

He couldn't do this. *Couldn't*. People thought excommunicating the Finders' Guild had been tricky? That was *nothing*! This situation wasn't just unprecedented, it was unimagined; nobody had ever seriously even considered it. The Church had no systems, procedures, even casual recommendations in place. Sicard didn't believe he had the authority to make a decision such as this, in part because he didn't believe *anyone* did!

When he'd made the offer, he'd known he was getting into a massive hornet's nest of liturgical law and debate that would have taken years to resolve!

His wildly flailing gaze turned rightward, settled on the congregation—and stopped.

A couple hundred people watched him—rapt, intent, awaiting his explanation of what had just occurred. Shifting, worried, curious, but calm. They trusted him to tell them what was happening, and how best to handle it.

He, who had been Bishop of Davillon less than two full years, who'd been assigned this charge in a dark period, when city and Church were nearly engaged in open, bitter conflict.

They trusted him now, and many of them had been given reason to trust—many of their lives saved, for all they didn't know it—by a deity not even their own.

And maybe that would be enough. Legalities, formalities, official decisions could wait. The belief of one congregation, the will of a single quorum of priests, might just be enough.

Sicard stepped back to the pulpit, clutching it with both fists.

"My friends, we have given thanks to Vercoule, to Demas, Banin, Tevelaire, Khuriel . . . All the great, all the blessed gods who have watched over us for so very long. Since before Galice was born, since we were nothing but savage tribes in the wilds, we have known the deities of the Hallowed Pact, and offered them thanks and glory.

"Now I am going to speak to you of another, a god of whom none of you have ever heard."

A cresting wave of shocked whispers and bewildered questions nearly swept him from the dais. He pressed on, raising his voice to be heard over the throng.

"A deity of the northern lands who was never one of ours, a deity with no reason to love Davillon, or Galice.

"Yet a deity who has, to the best of his ability, watched over every one of you!"

The sanctuary fell deathly silent.

Sicard felt his voice about to break. He wished he could move faster, worried that every second might be too late—yet he had to build them up to it. He *had* to make them believe!

A surge of contentment welled within him, despite those concerns, washing away the pain and fear yet lingering. This was the right thing to do; he knew it was.

Thank you, Widdershins. I wish I could have done something for you, too.

"Let me tell you, my friends, of a young woman some of you have heard of and *think* you know. A young woman named Adrienne Satti. And of Olgun, a god from so very far away, a god nearly lost to the world. Of how he saved her, and she him, and how they both risked all—yes, all, even the god!—to save *you.*

"And of all Olgun has done, I believe, from the depths of my heart and soul, to earn himself a place as the very first newcomer, the 148th god, of the Hallowed Pact."

❁

No longer did the clash sound anything like the impact of steel on steel. So swiftly and furiously did the two women strike, parry, and riposte, it now seemed a single, continuous tone. Shins's rapier flew, murdering raindrops in its travels. The blade moved faster, her wrist flexed in more directions than were humanly possible. Sweat poured down her body; she felt it, in a layer somehow distinct from the rain.

If Lisette had tired at all, she did a masterful job of hiding it.

She stood almost at ground level, now, the shadowy limbs holding her perhaps a foot or so above the street. Night oozed down her face in ever thickening torrents; the phantom children laughed until they shouldn't have been able to breathe, then laughed longer; her sword and dagger never slowed, kept from Widdershins's innards by only the greatest efforts of thief and god.

And then even those efforts weren't enough.

Shins staggered and fell to one knee, crying out in agony as the tip of one blade ripped through her left arm. It was a shallow wound, a long gash across the bicep, hardly crippling in and of itself. It *hurt*, though, and was doubtless only the first of—

Something deep inside Widdershins tore. Not physically; this was nothing so simple, so benign, as a wounded body, no. Something mental. Emotional.

Spiritual.

She felt hollow, as if she'd been scooped out with a spoon. The dark of night was suddenly crushing, oppressive; each drop of rain a tiny thorn. She felt *alone*, alone as she could scarcely remember. Not since she'd lost her parents as a girl had she ever felt so alone.

It was a hurt that made her arm insignificant. It might almost have been the end of the world.

"Olgun?"

Impossible as it was, she could have sworn she heard her words echo in the newly emptied recesses of her mind.

"Olgun?!"

Nothing. Silence.

Widdershins sobbed once, a primal sound, wracking, despairing. Then, though her legs threatened to collapse at any instant, she placed a hand on the nearest wall and dragged herself to her feet.

Turning, she saw Lisette watching her, her grin so inhumanly wide that trickles of blood mixed with the black sludge at the corners of her lips.

Of course. Iruoch had been able to sense Olgun. The others probably could, too. Which meant they knew . . .

But he would live. And so would she, if only in his memories.

Remembered forever, literally. Not that bad, all things considered.

Sicard, Faustine . . . thank you.

Though her fist shook, her grip on the drenched hilt seemed terribly slick and unstable, Widdershins raised her rapier. Olgun or no, if she was going to fall at Lisette's hands, then by all the gods she'd go down fighting!

And celebrating, through her grief, the fact that she fell alone.

Nearly blinded by rain and tears, Shins dropped back into her most natural defensive stance and waited for the end to come.

CHAPTER TWENTY-TWO

It all happened so very fast.

In a matter of instants, he had been yanked away from, so far as he was concerned, the most important mortal since the beginning of time. The one, above all others, he had and would always love.

When he'd first felt the tug of new souls, new worshippers, he'd been stunned. Whole seconds were lost to his shock, his disbelief. The call of the *others*—no words, not even song, just a divine *sharing*, a bond such as he hadn't known since long before he'd come to Davillon—overwhelmed him. He couldn't think, couldn't act.

It was everything, everything he'd ever wanted, everything he'd missed, everything he'd been terrified he would never have again.

In that moment, he'd have chosen to die, to give it all up, if it meant another minute with her—but some things even the gods cannot have.

Other mortals believed—more than believed, had begun to revere. The gods of the Hallowed Pact, whatever the Church might or might not "formally" prefer, accepted him with open arms, aware of everything he and Adrienne had done for their people. Between his newly divided attentions and the laws of the Hallowed Pact itself, Olgun had no choice.

No matter how he fought, how he wished, how he even *prayed*, he couldn't stay. He had only one more second with her, no more.

A deity can do a lot, though, with one second.

For that one sliver of an instant of overlap, he had a foot in both worlds. A connection to Adrienne like no god had with any other mortal, *and* his first access to the power and the authority of the

Hallowed Pact. Not all of it, not enough to whisk her away or strike dead the creatures who threatened her. Not enough to alter the physical world.

But the fae weren't creatures of the physical world, not entirely. At their core, no matter how they manifested, they were creatures of spirit. And *spirit* . . .

That was an area where the gods had tricks—and, in Olgun's and Adrienne's case, *allies*—of their own.

Just before the last of his conscious essence vanished from Widdershins's presence, Olgun drew on his new powers, his new knowledge. Between the worlds, he yanked open a door that normally swung only one way, and with everything he had, he called out his need.

He called, and they answered. Not for him.

All four of them, for love of her.

❋

She couldn't begin to tell, at first, just what she was seeing. She assumed it to be some optical illusion, some combination of the dark and the storm, the pain and the tears. Some random lights and movement, blurred into the illusion of something more.

Until it occurred to her that she wasn't dead. That Lisette hadn't moved in for the kill, was . . .

Was backing away.

Utterly confused, Shins wiped the back of her hand over her eyes—wincing at the pain as she used her injured arm but unwilling to relinquish the rapier—until she was able to see.

And she saw, but had her unnatural enemy not been retreating before them, she would never, *ever* have believed.

They were scarcely visible, merely shimmering forms in the glow of the lamps and the lightning. Rain and wind passed through

them, rippling slightly but otherwise unaffected. First two, then a
third, and a fourth appeared in the road between the two combatants.
Somewhere, from no direction she could name, Widdershins heard
the slamming of a distant gate.

Lisette was screaming something, her voice still coiled and slithering around those of her unnatural allies, but Shins didn't catch a
word of it. She was too busy staring, trying to make out some sense of
detail among the nebulous figures. And though she should have been
able to see no such thing, she did.

Widdershins choked, having literally forgotten to breathe. Her
rapier clattered on the cobblestones, and it might only have been the
wind that still held her upright.

The first of the phantoms looked her way, raised a hand to tip his
broad-brimmed hat in a friendly, informal salute. He drew his own
rapier from beneath a dark tabard, which flapped about him without
the slightest relation to the gusting winds. A tabard on which Shins
could spot the faintest hint of the fleur-de-lis, ensign of Davillon's
City Guard.

He *couldn't* be here. But she'd have recognized him anywhere.

"Julien . . . ?"

He didn't seem to move, took no obvious steps. Yet suddenly he
was elsewhere, no longer standing before Shins but beside Lisette.
With a high-pitched, buzzing keen, a thick slab of shadow detached
itself from the swirling darkness around her, briefly assuming a
humanoid form with misshapen, frog-like legs. The shriek ended;
the two figures clashed, slamming together in absolute silence. They
were still dueling, ghostly blade against inhuman hands and tongue,
as they faded again from sight.

And if that had truly been Julien, the others must be . . . *Oh,
gods . . .*

She felt it, then; Widdershins knew that smile, even if she
couldn't make it out. A second apparition, its long transparent hair

tinged with gold, raised a hand in greeting, her invisible smile widening further still. She stood at the slightest angle, as though one leg supported her weight less well than the other. Then, like the first, she flickered and was gone, stripping the leaf-and-thorn-clad fae from Lisette as she passed.

Widdershins, Lisette, the entire street began to glow, bathed in a wave of haunting light. It emanated from a heavy staff, shaped like a shepherd's crook, held in the hands of someone clad in heavy—perhaps ecclesiastical—robes of office. He didn't even approach Lisette, this one. He laid a gentle hand on Shins's shoulder; she knew, somehow, that it was gentle, even though she couldn't feel a thing. A single step, and he raised his staff on high, until the light grew blinding. He was gone when it faded, but so were the bulk of shadows around Lisette, all the many lesser fae who had served her along with the most terrible three.

That left only one. Shins cried openly, now, reaching out for him no matter how futile she knew the gesture to be. He reached out, too, his fingers passing through her own. He straightened, then, tugging the hem of a nigh invisible vest, smoothing out the unseen wrinkles. The rapier he drew was familiar, oh so familiar; Shins had carried it— or the "real" version of it—for a very long time.

Then he, too, was gone—as was the last of Lisette's power, the Prince of Orphan's Tears wrenched from her body and soul by the man who, however briefly, had replaced the parents Widdershins had lost.

Lightning flashed. Thunder roared. And Shins, after wiping her eyes clear once more, bent down to retrieve her fallen weapon. Her steps slow but steady, she followed in the path of the now departed ghosts, until she stood beside the only other soul, living or dead, who had also been left behind.

Whatever the fae had done to Lisette, however they had wound themselves through her, it had reduced her to something that couldn't last on its own. Her skin hung in folds around her bones, like newly emptied burlap sacks. Hair fell from her head in clumps; nails slid from her fingertips, leaving glistening trails behind. With every breath she gurgled and choked, struggling to breathe through the inky sludge that, only now, had begun to melt away in the rain.

Her eyes, though yellowed and sunken, had reappeared in their sockets, glaring up at Shins. And in them, still, the young woman saw absolutely nothing but hate.

When Lisette spoke, it was with such a crumpled-paper rasp as to be nigh incomprehensible. "It's not . . . fair . . ."

Shins could only shrug. "I don't think it was ever meant to be."

The single thrust of her rapier was an act of pity as much as anger. Then, leaving the blade in the corpse, Widdershins stumbled to the nearest stoop and sat down, hard. There she stayed, curled tight around the gaping hollow in her soul, and wept until long after the rain had finally, *finally* stopped.

※

"Is that safe?" Igraine asked doubtfully as she strode across a rooftop still speckled with puddles and scattered leaves left behind by the storm.

At least most of the dried bird guano had been scoured away.

"Not really." Shins watched her approach or rather watched her legs and hips approach. She didn't have much of a view of the rest of the priestess, given that she was currently balanced in a precarious handstand at the building's edge. "I can still do it, though. Surprisingly easy, actually. Not sure what to make of that."

"A really big, goopy mess, if you're not careful."

Widdershins chuckled softly (secretly pleased that she *could* laugh, a little) and allowed herself to slowly topple. One foot kicked out, toes striking rooftop, and she rolled herself upright.

Her head swam, just a bit. She tried to ignore it. It had never done that, before she was . . . alone.

"Pretty sure it's safer than where *you've* been, yes?" She knelt sideways, one knee tucked in tight, letting the other leg stretch. "How's it going?"

Igraine's answer began with a very unpriestly snort. "Same as yesterday: It isn't. Far as we can tell, there's not a single member of the Luchene bloodline left. The duchess hadn't returned power to the Houses before she died, so nobody's entirely sure who should be in charge."

"It'll all go back to status quo. I mean, the Houses'll be doing better working together than scrabbling for power that *nobody* had a week ago."

"Oh, sure. They just need to trudge through a bit more ambition and pride before they'll admit it." She drew breath to say more, but Widdershins beat her to it.

Mostly because she wasn't yet ready to tackle what she suspected Igraine's next topic of choice would be.

"How's the Guild?"

The priestess blinked, then glanced around the roof. Perhaps realizing she'd find no clean place to sit, she leaned against the chimney with a faint grumble. "It's going to take some getting used to the new order. The Finders have to learn to be a little more subtle. The priesthood of the Shrouded God is going to be a separate organization now, albeit with shared leadership, so the Guild won't have that protection any longer."

"I'm sure the new Shrouded Lord is just thrilled at the extra bureaucracy," Shins snickered.

"Lady," Igraine corrected.

"What?"

"The new leader of the Finders' Guild and the priesthood. The Shrouded Lady. Our first one, actually."

"Is that so?" Shins shifted sides, stretching the other leg. "I wonder who she might be," she said, without any question in her voice at all.

Igraine shrugged, but Shins was quite certain she spotted a glint in the priestess's eyes. "I'm sure I couldn't tell you."

"No, of course not." A sudden doubt clouded her face. "Renard?"

"Didn't want the post back, not that we'd have let him take it. Actually, he's debating whether he wants to remain in the Guild. I was actually hoping you might speak to him."

"Oh." Shins pondered a moment. "Sure, I guess."

"And maybe about a few other things, while you're at it." Then, at Shins's bewildered look, Igraine couldn't quite keep from grinning. "You're really blind sometimes, Widdershins."

"So I'm told," the thief replied, still absolutely clueless as to what that was all about.

Igraine tactfully changed topics. "What are *you* going to do?"

"Short term? Try to find Evrard. Or at least learn if he's still alive."

"Still no word, then?"

"Nope. Just the mess at his suite. Blood and broken furniture, but no bodies. Not my favorite guy, but he helped. I figure I owe him that much. After that, help Robin and Faustine rebuild the Witch.

"But long term? I honestly don't know."

"If they need a place to stay," Igraine began, "or if you do . . . well, with so many Finders in gaol, there are a few empty safe houses. I could—"

"Thank you. Really. But no, we've got a temporary place."

Igraine nodded, coughed at a puff of ambient cinders from the chimney—and then her whole face fell. "You didn't!"

"Why not? I mean, he's already paid for the place through summer. Until then, or if he turns up alive before then. . . . It's a *really* nice place. Or will be, once we get the blood cleaned up."

Shins decided she'd stretched enough—and *not* because her thigh was starting to ache, dogs grommet!—and stood. She took the opportunity to brace herself, emotionally and even physically, in the process.

"None of this is why you came looking for me, though," she said.

Igraine's expression was answer enough.

"Church stuff, then," Shins said. "Sicard?"

"Driving himself crazy, trying to keep the rest of the city's clergy calm. Nobody knows if he had the right to do any of what he did. And that's just locally. Once word reaches Lourveaux, we're probably looking at years of conferences, investigations, political wrangling . . .

"But none of it matters. It's all just face-saving. All of us felt it when the Pact accepted Olgun." Shins struggled not to wince at Igraine's use of the name. "At the end of the day, if the gods accept what Sicard did, the Church'll have to. To avoid open schism if nothing else."

"I'm glad." Part of Widdershins even meant it. The rest of her wished Igraine would go away so she could cry again. "He deserves their acceptance. He—"

"But that's still not why I'm here."

Shins's brow furrowed.

"The story of Olgun is spreading through Davillon. And with it, the story of Adrienne Satti. Between that, and the fact that half the city's priests woke up from dreams declaring your innocence . . . well, you'll have some legal hurdles to jump, and there may be a few aristocrats here and there who'll never accept it. But Adrienne can have her life back, if she wants it."

Widdershins didn't consciously decide to sit, didn't even *remember* sitting. One minute, she was standing a few paces from the priestess, the next her backside was in a cold puddle, her legs sprawled out before her.

"I don't . . . this . . . I never . . ."

"There's not much of the Delacroix estate remaining, but what's left has been put aside. We got enough of the Houses to agree on *that* much, though there may have been some legal threats made. You won't be anywhere near rich, but you won't go wanting for a good few years. When you decide, it'll be waiting."

"Is it me, or does it feel like this building's foundation might be made of old fruit?" Shins asked weakly.

The priestess's smile was genuine but brief. "That's *still* not the full reason I'm here."

"I'm pretty sure I'm not secretly a lost princess, and that everyone I think is dead . . ." She squeezed her eyes tightly shut, just for a moment, at the thought of the ghostly figures who'd saved her. ". . . really *is* dead. So I'm not sure what else you've got to surprise me with."

Igraine carefully crouched, so they were again on a level. "Your situation with Olgun was unique. So was his entry into the Pact. To judge by the omens and signs, he made a few—bargains.

"This can only happen once, Widdershins."

"I don't understand." Shins felt something turn over in her gut. "What *can* only happen—?"

The priestess's eyes rolled back in her head. She began to topple, just as swiftly caught herself. Gracefully she stood, beckoning Shins to do the same.

"Hello, Adrienne."

It came from Igraine. Her chest rose and fell, her mouth moved with the words. But this voice was deep, sonorous, and gently brushed with an accent Shins had never heard.

Never heard, but knew all the same.

"Olgun . . . ?"

Igraine—Olgun—smiled to shame the sun. "We both know that I *can* hear you when you speak so softly, but there is no reason to—*oof!*"

Shins slammed into him, arms wrapped desperately tight around him, and sobbed into his chest.

Only when she felt fingers running so very softly through her hair did she begin to calm—and only when she heard the soft but resonant sounds of a god softly weeping with her did she pull herself together and take a step back.

"I have to confess," she said, sniffling and quickly wiping a hand across her nose, "this is really *not* how I pictured you."

His laughter seemed too large for reality, felt as though it couldn't possibly be coming from Igraine's slender form. Finally, when he'd calmed, "It is a new outfit I am trying on."

Her turn, then, to laugh; no mere chuckle, as before, but *real* laughter. She felt a hundred times lighter. "Gods, there's so much I want to talk to you about. So much . . ."

She petered out as Olgun's expression sobered. He didn't need to say anything; she knew.

"How long do we have?" she asked with a quiet hitch.

"I am sorry, Adrienne. Only a few minutes. It would require longer than that for me to explain why, so let us say only that it is to do with the natural laws of divinity, along with a desire not to cause any harm to Igraine."

"Then why?" She knew it was a childish, bitter question, unworthy of either of them, yet she couldn't help but ask it. "Why even come back? What's the point?"

"To see you," he said kindly. "And because you saved me. So many times, in so many ways. I could not go without saying good-bye."

The rooftop grew blurry again as Shins struggled, and failed, to keep from tearing up yet again. "I shouldn't have said that. I'm sorry."

"No." This time it was he who stepped up to her, he who embraced her. "You do not need to apologize to me. Not ever. I do not believe a god has ever owed so much to any one mortal. We are all grateful for it, the whole of the Pact. Although none other so much as I."

"Even Cevora?" she sniffled, trying to smile.

"Even he. A savage and ambitious god, yes, but his Acolyte went much too far in his madness. Cevora would never deign to offer apologies to a mortal, but I believe he truly regrets."

A nod, another sniffle.

"I have to depart soon, Adrienne."

"*No!*" Again she clutched at him, hard, even as she struggled to calm herself. "I mean, I know you do, I . . . Olgun, please. Please stay."

"I cannot. Oh, dear one, I truly *cannot.*"

It came out a whisper, nothing more. "I don't want to be alone."

The god in mortal flesh stepped back, so he might look at her, and she at him, even as he kept a tight hold on her shoulders. "You will never be alone. Not ever.

"You have spoken to Igraine, to Ancel, to William. You know that our priests have a connection with us. They are favored by chance. They receive word through signs and omens. And we speak to them in dreams."

"I'm not a *priest!*" she squealed.

The god laughed once more. "Amusing as it would be to see you try, no, you are not. But I can grant you as much. You are strong, fast, already, if less than you were. After our years together, I think you always will be. And I shall always watch over you, as though you *were* my highest priest. I will grant you what luck I can, and I will visit, on occasion, in your dreams."

Better than nothing, perhaps, but it wasn't enough, not nearly. "It won't ever be the same, though, will it?"

His fingers tightened on her shoulders. "Nothing ever is."

Olgun's—Igraine's—eyelids trembled. "It is time," he said.

"I know. Olgun, thank you."

"No. Thank *you.* And Adrienne . . . I love you, too."

Shins stared into what she knew to be Igraine's eyes. Olgun was gone.

The priestess said not a word, only offered Widdershins a brief hug of her own before turning away and disappearing back across the rooftop.

Widdershins turned, too, striding up to the very edge. From there she could see Davillon, bustling along as though it were just another day. The sky remained choked with clouds, but it felt as though there would be no more rain, for a time.

"It'd be nice to be dry for more than a few hours at a time, wouldn't it?"

The lack of response surprised her for only an instant, and she couldn't quite repress a smile, wondering if she'd ever break the habit of talking to herself.

"Maybe Widdershins and Adrienne can exchange a few words," she muttered.

Widdershins. Adrienne. She had more than her life still ahead of her; she had two to choose from.

She had the Flippant Witch to rebuild. Whether she would stay with it after that, or return to the Guild, or both, or neither, she couldn't say. But the choice would be hers.

She had Robin, Renard, Faustine, and others. People who loved her and whom she truly loved—and if it was not always in the precise way they might *wish* she loved them, she knew they would still be there. Her family.

She had a god watching out for her, to the best of his ability. For her, more than any other man, woman, or child. Because he loved her, too.

And that was a lot. It wasn't enough, not yet.

But it would be.

AUTHOR'S AFTERWORD

Some of you hate me right now.

It's okay to admit it. Not only do I understand, but I kind of hate me right now, too.

I always struggle with good-bye-type endings. They make me sad, even the ones that aren't written to be; the closer I've felt to the characters, the sadder. So you can imagine how upset I was writing these last couple of chapters.

What you may *not* realize is that Widdershins has been more a part of me—my creative process, stories, plans, my imagination—than any other character. Technically, I created Corvis Rebaine (*The Conqueror's Shadow*) earlier, but only by a year or so. And Shins has, at the time I'm writing this, more word count devoted to her than Corvis does.

The first draft of the book that would eventually become *Thief's Covenant* was written way back around the summer and fall of 2000. It's been *massively* rewritten since then, multiple times, but throughout all of that, Shins herself didn't change much.

Yeah. A long time. She feels real to me, and that means her losses do, too.

So, as I'm sure some of you are asking, why do it?

Truth is, I almost didn't. The planning stages, outlining stages, writing stages; during each, there was at least one point where I nearly chickened out. If I'd been writing this book *just* for me, tailoring it to my own enjoyment, I probably would have. This is the first time what I've wanted emotionally, and what I've wanted creatively, have differed to such an extent.

In the end, though, I'm *not* writing this just for me. I'm not even writing it just for my audience, though you guys are one of my greatest motivators.

I'm writing it because I have things I want to say and stories I want to tell. And this? This is what was right for the story and the characters.

It was *dramatically* appropriate. Ending it this way made Widdershins's tale far more powerful and compelling than it otherwise would have been.

It was *creatively* appropriate. After four books, I felt like I was on the verge of starting to repeat myself. Nothing's more disappointing than a good character or series that hangs around too long, becomes a shadow of what it once was. I'd much rather I—and Shins—take a bow before that happens.

And it was *thematically* appropriate. You see, it was time for Shins to grow up.

I didn't *intend* to make the series a metaphor about growing up. Heck, when I wrote the first book, I didn't even intend it to be a series; I hadn't decided if I even wanted to write a sequel or not. It became very clear to me, however, as I was writing *False Covenant* and planning *Lost Covenant* and *Covenant's End*, that that's exactly what it had become. It was, my own intentions notwithstanding, a series about Shins maturing and learning to stand on her own.

Parents, whether they want to or not, have to eventually let their children go. Children, whether they like it or not, have to eventually stop relying on their parents. Oh, the family's still going to be there—special occasions, emergencies—but no longer a part of everyday life. No longer something to lean on.

Like Olgun and Shins.

So that's where I found myself. I've known since book two how book four had to end. I'm not one of those authors whose characters speak to them or anything like that. But in this case, the story really did demand to go only one way, and it would have felt dishonest of me—as a storyteller, as an entertainer, as an author—to do otherwise.

What does that mean, then, for Widdershins? Is this really her last book, the last time we'll be seeing her?

Well . . . yes, no, and maybe. Isn't that a helpful answer?

Yes, this is the end of the current series, what I guess you could call "The Covenant Cycle." Four books, over and done. There won't be any more of these, specifically.

No, it's probably not the last time you'll see her. While I have no more Widdershins books currently planned, I *do* intend—circumstances permitting, of course—to write more stories set in this world. If you think Shins isn't going to pop up occasionally in those, whether as a supporting character or just a cameo, then you haven't been paying attention. Shins doesn't keep her nose out of *anything*.

And maybe. I never know what ideas are going to come to me, and I don't rule anything out. The Covenant Cycle is done—any future Widdershins book will be a very different beast, given that she's no longer got her divine companion—but if the right story hits me, something that really feels Widdershinsy, I'll certainly write it. I'm not sure what it'd be like to write her without Olgun, but I'm not unwilling to find out.

(I do *not* anticipate ever putting them back together. I feel like that would be a cop-out and would cheapen the stories that have come so far. I guess it's possible that an absolutely genius idea for doing so might someday come to me, so I won't *swear* never to do it, but it's *highly* unlikely. Shins—and her writer—need to keep moving forward.)

I want to express my heartfelt gratitude to each and every one of you who came along on Shins's travels with me. This could never have happened without you, and you've made it an incredibly rewarding experience. I hope you'll join me on some of my other journeys, as well—if you liked the Widdershins books, I think you'll enjoy a good portion of my other works—but even if you don't, thank you, truly, for sticking with this one.

Ari "Mouseferatu" Marmell

May 12, 2014

ABOUT THE AUTHOR

Ari Marmell would love to tell you all about the various esoteric jobs he's held and the wacky adventures he had on the way to becoming an author, since that's what other authors seem to do in these sections. Unfortunately, he doesn't actually have any, as the most exciting thing about his professional life, besides his novel writing, is the work he's done for *Dungeons & Dragons* and other role-playing games. His published fiction includes the Widdershins Adventures YA fantasy series, along with *The Goblin Corps*, from Pyr Books, as well as multiple books from other major publishers, including the fantasy-noire Mick Oberon series, the Corvis Rebaine duology, and the official computer game tie-in novel *Darksiders: the Abomination Vault*.

Ari currently lives in an apartment that's almost as cluttered as his subconscious, which he shares (the apartment, not the subconscious, though sometimes it seems like it) with George—his wife—and a cat who really, really thinks it's dinner time. You can find Ari online at http://www.mouseferatu.com and on Twitter @mouseferatu.